THE
Corpse
WITH
THE Golden
Nose

CATHY ACE

TouchWood
Editions

TouchWood Editions
touchwoodeditions.com

LIBRARY AND ARCHIVES CANADA CATALOGUING IN PUBLICATION
Ace, Cathy, 1960–
The corpse with the golden nose / Cathy Ace.

(A Cait Morgan mystery)
Issued also in electronic formats.
ISBN 978-1-927129-88-3

I. Title. II. Series: Ace, Cathy, 1960–. Cait Morgan mystery.

PS8601.C41C66 2013   C813'.6   C2012-906790-3

Editor: Frances Thorsen
Proofreader: Lenore Hietkamp
Design: Pete Kohut
Cover image: Kevin Miller, istockphoto.com
Author photo: Jeremy Wilson Photography (www.jeremywilsonphotography.com)

Canadian Heritage   Patrimoine canadien   Canada Council for the Arts   Conseil des Arts du Canada   BRITISH COLUMBIA ARTS COUNCIL

We gratefully acknowledge the financial support for our publishing activities
from the Government of Canada through the Canada Book Fund, Canada
Council for the Arts, and the province of British Columbia through the
British Columbia Arts Council and the Book Publishing Tax Credit.

RECYCLED
Paper made from
recycled material
FSC
www.fsc.org   FSC® C103567

The interior pages of this book have been printed on 100% post-consumer
recycled paper, processed chlorine free, and printed with vegetable-based inks.

1 2 3 4 5 17 16 15 14 13

PRINTED IN CANADA

This book is dedicated to
Ella, Evelyn, and Trevor

Champagne and Orange Juice

BUD SLAPPED THE PHOTOGRAPH ONTO the table in front of me as though it were a gauntlet.

"This photo showed up in my email a few days ago. From someone I...know. What do you read in it, Cait?" He looked grim.

I held the photo at arm's length and squinted at the blurry image. I could make out two women, both with dark, curly hair. They were smiling.

I felt my multi-purpose right eyebrow shoot up as I asked, "Is just one of them dead, or both of them?"

"How'd you guess?" Bud asked, grinning.

"Oh, let me see, now . . . maybe it's something to do with me being a criminologist who specializes in victim profiling and you being an ex-homicide detective. *And* the hope, on my part, that you're unlikely to show me a photo of a woman, especially *two* women, in whom you have anything other than a *professional* interest. Those facts, when taken together with my amazing powers of deduction, have helped me reach the conclusion that I'm looking at either one or two victims, or, if not victims, then at least people who are now dead." I hurled a bright smile toward Bud and waited for him to tell me off for my cheekiness.

Bud shrugged. "You know me too well, Cait." His voice warmed, and he looked pleased about something. Then his smile faded. "The taller of the two died about a year ago. The other one's her older sister. But that's all you get."

"So there's no point my asking if it was an accident, a suicide, or a homicide?" I asked.

Bud paused, refreshed our glasses, and took a sip from the champagne flute that looked almost too delicate in his large hand. "I can't tell you that, because I don't know, Cait, I can only be certain it wasn't an accident. The whole local community, the cops, *and* the coroner, all say suicide. The sister says no way. I have no idea. There *was* a note, and the sister says the cops won't look into it any further as there are no grounds to suspect anyone else was involved."

Ah—so *that* was it. Bud had found a damsel in distress and he wanted to help her. Immediately, I wondered why he felt he owed this unknown woman anything. I mentally kicked myself for allowing a pang of jealousy to clutch at my satisfyingly full tummy. I swallowed deeply from my glass, and decided to play nice.

Bud and I had chattered happily through the delicious brunch I'd prepared in the small kitchen of my little house on Burnaby Mountain. We'd already managed to solve the world debt crisis *and* the problems in the Middle-East before I'd made the second pot of coffee. *We're good like that.* Throughout the meal of creamy scrambled eggs draped over golden, buttered toast, Marty, Bud's tubby black Lab, had waited patiently under the table, never taking his glorious amber eyes off us for a moment. Finally, his steadfastness had been rewarded, and I congratulated myself on saving at least a dozen calories by allowing him to lick my plate. It was then, when I was enjoying the memory of the food, and therefore at my most vulnerable, that Bud had produced the photograph. *He knows me too well.*

"You know I don't like to assess individual photographs. They're unreliable sources of insight," I snapped, possibly a bit too sharply.

"Well, you might not *like* to," Bud spoke slowly, "but you're good at it. You were good at it when I hired you to consult for my integrated homicide team, and, even though I'm retired now, I reckon you're *still* good at it. So treat this as a challenge if you must, sweet Caitlin Morgan"—he was grinning wickedly, a sight that always makes my heart flutter and stutter—"and tell me what you can?" He phrased it as a question, but we both knew it was the sort of challenge I couldn't resist.

I scrabbled around under the copy of the *Globe and Mail* that lay on the table, hunting for my reading glasses. I don't need them all the time, you understand, but I do seem to be using them more often these days. Since I'm almost forty-eight, I guess it's to be expected. I believe they lend me an air of imperiousness when I glower over them. Frankly, if they help me to intimidate the students in my classes who need to be brought down a peg or two, then they're worth every cent I've spent on all ten or twelve pairs—*where do they disappear to?*—and the various cases, chains, and clips that are supposed to attach them to my body and prevent them from being lost.

I looked at the picture again: the frozen expressions, the way the women had been relating to each other at that point in time, and their setting. Both were around forty, and they bore a sisterly resemblance to each other; each was casually dressed in shirts, pants, and sandals; one had her arm around the other's shoulders. They were standing at the foot of a grass-covered, stony hill between rows of vines.

Bud petted Marty as I studied the photo. As I began to speak, he turned his attention to me.

"Okay. Sisters. The taller one, the dead one, is, or *was*, the more dominant. She's clearly the more confident person, and she knows how to present herself to the camera. She's better dressed, except her bra's too small for her. She has a better haircut, good makeup, and she's draping her arm around the shorter sister as though to push her forward. So, one confident and supportive, one less so, but loved. I'd say the tall one has, or *had*, some sort of public-facing role in life, the other some sort of backroom job. They're in wine country, among vines, early in the fruiting season, but are not wearing vacation clothes, so I suggest that's where they live, or at least spend a lot of time, and where they feel comfortable. In fact," and as I thought it through it became clear, "the tall one looks proprietorial. Is this their land? Is this *their* vineyard?"

I glanced at the champagne bottle on the table. MT DEWDNEY FAMILY ESTATE WINERY ANEN ANGEL SPARKLING N/V. I wondered if I was looking at women who had some connection with the wine I was drinking: after all, Bud didn't usually bring alcohol for brunch.

Bud shook his head. "No more questions. Keep going."

Sometimes Bud can be a bit of a devil! I love it.

I allowed my eyebrow to arch disdainfully in Bud's direction for a moment, but I think my smile lessened the effect somewhat. I returned my attention to the photograph.

"No rings on the left hand of either sister, so both single, though it wouldn't surprise me to find that the taller sister was divorced, or maybe even had several relationships behind her: she's worldly and she's comfortable in her own skin, something that only really develops when you've been in relationships where you get to know yourself in a positive way. To be honest, Bud, it's difficult to say more. I can't tell exactly where they are, geographically, though I would suggest they are North American, given the way they are dressed, so maybe the Okanagan or Niagara, or maybe Sonoma or Napa. I can't see the terrain, so I can't say more. Age? Close to each other and around forty, I'd say. But a photograph is difficult to analyze more than that. It captures just a tiny fraction of a second and people adopt unnatural expressions in front of a camera. They're both smiling at the photographer, but that could . . ." I paused, and held the photograph closer, peering through my specs. I'd spotted something in the women's expressions.

"What is it?" asked Bud. His tone suggested urgency, which surprised me. But I let it pass.

"I don't know who took this photograph, but I can tell you that the dead sister liked the photographer a great deal, and the shorter sister didn't like them at all. Yes, they're both smiling, right *at* the camera and hence the photographer—but the tall one has a very positive connection with whomever they are seeing behind the camera. Her expression is soft and warm. But the short one, well, she's smiling too, but there's hardness in her face. She's almost literally gritting her teeth. And there's defiance in her eyes. She really doesn't like what she's seeing."

"Now that's interesting, Cait. And puzzling," observed Bud.

"So—who took the photograph?"

"No one. The sister who sent it to me told me they took it themselves. They're looking at a camera on a tripod. Odd that you should infer such emotions regarding a tripod." He smiled. It wasn't an unkind smile.

I had to agree that it sounded odd but I could *see* those feelings on their faces. I was in no doubt.

Bud petted Marty absentmindedly as he thought about his next words. Marty didn't care that Bud was thinking about something else, and reacted with licks and vigorous tail-wagging. I'm pretty sure he was smiling up at Bud, too.

As Bud wiped his Marty-dampened hand on his pants, he looked at me with a curious glint in his eyes. I knew that look. As a psychologist with a master's degree in criminal psychology, who then wrote a pretty controversial PHD thesis about victim profiling, I had been bravely retained by Bud in the past to work with his integrated homicide team on many cases. I'd had the chance to see that same expression on the faces of various suspects he'd interviewed, as they tried to decide how to balance truth with lies before they answered their interrogator. Bud was weighing how to proceed. I trusted the balance would be in favor of the truth.

He sighed and sat back in the kitchen chair. The decision had been made. "Okay, I'll come clean. The short one, she's Ellen. I've never met her face to face, but she's been my online 'grief buddy' for a few months now. After Jan was killed, I went for counseling . . ."

As the words left Bud's lips I could feel myself stiffen. I couldn't help but be surprised. This was the first I was hearing about counseling, and we were supposed to be getting to know each other as a proper couple—or so he said. Not much chance of that happening if he kept things like counseling from me.

"Don't get cross, Cait," snapped Bud, correctly interpreting my expression. "I haven't told you about it because I'm not really comfortable with it. I think the best way to get over the loss of a loved one is to dust yourself off and get on with life. But my wife was killed because some low-life scumbag thought she was *me*, so the Force didn't *suggest* therapy, they *insisted*. I suspect it was some sort of liability thing in case I killed myself."

I couldn't let *that* pass.

"You told me that you'd only ever thought about . . . you know . . ." I couldn't bring myself to say the words, ". . . for a fleeting second. That it wasn't something you'd ever *seriously* considered."

I wondered if I knew Bud Anderson at all. This brunch was turning out to be something quite extraordinary.

He continued, looking grim. "Look, the therapist I saw—the therapist I *had* to see—got me to join up with this online community for people who've lost a loved one through violent or unexpected circumstances. They get you to buddy up as well as share anonymously in a blog. None of this was what I *wanted* to do, Cait. All of it felt strange and unnecessary. Ellen and I gravitated toward each other and became 'grief buddies' because she said she felt the same. As you know, I'm not a big sharer, and I'll admit to you that I wasn't very forthcoming with personal details. I even used a fake name. Ellen and I seemed to reach some level of quiet acceptance of each other, in writing. Online. Then, when the trial of Jan's murderer was all over the news, Ellen put two and two together and worked out who I was: that Jan was the wife I was mourning. So I opened up a bit more to her. Not emotionally. I talk to *you* about my feelings," he patted my hand, much as he'd been patting Marty's head, "but it seemed to give her the green light to write more about the facts of her sister's death, and how unhappy she was about the suicide verdict."

I nodded. I've seen how finding out that Bud was a cop, even a retired one, changes the way folks relate to him. We'd been to a few functions at the University of Vancouver, where I teach, and everyone had acted quite naturally when I'd introduced Bud as my "plus one." When they'd found out he was a retired cop, their body language had changed completely. Trust me, I'm really good at reading people, and I can spot a telltale sign a mile off. For some, it meant they just watched what they said—all the jokes about drinking and driving would stop, for example—but for others, they'd literally walk away, smiling politely, but, essentially, escaping.

Bud kept going. He knew I understood what he meant. "A few days ago Ellen emailed me this photo and wrote much more about her sister's death. Now she's invited me to visit her next weekend, over Easter, in Kelowna. I thought I'd let you use your deductive powers on the photo before I gave her a reply. I'm not sure what to do. I'm pretty certain that she wants me to look into how her sister died, but I'm not comfortable with that. Besides, I've retired, I have no standing, no ability to get hold of official reports or anything like that. I thought I'd turn to my Best Girl, and see what she has to say about the whole thing."

Bud smiled and looked thoughtful as he took the photograph from me, folded it carefully, and put it back into his wallet.

I suspected that I, too, looked thoughtful as I studied Bud: his rugged features; his once fair hair, now almost completely snowy; his heavy, silvered eyebrows, brilliant blue eyes, slightly snubbed nose, and weathered complexion. Out of the corner of his he probably caught me looking at him, but if he did, he didn't seem to mind. I sipped my champagne, grateful that this wonderful man wanted anything to do with short, overweight, indulgent, insecure, bossy me. *At least I know some of my shortcomings.*

They say you never truly *know* another person, but some of Bud's words had really stung. Of course I'd known Bud's wife, Jan. Not well, but in the way you come to know the wife of a colleague. You hear about their interests, their habits, their lives, *through* your colleague. Your colleague filters their being and presents it to you. Bud did that with Jan. He spoke of her frequently, and always with warmth and admiration. Every time Jan and I met, which was quite often, we got along well. Of course, we differed from each other: Jan was into groups, activities, hobbies. Me? Bit of a loner, I suppose. At least, that's how I've heard folks describe me. Jan reveled in mixing, and Bud enjoyed hearing about what she'd been up to while he'd been chasing down villains. They had a well-balanced relationship. Bud always referred to Jan as his "soulmate," which used to make me wince. It came as no surprise to anyone, therefore, that when Jan was shot and killed, the shooter believing he was targeting Bud himself, Bud's life, and even the way he looked at life, had changed completely. When Jan was shot and killed, the shooter having believed he was targeting Bud himself, it came as no surprise to anyone that Bud's life, and even the way he looked at life, changed completely. He'd tried to carry on in his then-role heading up a Canada-wide gang-busting police force, but he'd felt he was endangering his colleagues because he'd lost focus. So, with a hefty pension, and unwanted but huge insurance and compensation payouts, he'd taken early retirement from the Force to which he'd given his entire professional life, and now he was "reassessing," as he called it. A part of that "reassessment" had been to take himself off on a vacation last September, from which he'd returned and asked me to marry him.

Yes, *marry* him! That's a good example of what I mean when I say you never *truly* know another person. He asked me to marry him, and I was completely floored! And as a psychologist I'm *supposed* to have a deep understanding of why people do what they do. But it seems that sometimes I don't. We'd only ever worked together before that. I mean, we were friends, of course. I have to admit that I'd had quite strong feelings about Bud even before Jan had been killed, but only as far as a person can about someone with whom they work and who is totally, blissfully, happily married. It's safe to admire, respect, and come to rely upon the advice of someone like that, because they're completely involved, emotionally, with the person they are *meant* to be with. But when Jan was killed, all that changed. For Bud, *and* for me. Yes, I know it was nuts of him to ask me to be his wife just months after Jan's death, but to him it made some sort of sense.

Of course I'd turned him down. I didn't think he was in any fit state to make such a big decision at that time. I told him that he could ask me again in a year, if he still wanted to, and that during that time we'd work on getting to know each other differently. He'd agreed, which is where we are now. Well, we're six-ish months down that road. If we weren't the age we are, you'd probably call it *dating*. "I'm *dating*. He's my *boyfriend*." It even makes *me* want to barf! There needs to be a new vocabulary invented for all those of us over forty-five—or, in Bud's case, over fifty—who are beginning new relationships. It's not as though there aren't a lot of us, after all, and it can't be just *me* who feels uncomfortable about it.

"So, will you go?" I asked. I was very curious.

"Would you come with me? Your university'll be shut for the weekend, right? Easter, and all that? You *could* come," he replied softly. Bud's not a man to ask for help. *Normally.*

"What has she said, exactly?" I wondered if Bud had told Ellen about me.

"She's invited me to stay at her B&B, which is housed in her dead sister's old home . . ."

"Oh, cheery!" I interrupted. I couldn't resist.

Bud carried on, ignoring me., ". . . The *family* home she has turned into a B&B to save herself from having to sell it. And she wants me to join her on something called a 'Moving Feast' or some-such . . ."

"Do you mean the "Moveable Feast?'" I interrupted.

"Yes," replied Bud cautiously, "*that's* what she said. Does it make a difference?"

I could feel the excitement grip my tummy. "Of *course* it makes a difference, Bud, but the Moveable Feast is private. It's a closed event. Or set of events. It happens every Easter, hence the borrowing of the religious term 'moveable feast.' At least, I expect that's why, because there can't be a good reason for using that term in relation to the Hemingway diaries . . ." I could see Bud looking puzzled, so I decided to get back to the point I meant to make in the first place. "It's one of the most talked about gourmet happenings in British Columbia each year. But it's all rumors and whispers, because you can't just attend or buy your way in, you have to be invited to host an event, and then you get to visit the other events. It's really only for great chefs and vintners, and those with the money to put on an amazing spread. So . . . oh, my God, Bud—you should go. You *must* go. And, yes, if *I* can come *of course* I will. It would be the culinary experience of a lifetime. Tell me *all* about it. What did she say *exactly*. Word for word. Come on, spill!"

Okay, so I got a bit over-excited. Bud looked rather taken aback, but he rallied and explained coolly that Ellen had invited him and an "accompanying other" as her guests for the weekend, "to stay at her B&B, where she'll be hosting some of the meals, to accompany her to the other events and to meet some folks who played a big part in her sister's life, and still do in hers."

"So, to be clear," I began, reining in my horses as best I could. "Ellen thinks her sister was murdered, and she's invited you to one of the most exclusive foodie events in BC to introduce you to the people she presumably sees as suspects. Is that right?"

"Hmm . . . I guess you could put it like that, though I hadn't thought of it quite that way before," replied Bud, looking slightly alarmed. He scratched his head, as he does when he's bothered about something. "You know, I don't think I *should* go. I don't want to get dragged into something I don't understand. I'm not a cop anymore." Bud was sounding less Bud-like by the minute.

I began to panic, seeing my chance to indulge in some of the finest food and wines in the province receding into the distance. "Oh come on Bud, nothing ventured . . ." I allowed the sentence to hang above the table.

"But Cait." Bud had made a decision. "I can't. It's not right. Like I said, I'm not a cop anymore. I know how much *I'd* have hated it if an ex-officer had turned up on *my* patch and started nosing about. Besides, from what she's told me, I think it probably *was* a suicide. I suspect she's just grappling with guilt and grief and not doing a good job of it. We both know that those left behind by a suicide find it tough to come to terms with what's happened: the guilt is tremendous."

"Bud, why do you believe it was a suicide? What were the exact circumstances of the dead sister's demise? What's her name, by the way? The dead one, I mean."

"Annette. Annette Newman. They were Annette and Ellen. Hence, Anen Wines—their parents named the wines after their daughters—Annette Newman and Ellen Newman, A.N.E.N. Anen Wines. Sweet, eh?"

I felt my eyes roll. "If you say so. Sweet." *Honestly, sometimes for a pretty tough guy you can be a right sentimental old fool.* I didn't say that out loud, of course.

"When their parents died, they inherited the winery and made a go of it. Ellen ran the business, putting her background in accounting to good use, and Annette was the 'nose'—the vintner—and she was damned good at it too. Won gold medals pretty much everywhere for her tasting skills and the blends she created. Gained a worldwide reputation for herself, the vineyard, and their wines. I gather it was pretty tough at first. They lost their mother and father in a car accident when Ellen was twenty-five and Annette was only twenty. Sorry Cait, I know you know how that feels." He patted my hand again.

Almost a decade had passed since my parents had died in a tragic car accident, and the passing of time hadn't made the loss any easier to bear. Their ashes are still sitting on my mantelpiece in two matching urns, for goodness' sake. The presence of those urns speaks volumes about how well I've come to terms with their deaths.

"Okay then,—Annette," I continued, determined not to get lost in sad memories, "how did Annette die, exactly? And why do *you* think that it was a suicide?"

"Look Cait," began Bud seriously. "You know as well as I do that the statistics for female suicides show certain trends: pills, not guns, for example. They tend to use passive methods, not violent ones. This was a classic scenario. She was found in the cab of a truck, with a hose leading from the exhaust and the windows sealed with duct tape. There was an empty bottle of wine on the seat beside her, along with a note that made her intentions pretty clear. Of course I haven't seen the note, but Ellen told me that it kicked off with 'I can't do it any longer. I can't go on.' It sounds to me like a pretty open and shut case."

"And that's how the local cops treated it? And the coroner? Clear-cut suicide?"

Bud nodded. "If it were my case, that's how I'd see it."

I was intrigued, and that can be dangerous. I had just a few more, telling questions. "And why does Ellen insist it was *murder*?"

"She says there's no way that Annette would have killed herself. No way. She said that Annette was in fine form on the evening she died, and that they would have talked about any problems she might have had. They got along well. In fact, Ellen reckons no one ever had a bad word to say about her sister. Obviously, she thinks that someone had it in for her."

"Has she said who it is she thinks killed her sister?" I was very curious about this one.

"That's another reason why I think it's just Ellen trying to manage her guilt. She hasn't the faintest idea of who would have done it or, indeed, who *could* have done it. She admits that much." He paused, took a drink, then looked at me resignedly.

I gave what he'd said some thought, sipping the last dregs of my champagne as I did so.

"By the way, are you ever going to drink that glass of orange juice I poured for you?" asked Bud quite caustically. "I get it that you might not want to mix the two, but you should probably drink some of it. Marty won't have it, and I've finished mine. So, go on, spoil yourself with some vitamin C, why don't you?"

Sometimes Bud can be a bit of a nag. *But only in a caring way.* I drank the whole glass of juice in one go.

Wiping my juicy lips with the back of my hand, which Marty then thoughtfully cleaned up for me, I said purposefully, "Well, that's it then, Bud Anderson. We'll both be going to the Moveable Feast next weekend, and we'll be doing our best sleuthing too. Whatever *you* and the rest of them might think, I agree with Ellen. I believe her sister *was* murdered."

Bud looked taken aback. "But the facts don't support murder at all. It's *clearly* a suicide."

"No, Bud. You've told me that a woman blessed with an incredibly fine, and presumably trained, sense of smell—a sense of smell and taste that made her a star in her field—chose to kill herself by inhaling noxious fumes. It makes absolutely no sense, psychologically speaking. The level of self-loathing it would have taken to have killed herself that way *couldn't* have gone unnoticed by a close and loving sibling. Okay, okay, before you say it, I know that carbon monoxide is odorless, but the exhaust fumes in which it would have been present certainly aren't. To be fair, I suppose I can't say with *certainty* that she *wasn't* suicidal. She *could* have hidden such thoughts from those who loved her. People do. Sadly, all the time. I just don't believe she'd have killed herself *that* way. We'd better get off to Kelowna and find out what really happened. Let's hope you still have some clout and some contacts in that neck of the woods, because I think we might need them."

"Oh dear Lord," sighed Bud, "I've created a monster! Or is that the Welsh avenging angel syndrome rearing its head?" He smiled, though a little apprehensively.

"I don't know what you mean, Bud." I sounded as wounded as possible at the cultural slight. "Yes, I'm Welsh through and through, though what that's got to do with anything I don't know. It doesn't mean I'm particularly foolhardy or anything. You're the one who retained me as a consultant on victim profiling—you knew I was good at it, and you know how many cases I helped with. In fact, I'm not sure what you mean by throwing my Welshness out as some sort of insult." Bud rolled his eyes and smiled, rather weakly, I thought. "And I'm no 'avenging angel.' I don't know Ellen or Annette Newman from a pair of holes in the ground. But if there's something amiss, and a murderer has got away with it so far, shouldn't *someone* do *something* about it? Shouldn't we apply ourselves and find out the truth? You've spent your whole career upholding the law, and bringing those who break it to justice. You might have retired from the Force, but you haven't stopped being a person who knows the difference between right and wrong who's prepared to do something about it. You *know* we should step up."

Bud held up his hands in mock surrender. He looked sheepish. "I didn't mean to use your Welshness against you . . ."

"Good!"

". . . and I *do* see the sense in what you're saying about doing the right thing. But I'm still convinced this was a suicide—that Ellen doesn't *want* to see things the way the authorities do. And you *do* have to admit that the Welsh can go rushing into things with hot heads sometimes. You've only got to see them on the rugby field to know that. Don't forget, I've had quite a few Welsh colleagues in my time, so I know how your lot can get."

"Oh, come off it, Bud. '*Your lot*?' That's like me saying that you can be a miserable old sod at times simply because your parents are Swedish! I get it that not all Swedes walk around gazing bleakly into the distance, constantly contemplating the grim mysteries of life, whatever some popular fiction would have us believe. In the same way, we Welsh are not all short-tempered bulls constantly pawing the ground and snorting in close proximity to china shops."

"Singing or swinging, Cait. That's what one of my old colleagues used to tell me about the Welsh: when they're backed into a corner, it's always fifty–fifty whether they'll burst into song or come out fighting. I've never had any reason to doubt that he knew exactly what he was talking about. He was Welsh himself."

"*Bud!*" I gave him my sternest look. "The *Canadian* Cait—and don't forget that I've been a Canadian for a decade now—says let's go, let's help this woman, let's try to sort it out. Okay? Or it's four choruses of my favorite Welsh hymn for you! Don't take this lightly, Bud. *I'm* not. The last time I went to Kelowna, I got snowed into a hunting lodge with a corpse and a hotbed of suspects. Believe me, I don't want to face that sort of thing again. It was a nightmare. Hopefully, since this poor woman died a year ago, a cold case like this should be pretty safe. More of an academic exercise, the sort of thing I'm used to. So, yes, I think we should go, and, yes, I think we should look into it. And if you could promise me no more dead bodies, I'd be grateful. Right?"

Bud smiled a tired smile. "Okay, Cait. We'll do it. And we'll do the best we can. I'll sort it. *And no more fresh corpses.* I promise. We'll just help Ellen with Annette's case, as we can."

I felt relieved that Bud was back to being Bud-like again, and knew I had nothing to worry about with him in charge.

As I cleared the dishes and allowed Marty to lick the bowl I'd used to scramble the eggs, I thought about what clothes I possessed that could both stand up to an entire weekend of enjoying some of the best food and wine that British Columbia had to offer (*so, stretchy then*), while still being smart enough for the occasion. Sweat pants wouldn't cut it, and there's only so many times you can wear bouncy, drapey black outfits and still make an impression. I sensed some panic-shopping in my very near future.

Coffee with Cream

I'M NOT A HEARTLESS PERSON, but if I'm honest, the unfortunate death of Annette Newman was not foremost in my mind as Bud collected me in his shiny new truck to drive to Kelowna the next weekend. Given the rain that pelted us sideways for two hours, and the semis that were laboring up the long hills at no more than a crawling pace, the journey went quite smoothly, thank goodness. The Classic Vinyl radio station cut out a few times, but it didn't stop us singing at the tops of our voices for long periods. Even though some of Bud's memories of the music inevitably included Jan, we talked it through, and overall, it was great fun. All very important in a burgeoning relationship. Honestly.

It was almost eleven o'clock. I knew there'd be no stopping again until we reached our destination, so I suggested a loo and coffee break. Understanding well enough what that meant, Bud pulled off the main road, and we swept down toward Merritt. We stopped at the first coffee shop we spotted. Within moments, I'd used the facilities and was nibbling on a delicious lemon and cranberry scone, while managing to slurp gingerly from a steaming vat of coffee with as much cream in it as I could fit into the paper cup. It was just what I needed: delicious!

"Road trips make you hungry?" asked Bud, with a chuckle in his voice and a twinkle in his eye.

I didn't stop nibbling or slurping to answer. By way of an acid retort, I simply looked in his direction.

Eventually I mumbled at him through cakey crumbs, "I haven't eaten since breakfast, and that was four hours ago."

"I seem to remember you polishing off that packet of cookies a couple of hours ago, not too long after we'd dropped Marty at Jack's acreage in Hatzic," he replied, not unkindly.

"Blood sugar was low," I muttered. It's a phrase that allows for a fair few snacks each day.

Bud smiled broadly as we ambled back to the truck, then, while I settled myself and brushed crumbs off my "ample bosom," as we large-chested women like to refer to our boobs—*well, I do, anyway*— he wiped off the worst of the insects that had splattered themselves across his shiny new number plate.

"Well and truly christened," he observed wryly. I think he was a bit sad that the brand, spanking new-ness was now marred.

With another coffee in hand for the next leg of the journey, Bud hauled himself back into the truck, then handed me a blue cardboard folder that he pulled from behind his seat.

"Here you go, some reading for you," he said, smiling wickedly. "You can interpret it for me."

I leafed through the contents of the folder: sheets and sheets of notes spread across my lap.

"And this is . . . ?"

"It seems that Ellen Newman thought we'd like some background on our fellow attendees at the Moveable Feast. That's what she emailed to me. I printed it out before I left my apartment this morning," replied Bud as we pulled back up the incline toward the highway.

"She's very thorough," I observed dryly. "But then, she's an accountant, so I suppose she's one of those 'all detail and no perspective' people," I added. It seemed like a reasonable comment to me.

"Oh come on now, Cait," chastised Bud, "don't be so judgmental. We haven't even met the woman yet. You're always doing that."

"What?" I bit back. Miffed.

"Reaching snap decisions about folks, two seconds after you've met them, or worse still, *before* you've met them, and based almost solely on what they do and where they live," he replied.

I suppose he was right, but I've never been any different, and I just can't help myself. To be fair to me, what people do for a living and where they live their lives have a huge impact on their behavior, and are significant indicators of both personality type and social standing as well as beliefs and desires. But, on this occasion, he had a point: I was judging Ellen Newman on a pile of papers I hadn't even read yet, and that probably wasn't fair.

"Okay then," I sulked. "I'll withhold my opinion until I've seen what she has to say, and maybe even until I've met her."

"Radio on or off?" asked Bud kindly.

"Off, thanks, it'll make the job quicker."

"Right then. Get on with it," he quipped.

I pulled my purse from between my feet, scrabbled about searching for my reading glasses, pushed them onto my nose, took them off again, cleaned them, poked them back into place, and began to read. There must have been about thirty pages in all, so it took about five minutes.

When I'd finished, I gave their contents some thought for a moment or two, then pronounced, "Okay, I'm ready. What do you want to know?"

Even from his profile I could tell that Bud was surprised, and amused.

"It still freaks me out a bit that you can read and digest so much information so quickly," he commented. "I wish I could do it. Over the years, I bet I could have saved *months* of my life that way. You're lucky."

"Lucky, *and* I work at it, Bud," I retorted. Having what some call an "eidetic memory," and what others call "a quick eye and a fast brain," because they don't think that eidetic memory exists, means I'm pretty good at this sort of stuff. I can see, understand, interpret, and encode information into my memory banks at great speed. It's been a phenomenal help to me in my academic life. It also means that I carry with me images and sensations I'd really rather forget. Sometimes they haunt my dreams, as vivid as when I first saw, felt, and smelled them. I don't just hold on to words on pages, I do it with everything that surrounds me. Insofar as I've been able to encode it accurately in the first place, of course. That's the problem with my "ability." Sometimes I encode things, or remember them, wrongly. I overlay them with my own, sometimes erroneous, interpretations. I color them with my attitudes and biases, often based upon my own incomplete knowledge. Because not even *I*, well read though I might be, know *everything*. It's something that's landed me in trouble in the past.

"So shall I tell you what I think about the writer before I tell you about what she's written?" I asked, a bit testily.

"Sure. Whatever you think, Cait. I'll take it all in, as best I can with my poor, feeble, non-superhuman brain." Bud chuckled, and I had to stop myself from giving him a friendly slap on the arm.

"Okay," I began, "Ellen Newman has written up a list of the people we're going to meet through the weekend, with some background on each person. It's a very thorough list. And I *mean* thorough. She's obviously given it all a great deal of thought, and of course, she knows the people she's writing about. So, what does this tell me about Ellen?"

I paused, for effect.

"Oh come on, Cait, just get on with it," Bud said with a smile.

"Ellen likes to organize. Here she's organized her thoughts, but I suspect she likes to organize everything around her, including people. Don't get me wrong, Bud, I wish *I* could be a bit more like her in my own life. You know what I'm like with the piles of papers, textbooks, and reports I have to read and grade—I like to use the 'strata method' of filing, where the oldest things are at the bottom of the pile. It doesn't matter so much for me, because I can recall when I put something onto a pile, so I can *usually* find it right away. But

Ellen? I suspect her sock drawer has those little divider things in it, and she probably fills her kitchen cupboards with items in height order. You know the type. Right?"

"You mean she's very tidy?" asked Bud.

"More than tidy," I replied thoughtfully. "Highly ordered, I'd say. Who knows, maybe she's bordering on OCD, or maybe not. The process she's undertaken here is, after all, one that requires order. Let's give her the benefit of the doubt, eh?"

Bud nodded, which I took as a sign to continue.

"Moving on, let's consider the cast of characters she's detailed. Well, they're an international bunch, with a variety of origins and some interesting stories behind them. I think the best way to help you understand is to explain the context in which we're going to meet them first."

Bud bobbed his head again. He was beginning to look like one of those nodding dogs!

"So . . . the Moveable Feast takes place every Easter and is attended only by those who are hosting meals and their invited guests—of which they are allowed two, maximum. Which is where we come in. Each host is responsible for providing food and drink, as appropriate to the meal they're hosting, for all the guests. *Everything* is up to the host to arrange and supply. There are no budget limits. No sponsors are allowed but otherwise, there are no rules. There *is* a timetable. This evening we'll attend a 'cocktails and canapés' reception, which differs from most of the rest of the weekend in that every host will have contributed something to tonight's soiree, and it'll take place at a venue they've hired. No one person is responsible for tonight."

"Tomorrow and Sunday we have a breakfast, lunch, and dinner each day, and there's a final breakfast, again un-hosted but contributed to by everyone, on Monday morning. After that, if we can still move at all, we're free to leave."

"Oh good grief," said Bud, looking a bit taken aback. "I don't even eat three times a day, let alone three special, probably very rich, heavy meals. At least I packed the Gaviscon," he added, smiling.

"I packed Tums," I chuckled, reflecting happily on how, for all our differences, we're really very similar in some respects.

"Other than lining our arteries and broadening our beams this weekend, it seems that the other thing we'll be doing is mixing with some pretty well-heeled folks." As I spoke, I began to worry that my wardrobe wouldn't stand up to the scrutiny of the people with whom we'd be mixing.

"Go on then, I can take it," urged Bud. "Tell me all about them. But bear in mind I'm going to need the potted version."

"First, then, let's talk about where we're staying. The Anen House Bed & Breakfast is the old Newman homestead. The late Annette lived there after the death of the Newman parents, but, since *her* death, Ellen has set it up as a B&B with two double rooms and a restaurant that, obviously, supplies breakfasts, but not just for residents. Apparently it's *the* place to go for breakfast in the whole area. You even have to book! The chef there, Pat Corrigan, makes award-winning sausages. It seems that while Annette Newman might have had a lock on all the gold medals when it came to wines, your Ellen has found herself a chef with the same sort of stranglehold on the world sausage-making circuit. I didn't even know there was such a thing. I must say, though, that I like the sound of it. I suppose that's why breakfast will be served there on both Saturday and Sunday, which makes life a little easier for us in the mornings."

"True," replied Bud, "and I guess it must be *very* good." He sounded quite excited.

"Anyway—there's the married couple who live at Anen House. They've been there since the place opened about eight months ago. Pat Corrigan is, as I said, the chef, and his wife, Lauren, is the housekeeper. Ellen hired them from a restaurant near Dublin, when it closed down. Clearly, she likes *him*, but merely tolerates the wife, whose cleaning standards are not quite the same as her own it seems, which is a bit alarming, since we're staying there. Mind you, it's unlikely we'd either of us notice the odd cobweb?"

"True," Bud replied. "I've got the excuse of having a muck-loving dog living in the apartment with me. I'm not sure you feel the need to have an excuse for not owning a long-handled feather duster, right?" He grinned.

"Oh, I *own* one," I countered. "I'm just not sure I *remember* where I left it . . ."

I grinned back, though Bud didn't see me because, very sensibly, he kept his eyes on the greasy road ahead.

"And there's me thinking you remember *everything* . . ." Bud smiled. *Bud's smile can be very distracting.*

"Possible cleanliness issues aside," I continued, "Ellen seems content that she has the right people running the B&B, but, from our point of view, as murder suspects—"

"Hey, they're *your* suspects, Cait, not mine. I'm still not convinced this wasn't a suicide."

"Okay, from *my* point of view," I conceded, "as murder suspects, the Corrigans, who I'm assuming are not just from Ireland but are in fact Irish, cannot be considered to be in the frame at all. They weren't in the country when Annette died."

Bud looked disgruntled, even though I'd given in to his rather sharply made point.

"Onwards and upwards," I continued, as our route did exactly that. "There's a whole collection of people listed as 'suspects'—Ellen's word, not mine, before you get on your high horse again, Bud Anderson. Saturday lunch will be hosted by the MacMillan family at their home, Lakeview Lodge—which I'm going to go out on a limb and guess overlooks the lake. He's something big in oil in Calgary, and she lives in Kelowna, in fine style by the sound of it. Ellen seems to think that Sheri MacMillan spends all her time wandering from day spa to day spa, sitting on committees, shopping, lunching, and spending her husband's money. She refers to her as 'vapid and fussy, but harmless.' Apparently, Rob MacMillan shows his face from time to time but basically spends the year in Alberta, where they have another house. Ellen admits to not knowing him very well. They have a seventeen-year-old son, who lives with his mother and attends high school in Kelowna, who Ellen describes as 'weird': she says he's quiet, lacks social skills, and is known for cycling around the area too fast. All three MacMillans were in town at the time of Annette's death, though Rob left on an early flight to Calgary the morning Ellen discovered her body. Ellen doesn't give any reasons for why any of these people might want Annette dead, so don't hold your breath waiting for motives to emerge," I added. I thought I'd better tell Bud sooner rather than later.

"I wasn't actually *expecting* any motives to be forthcoming," he replied calmly. "Ellen's told me on several occasions that Annette was universally loved and respected."

"Hmmm . . . well, that's not true about *anyone*," I replied, "except you, of course," I chuckled.

"Oh Cait—now you *know* that's not true . . ." Bud sounded sad, and I realized, too late, that I'd just said something stupid, thoughtless, and painful. The guy who'd shot Jan, Bud's late wife, had meant to kill Bud himself—*of course* there were people who hated him and wanted him dead.

"Oh Bud . . . I'm so sorry . . ." I faltered. At that moment I was terribly aware that Jan would always be with us, in some way.

"It's okay, Cait. It can't be helped," replied Bud, still sounding grim.

"Yes it can. I can be more damned thoughtful!" I was cross with myself, not Bud, but it didn't sound that way.

"Alright then, if it makes you feel better, go ahead and beat yourself up about it. But I won't do it for you, Cait. Blame. Guilt. 'Would-have. Could-have. Should-have.' None of it gets a person anywhere. Trust me on this: I've become something of an expert."

I didn't say anything for at least two minutes, which, for me, is a very long time indeed. I watched the road wind far ahead of us. I reasoned that I couldn't always walk on eggshells. I allowed the millions of trees covering the rolling mountains surrounding us to become a soothing blur.

Finally, Bud said, "Are you going to tell me about these people, or what? We're almost at the summit, so not much longer now. You'd better get a move on. I know you're bursting with it," and he smiled a warm smile that dissipated the tension and freed me to continue. *Bless him.*

"Right. Next up are the fabulous Sammy and Suzie Soul," I announced, rallying.

"*The* Sammy Soul?" queried Bud.

"Yep, *the* Sammy Soul who famously took every drug, drank every drink, and bonked every groupie available through the '60s and '70s."

Bud looked confused. "Bonked?"

"Yes, you know, 'had biblical knowledge of.' Though I cannot imagine there was any sort of ecclesiastical element involved."

Bud nodded. "Is that a Welsh-ism? Bonked?"

"No, but I suppose it's very British. *Bonk* means hit. You can *bonk* someone on the head; or cyclists *bonk* when they're tired, because they've hit a wall; and we Brits use it to mean hit in the sexual sense. But not like when North Americans say 'he *hit* on someone'—that just means chatting them up, not bonking them . . ."

"Ah, the joys of being separated by a common language," mused Bud, smiling. He often said that, especially when I lapsed into Brit-speak, as he liked to call it, or, even worse in Bud's book, Wenglish—a sort of middle ground that exists between Welsh and English, which really only exists around the Swansea and Swansea Valleys area, where

I'm from, so it's hardly surprising he can't make head nor tail of it!

I pressed on. "As I said, yes, *the* Sammy Soul who was well known for hell raising and womanizing, when he headed up his band the Soul Rockers. God, he could play that guitar! I have to admit, I thought he'd be dead by now. He probably *should* be. It looks as though he bought a winery in the Okanagan, now called SoulVine Wines, and he's been there for about twenty years. Who knew?"

"Well, not me, for one," said Bud, playing along.

"And not me, for two," I added, grinning. "He lives there with his wife, Suzie. She must be quite the strong character to have put up with him for the almost forty years that Ellen says they've been married. They also have a daughter, Serendipity. Poor thing. Imagine growing up with *that* as a name."

"Seems to fit the bill for the child of a rock star. Weird names were quite the fashion, once upon a time, right?" said Bud.

I chuckled. "You know, it could have been much worse for her, I suppose." My mind wandered to all those bizarre names that are carted about by the children of the hip and wealthy. I mentally thanked my parents for being so traditional in their choice. "Ellen reckons she's turned out to be quite a star in the kitchen. She trained in France and has an excellent reputation as a chef. She runs the restaurant at her parents' vineyard, SoulVineFineDine, which seems to be quite a mouthful for the name of a restaurant, but maybe that's the point. Anyway, it's where we'll be having dinner on Saturday evening, so we'll have a chance to see if Serendipity is all she's cracked up to be. Ellen only has good things to say about her, but her less than flattering comments about Serendipity's parents seem to indicate that Ellen's not too keen on *them*. She calls Sammy Soul 'drug-addled' and 'lacking a moral compass,' and she refers to his wife as 'a man-eating whore.'"

"Good grief." Bud seemed shocked. "I had no idea Ellen could be that—well, *bitchy* is the only word, right?" *Was Bud checking if my female perspective allowed for that word to be used?*

"Well, maybe *catty*," I replied, "but, you know, I'm trying to not be *too judgmental*, Bud."

"Oh, okay, touché!" He grinned. "I guess I can be a bit judgmental, too, under certain circumstances."

"Hmmm, right. Well, we'll both have a chance to assess *Ellen's* judgment tonight, when we meet these folks at the cocktail party, but, in the meantime, on to the next hosts. After another breakfast at our own domicile on Sunday morning, we'll be heading off to the Faceting for Life Restaurant on Pandosy Street in downtown Kelowna, where the owners, Grant and Lizzie Jackson, will be our hosts, and where Ray Murciano is the resident chef. Ellen says that Lizzie Jackson is an alarming woman originally from Phoenix, who met Grant Jackson at a 'Faceting Camp,' whatever that is, about five years ago. It's his second marriage, but it's Lizzie's first. He's originally from Vancouver. It seems that the Jacksons are into that whole sustainability/organic movement, as well as this Faceting thing, which Ellen reckons is the 'crack-pot scheme of some flaky so-called guru in Sedona'—her words. Bud raised an eyebrow-in-training. I chose to ignore him. "Lizzie Jackson is a 'healer.' Ellen says she practices hypnotherapy and aura alignment. She uses crystals, which is all bound up with the Faceting dogma, apparently. Sounds interesting," I added, pulling a face that Bud couldn't see.

His eyes were locked on the road ahead, which was a very good thing because we were at Pennask Summit, and swathed in icy fog. The road was slick and challenging, the winter's snow piled so high at the sides of the road that it towered over the huge trucks we carefully passed as they crept along. I inwardly praised Bud's insistence upon packing a shovel, warm blankets, a thermos, and lots of snacks.

From that point on, the journey was, quite literally, all downhill. It wouldn't be long until the landscape would open up ahead of us and show us the Okanagan Valley and the beauties it held. But there was a way to go yet. I carried on with my assigned task.

"In summary, we have the Irish Corrigans who live at the B&B; the Canadian and American Jacksons who live at Anen Close, located immediately below the B&B, and who run a shop and restaurant in Kelowna itself; the all-Canadian MacMillans who live in Lakeview Lodge, farther along Lakeshore Drive than Anen Close and the all-American Soul family, at SoulVine Wines in West Kelowna, the other bank of the lake. Other residents we'll meet are Gordy and Marlene Wiser, who also live in Anen Close, opposite the Jacksons, and have been there about four years. Both the Jacksons and the Wisers have lived in the two houses that comprise the Close since they were built, on part of the land that used to belong to the Newman homestead. Ellen says that the Wisers are very nice people, old, reliable, and trustworthy, but that he's a real nosey parker and she's fixated on her garden. Take that as you want."

"Then there's the du Bois family—parents Marcel and Annie, and their two daughters, Gabi and Poppy—they own and operate C'est la Vie, the French restaurant where we'll be dining on Sunday night. It seems that the parents had a background together in the food business in Montreal before they arrived in Kelowna, when they bought a rundown hole-in-the-wall and upgraded it to become a very well-respected brasserie-type restaurant, with a traditional menu and a reputation for fine ingredients and good cooking. He runs front of house, she's the chef, and the two girls wait tables. I must say, that's probably the meal I'm looking forward to the most. There's just something about French food . . ."

"That's not what you said when you got back from France last year," quipped Bud, still concentrating.

"True . . . but those *were* extraordinary circumstances, you have to admit," I added. "And in any case, I'm over all that now. And I mustn't let myself be sidetracked, even if I am hungry. Our final group are those Ellen describes as 'latecomers/others.' By 'latecomers,' I gather she means those who have been in the area for less than five years or so. I suppose that having grown up in the area she thinks of everyone who's been there for less than a lifetime as a latecomer, but this is her term so I'll use it. But, as far as her use of the word 'others' is concerned, well, it seems to me that she's discounting these people as suspects. First there's a guy called Vince Chen, who's the new vintner at SoulVine Wines. He's been in town for less than a year, so wasn't there when Annette died, and was brought in by Sammy Soul from a winery in Niagara, though he's originally from Vancouver. It seems that Sammy Soul's last vintner had to leave, because Ellen's sister Annette left him *her* half of the family wine business in her will."

"You're kidding," Bud responded sharply. "Ellen never mentioned that to me."

"Well, she's mentioned it in her notes. She says that Raj Pinder was the vintner at SoulVine Wines for about three years, then, when Annette's will was read, it came as a great surprise to everyone that she had left her entire interest in the business, which was fifty per-cent, to this relative stranger. Then she writes that she's very pleased her sister did that, because he's the best vintner in the business, now that her sister's no longer around."

"Weird," said Bud.

"Yep, definitely odd. Especially since she's put him into the non-suspects category. I think I need to poke around *that* a bit when I meet everyone."

"Poke away, Cait. Poke away," was Bud's rather patronising reply. I didn't rise to the bait.

I left it at that, because we'd finally rolled into West Kelowna. The picturesque highway was behind us, and endless strip malls now hedged both sides of the road. The highway had been busy with an unexpected number of trucks, given that it was Good Friday, and now the local roads were laden with folks hurrying from A to B, presumably stocking up for the Easter weekend's family feasts.

"How much farther, exactly?" I asked.

"I guess about half an hour or so, depending on the bridge," Bud replied. "It might be busy because it's lunchtime, or maybe not, because it's a holiday. It'll be what it'll be. Ellen is expecting us when we get there. I didn't say we'd be there at a certain time, just some time after lunch, which I guess it is, now," he observed.

I wondered if he assumed that a few cookies and a scone would hold me until dinner time, but I thought it best not to say anything. We were, after all, about to jump headlong into a gourmet weekend. Besides, it was clear from Bud's expression that the carefree road trip had now become a journey to a specific destination. I imagined he was not looking forward to meeting his "grief buddy." I knew I wasn't, but I didn't really know why.

As we wound down through West Kelowna and approached the Bill Bennett Bridge, the sun finally poked through the clouds, glinting off the sparse ribbon of vehicles below us. On the opposite side of the vast lake, the rapidly growing city of Kelowna nestled beneath the hillsides, which were yellow with wintry grasses and still showing patches of snow on the ground. Here and there were copses of pines that had survived the terrible forest fires a few years earlier.

"Gonna keep an eye out for Ogopogo as we cross the lake?" quipped Bud.

"Sure," I replied, smiling, "but give me a minute while I get my camera out—just one photo of the Loch Ness Monster's Canadian cousin, and we'd be worth a fortune." I love monster myths. The human distrust of deep bodies of water allows us to populate them with all sorts of terrifying creatures. Okanagan Lake, at almost eighty-five miles long and with water as deep as seven hundred and seventy feet, is prime monster-story territory. Of course, no one knew that the giant squid was a reality until the early twenty-first century. Out there somewhere, in one of the world's deepest and oldest lakes, there might actually lurk a creature descended more directly from the dinosaurs than even our feathered raptor friends. The world's such a fascinating place.

We zipped across Okanagan Lake and headed through the knots of traffic that jammed each of the city's crossroads, finally heading south along the edge of the lake. We passed undulating hillsides planted with neat rows of bare vines, but I could glimpse the white fuzz of blossom in apple orchards in the distance. The clouds had already broken, and it promised to be a golden afternoon.

"Okay, keep your eyes peeled," said Bud, as the pinging on the truck's GPS told us we were close to our destination. Clearly, we hadn't actually reached it, because we were on a bit of road that, while it gave us a wonderful view of the lake, didn't offer much else. We pulled over and looked around.

"There," said Bud with surprising certainty, given the narrowness of the track he was indicating.

We turned sharply away from the lake and the track soon presented a wider vista. To our right was a large, traditionally-designed, newly built house, to our left its mirror image—except that one was cream with blue trim, the other cream with red trim. Each house was set on about an acre of its own land. Between them, the track widened to a road that wound in hairpins up a steep hill to a small, older home, which sat atop the weird, knobbly hill. It looked rather like those houses that children draw, even to the picket fence that surrounded it.

A large sign at the foot of the winding road announced ANEN HOUSE B&B. As Bud changed gear to take the steep road ahead, I saw the curtains in the front window of the house to the right of us twitch. It must be the Wisers' house; anyone living there would have a great vantage point for keeping an eye on things in Anen Close, and at the B&B.

"So, there it is, then," I said to Bud solemnly as we wound upwards.

"Yes, and here *we* are," he replied.

"From now on, almost everyone we meet might be a possible suspect," I added.

"*If* Annette was murdered," he replied, pointedly.

A sign directed us to the RESIDENTS' GARAGE, a separate structure built for two large vehicles, set away to one side of the house. Soon Bud was carrying his bag, and I was wheeling my suitcase, along the narrow path that led from the picket fence toward the front of the house. Before we reached it, the red door flew open and a long-faced, lean woman of about thirty, with a sallow complexion and dark hair piled high on her head, came toward us.

"You must be Bud and Cait!" she exclaimed, almost by way of an accusation, scooping my suitcase from me as she limply shook Bud's free hand.

"Ellen told me you'd be here after lunch some time. Of course, we're happy you had a safe journey." She sounded like she wasn't happy about it at all. "Let me get you settled, then I'll call and tell her you're here." She was now holding open the front door and trying to usher us into the house, impatiently waving us in.

"Thanks," replied Bud hesitantly. I decided to let him take the lead on this; after all, I wasn't the *real* guest, he was. I was just his accompanying other.

Immediately I stepped inside the house, I fell in love with it: a symmetrical layout, sunshine-hued walls, vases of flowers dotted about. It felt like a home, not a temporary residence for nomadic tourists. The smell that filled the air made my tastebuds ache: some sort of beef and vegetable soup. I was instantly ravenous. I couldn't help but wonder if the food might be for us.

As if she were telepathic, the woman announced, "Pat, my husband, made some soup for you. *He* thought you might be hungry." She said it as though it were a very stupid idea.

Bless you Pat—I like you already!

"Oh, and I'm Lauren. Lauren Corrigan, general helper and chief dogsbody." The woman held out her hand to me, having balanced my battered suitcase in the entryway.

I shook her small hand and felt it crumple in my own. Closer to her now, I could see a network of fine lines on her face that suggested she was more used to frowning than smiling. She smelled of plain soap, and seemed haggard for her age. Not a happy woman, I suspected. Her body language backed me up. Every movement was filled with anger. She wrenched my suitcase back onto its little wheels and pointed toward the staircase that headed from the front door to the upper level.

"I'll take your bags up, you have something to eat." It sounded like an order. "Unless you want to freshen up, of course." She made "freshening up" sound sinful. "*Pat, they're here!*" she shouted, making both Bud and myself flinch. She wasn't the most welcoming of people.

Bud tried to get Lauren to allow him to take the bags upstairs himself, but she declined. "No, no, it's my job," she said. She was not very enthusiastic about it. Her accent was clearly Irish, and without many of the edges knocked off.

As Lauren began to clatter and bump up the stairs, huffing and puffing a short, red-headed man, in full chef whites appeared from a back room. He grinned broadly, almost wickedly.

"Ah-ha! Our esteemed weekend guests. You must be Bud." He shook Bud's hand politely but firmly. "And you must be Cait." He took my hand in both of his and shook it warmly. "I've been looking forward to meeting you. Ellen has spoken very highly of you, and with good reason, I'm sure." His lilt was even more pronounced than his wife's. Certainly a southern accent, but not Dublin, although Ellen had written that that was where she'd found him. Maybe Cork?

"You'll be wanting something to eat, I'm sure," said the chef, as though nothing could be more natural, or make him happier. "I've made a lovely soup for you, hearty but not too heavy, just right to get you through to dinner. You'll be glad, later on, that you've had it

now, given all the drinking you'll be doing with your food tonight."
Definitely Cork. Lovely accent.

Bud and I happily allowed Pat to seat us at one of the several
tables in what was clearly the breakfasting area. We greedily tucked
into the steaming, aromatic soup that he served to us, accompanied
by large chunks of fresh, homemade bread, and curls of yellow, salty
butter. It took us a while. Neither of us spoke, except to make little
noises that showed how delectable we thought the meal was. I love
the way that "*Mmmm . . .*" can speak volumes!

When we'd finished, we both pushed back a little from the table
and looked equally satisfied. Almost immediately Pat reappeared and
asked if everything was alright. Bud and I nodded.

As Pat collected our dishes, Bud asked, "Do you know what the
exact plan of action might be, Pat? Ellen's very kindly sent us an out-
line of what the weekend will hold for us, but she left us a bit in the
dark about where to be, and when, for this evening."

"Hmm—that's not like Ellen," remarked Pat with an impish
grin. "I reckon she'll be here very soon to tell you herself. Lauren
called her, and she said she'd be right over. Her office is at the vineyard, which is only about ten minutes along the road. You'll have
passed it on your way. I *do* happen to know that Ellen's booked a
taxi from her place to here, to collect you at six, and take all three of
you to the cocktail party at the Arts Centre downtown, which kicks
off at six thirty. And it's formal dress. Although it's only canapés,
you'll sure have plenty to eat there. The car'll bring you back here
afterwards. Knowing that lot, I think midnight'd be about right.
There's breakfast here at eight tomorrow morning, so we can't
come tonight. It'll be a busy night for me, and a busy morning
for me and Lauren both. Good fun, mind you. It's my first time,
you know. First time. Very exciting. Truth is, I'm a bit nervous,
all those folks eating my food, like? Used to some fancy fare, they
are. But not here. Ellen agreed—keep it simple, keep it plain. So

it's a traditional Irish breakfast you'll be getting tomorrow, and an Irishman's version of a 'North American' start to the day on Sunday. So think on that when you're noshing it up tonight, and save some room for my famous, award-winning bangers."

I asked, "How formal will it be tonight, Pat? Do you know?" Whatever I was going to wear I'd need to unpack it, check it over, possibly iron it. I'd need time to clean up, redo my hair . . . The list went on and on, and I could see that it was already past three in the afternoon.

"Compared with the old country, nothing seems very formal around these parts at all," replied Pat, smiling. "Unless it's a wedding, they all seem to make do with open-necked shirts, and even trousers for the ladies. But tonight . . . well, maybe you'd better ask Ellen. She'd know better than me."

As though on cue, Ellen Newman walked quietly through what had been her family's front door as she grew up, into what had, more lately, been her dead sister's home, and was now a place for fee-paying guests. I thought it odd that she looked around as though *she* were the guest, uncertain if it was acceptable for her to enter. I knew from her notes that about five years after her parents' deaths, she had chosen to move out to an apartment closer to the downtown core. Maybe that accounted for her manner: this *hadn't* been her home for a very long time.

Pat melted back into the kitchen bearing our bread-mopped bowls, a smile on his face.

Bud stood up and moved to greet Ellen. Of course we both recognized her from the photograph she'd sent, but I saw a woman who'd aged at least five years since that shot had been snapped. I knew from her notes that it had been taken just about a year earlier, a few days before her sister's death. Her once bouncy dark hair was now lank, with unflattering yellowish-gray strands popping up like little wires; there were dark circles under her once-bright eyes, and her mouth was set in a grim line. Her general size and shape didn't differ too much from the photograph, but she seemed to stoop, and looked frail. A couple of inches taller than me, so about five-five, she might have been five-six or -seven if she'd straightened her back. Bereavement can take its toll physically as well as emotionally.

"Ellen. It's good to meet you . . . at last," said Bud with feeling, as he strode across the hardwood floor to gather her in his arms in a warm embrace. She hugged him back. After a moment, they pulled back to look at each other smiling a rather awkward smile. Bud turned toward me and announced, "This is Cait, Ellen. The woman I love. I've spoken to you about her, I know."

I actually felt my jaw drop. "*The woman I love?*" Bud's told me he loves me many times and I have admitted that I love him too. But to hear it proclaimed that way? I was gobsmacked.

"It's just delightful to meet you both. Thanks for coming. I know it's going to be alright now. I trust you, Bud. *You'll* find out what happened to my Annette, won't you?"

And there it was. The *real* reason for us being here. Not the food, not the scenic drive, not the weekend together knowing that Marty was happily visiting doggie friends on acreage so he wouldn't bounce all over us when we were getting close. No, we were here to help Ellen.

Bud looked at me. We locked eyes for a moment, exchanged a slight smile, then he said, "Right, Ellen. We'll do what we can. So where do you want to start?"

And that's when the mood of the weekend *really* changed.

Listerine

"COME WITH ME," SAID ELLEN as she started up the stair-case. Bud nodded and we dutifully followed Ellen up the stairs. I took her cue to walk into the room that led off the righthand side of the landing. It was a beautifully decorated double guest room. Tastefully elegant. Paisleys, good landscape prints, and plain walls allowed the real focus to be on the wonderful views.

Once Bud and I were inside, she closed the door. She gestured to us to sit on the sofa nestled in front of the floor-to-ceiling window, overlooking the hairpin road we'd ascended and the glinting expanse of the lake beyond. She pulled a slipper chair from the corner and sat between us and the window. She became not much more than a silhouette. It gave her a conspiratorial air, and rather put us at a disadvantage. It was tough for me to read the finer points of her facial expressions. I tried shifting to get a better angle, but failed.

Ellen hunched toward us. "Tonight you'll get to meet *everyone*," she said determinedly. "I know how confusing it can be to meet a lot of people all at once and to have to remember them all, so that's why I prepared those notes for you. Did you read them?" She seemed over-eager. "If you're going to work out who wanted to hurt Annette, you'll need to hit the ground running," she added, as Bud gave me a rather alarmed glance. Clearly, neither of us had expected *this*.

Bud scratched his head, but he didn't say anything. I looked at Ellen, then Bud, and decided I should speak.

"Yes, Bud let me have a look at your notes—I hope you don't mind?"

"Oh no, not at all. Anything either of you can do—really, any-thing—would be helpful. Thank you." She was very intense.

"Well, I do have a couple of questions for you, but if now's not a good time . . ."

"Oh no, now's fine. Just fine," she was almost panting with excitement.

"Okay then. Ellen, on the third page of your notes you've referred to Sammy Soul of SoulVine Wines as a 'drug-addled, ageing hippie with no moral compass.' Do you know for a fact that he still does drugs, or are we talking about all the acid he famously dropped in the '60s and '70s, when he was making his lead guitar bleed and scream as the front-man for the Soul Rockers?"

Ellen gathered herself quickly and replied, angrily, "No one ever sees him taking drugs, but he can't possibly be the way he is without them. Besides, he keeps going on about how it should be legal to grow cannabis for your own use and then to be able make wine with it, like they do in some places in California. In fact, I'm pretty sure he's doing it already." That seemed to settle it for her, and it helped me to build another layer of her psychological profile. I know Bud reckons I'm sometimes alarmingly judgmental—but I thought Ellen Newman might actually be more so.

"Have you lived here all your life?" I enquired, tactfully trying to change the subject to one that might infuriate her less.

"Why would I leave?" was her reply. Her tone spoke volumes. She didn't say it happily, but with a venom that suggested she'd be just as unhappy anywhere.

As I dwelt momentarily on Ellen's reply, Bud *finally* stepped up and asked, "You went to university in Vancouver, right?"

"Oh yes," replied Ellen coolly. "But I didn't like it there. The people were cold and hard. Always trying to get on. And the city was dirty and noisy." The straight line that was her mouth became thinner and more firmly fixed.

I suspected that Ellen had left her home to go to a city she'd been determined to dislike, and she'd done just that. People always seem to forget that they pack their own emotional baggage and lug it about with them everywhere they go.

Changing tack, Bud asked, "Ellen, who have you told these folks I am? How will you introduce me?" It was a good question.

"Well, I've thought about that and I'm going to say you are: Bud Anderson, my 'grief buddy.' They'll understand that. They all know about my online stuff."

I didn't know who was more surprised, me or Bud.

"That's all supposed to be *private*, Ellen. We've blogged a great deal about how it's the privacy that allows us all to write as we do. The anonymity that allows us to open up. You've written that yourself. *More* than once." Bud sounded frustrated.

"Yes, but it's different now. We *know* each other. We can be open about it all. Besides, I've already told Pat and Lauren Corrigan and *they* were okay with it."

"And what have you said about *me*?" I wondered. Aloud, as it turned out.

"Oh, I've just told them you're his girlfriend. No one knows what you do. Actually, Bud hasn't even told *me*. It never came up. What *do* you do? Is it interesting?"

I gave it a split-second's thought and blurted out, "Marketing professor. At the University of Vancouver. Business school!" Bud looked at me as though I'd had a stroke. "It's fascinating. I love it. Been there ten years."

"Nice," Ellen replied, smiling. "I studied at the UVan business faculty about twenty years ago. Is Professor Colling still there?"

Oh damn and blast! I had no idea who Professor Colling was, or whether he, or she, might still be at the university.

Luckily for me, Ellen answered her own question by adding, "Oh, but that's a silly question, of *course* she won't be. She was ancient when *I* was there. She's probably dead by now. And good riddance."

"Well, back to the matter at hand," I said, trying to escape from any more close calls. "I know that you're due to collect us here in a cab at six o'clock this evening and that dress is formal tonight, so I'm assuming a long dress will be okay for that?" I raised my eyebrow in query, and Ellen nodded. "Right, well, that means I'm going to have quite a bit of getting ready to do. I'd like to clean up a bit, and so forth, before I dress. Would it be alright if we meet you downstairs here at five thirty, in case we have any more questions before we leave? Could the cab wait?" I thought that my rapid exit strategy might be a bit abrupt, but Bud was raking his hair with frustration, looking worried, and seemed keen to get away. I knew I was.

"Oh, absolutely," agreed Ellen with enthusiasm, and she bounced up out of her chair, put it back in its place and started toward the door. "This'll be your room, Bud, and Cait's across the hall. Unless you'd rather be the other way around. It's just you two this weekend, so you'll have the place to yourselves—well, except for Lauren and Pat, of course. They live in. Well, out back, in the double-wide. But that was in my notes, right? Yes. They won't be a bother, though— they'll be pretty busy getting things ready for tomorrow's breakfast. Let's get tonight behind us first. See you, ready to go, at five thirty, and we can clear up anything you need to know before we leave. Byeee . . . lovely to see you both and thanks so much for coming." And she was gone.

I sat down again, hard, having risen to accept her parting words. We sat there until, from my vantage point, I could see her walking out of the front door. Then I turned to Bud and said, "Having promised in the truck to hold off with my opinions until I'd met the woman—I have now met her, and she's a *nut job*, Bud!"

"And that's your calm, analytical, professional psychologist's opinion?" he replied, shaking his head.

"Sometimes, Bud, I revert to the vernacular so that non-psychologists like you can understand what I'm talking about. The full two barrels of vernacular assessment are that anal, she's judgmental, she's closed-minded, she's *small*-minded. She's poorly read, hasn't been exposed to anything but a traditional, locally based way of life. She's unused to male attention, might have had a boyfriend or two when young, but nothing serious—not for them, anyway, but maybe for her. She's controlling, she's passive-aggressive, she's repressed—in every way. Do you want me to go on?"

"How about the fact that she's grieving her dead sister and can't see the wood for the trees?" asked Bud pointedly.

I sighed. "You're right," I admitted. "I'm being too harsh. *Too judgmental.*" I smiled guiltily at him. "She's operating under duress, and her sense of perspective is likely to be way off. This might be unusual behavior for her and then again it may not be. That's part of the problem. Everything's coming at us from *her* point of view, and we don't know how true, or off center, that is."

Bud nodded. "Talking about *off*—what was all that about being a *marketing* professor? You could have given me the heads-up on *that* one."

I shrugged. "I made a split-second decision, Bud. It might be too late for you to be anonymous here, and, given what you've done for a living, it was always likely that it wouldn't have worked anyway." Bud nodded his agreement. "But there's no reason for folks to know that I'm a criminal psychologist. That's *not* the sort of person a murderer usually opens up to, so I thought it was better to be something that no one would bat an eyelid at."

"Nearly got caught there though, eh?" Bud grinned.

Again, I shrugged. "Yep, I never thought of that. I'll be better prepared when I meet the other suspects. I'll draw on my time back in London when I worked for that advertising agency, and waffle on a bit about return on investment and brand building . . . if I have to talk about anything to do with marketing at all. After all, it's unlikely, right? I mean, we're both going to be trying to direct our conversations towards possible motives, opportunities, and all that. *Right?*"

Bud shifted uncomfortably.

"Come on, Bud. That's why we're here. That's why we've come. Well, Annette's death, *and* the food, of course."

"Diet on the back-burner this weekend?" he asked.

I patted my tummy. "I'll start again on Tuesday."

"Good luck with that." He smiled indulgently.

I dragged my thoughts away from the long days filled with little more than Greek yogurt and lettuce that I'd have to endure for weeks to make up for my forthcoming indulgences, and refocused on the matter at hand.

"Listen, Bud, about Ellen's notes: the physical descriptions and the factual backgrounds—you know, who does what and lives where—might be useful, but I don't think we should rely on any of the character assessments she's written. Maybe I should just call them what they are—character *assassinations*. People might not have had a bad word to say about her dead sister, but she sure as hell has a lot of bad things to say about everyone we're about to meet. Something I didn't have a chance to comment upon before we got here was that she says nothing at all about Annette in the notes, other than, as I just mentioned, that no one ever had a bad word to say about her. Now, if, as you say, she also told you that everyone loved Annette, I don't quite know what she expects us— sorry, *you*—to do. Why would *anyone* want Annette dead? Well, other than this Raj Pinder, the guy who inherited half of Ellen's family business . . ."

I suspected that Bud was desperate to gloat, but he didn't. "Yes, okay, I admit it's not looking too fruitful on the motive front yet," I continued, "but it's early days yet, right? Maybe we'll meet someone with clear homicidal tendencies at the party tonight. I really do want to clean up, and I'll need to take my time getting ready. First impressions are so important."

"Yep, me too. I could do with a long, hot shower, to ease the stiffness in my legs and back a bit. In my *own* shower, of course, in my *very own* bathroom!" He smiled. Naughtily. "You got all that, eh? The separate rooms?"

"Yes, Bud. Hence *repressed*!" The question of rooms, and sharing, hadn't even crossed my mind until Ellen had mentioned it. The weekend was about food, wine and probable murder, in that order.

"I'm fine with separate rooms. Then I can take as much time in the bathroom as I like. Okay with you?" I asked. Bud nodded, still grinning wickedly. "You'd better come across the corridor and get your bag, if that's where it is. Then I can jump in the shower and get ready for this thing we're going to tonight."

As soon as Bud had left, I brushed my teeth, twice, and gargled with Listerine until my eyes watered. It was the only alternative to having a cigarette, which wasn't an option, because Bud had made me promise I wouldn't smoke all weekend.

Finally, my fussing and primping, which seemed to take forever, was done, and Bud knocked on my door at five-twenty-five, with a warm smile on his face, and his arms open wide.

"You smell good," he said, reaching out to hug me.

"You too," I replied, as I tried not to get lipstick on his jacket or my hair caught under his arms.

He looked very handsome in his dark navy suit, crisp white shirt, and red and gold striped tie. In an effort to be more dressy I'd decided to keep my hair down, rather than tied back, which is my normal thing. I'd done my best with curling tongs, half a container of mousse that's supposed to give volume to fine hair, and enough hairspray to jeopardize the entire ozone layer. But I wasn't happy with the outcome. Something which Bud quickly deduced.

"Your hair looks great when it's down like that, Cait." He smiled again. "Honestly. I wouldn't say it if I didn't mean it and you look lovely in that gown. It's very flattering."

"It's plain black, with a jacket to hide my arms, and you've seen it before," I replied sulkily.

Bud pulled up my chin and looked deep into my eyes. "Caitlin Morgan. You're gorgeous. I love you. Do you care what other people think of you? I mean, *really*?"

I smiled back up at him. "I love you too. That you think I am gorgeous means the world to me." All of which was true. "And I *don't* care what anyone else thinks of me, you're right." We kissed. Gently.

"Are you two coming down?" called Ellen Newman from the bottom of the stairs, brightly enough, but I was convinced she thought we were up to something.

"Coming right down," I replied, just as brightly. Bud and I followed her into the little lounge area to the left of the staircase, the mirror image of the breakfasting area we'd been in earlier that afternoon.

The aroma of the wonderful soup had been replaced by something more oniony, herby, and porky, yet still pleasant, but the matter at hand was still murder. We settled into comfy chairs, and I opened with, "Thanks for taking the time to write all those notes— they've been most helpful," I half lied. "I don't think there's anything else we need to know right now except, maybe, one or two things." Bud was on the edge of his chair, probably worried about what I was going to say.

"Anything," replied Ellen, who seemed to think that a short, forest-green velvet skirt, with a too-vivid orange silk blouse worn loosely over it, comprised formal wear. I could tell by the way she was eyeing us that she felt uncomfortable about something, so before I started to ask questions about Annette's death, I thought it best to follow my instincts.

"Is something wrong?" I asked.

Ellen wriggled in her seat. "Not really," she replied, clearly not meaning it.

"Are you sure?" asked Bud, quickly following my lead.

Ellen sighed. "It's just that I thought that *you'd* be the one helping me, Bud. Not that I wouldn't want *your* help, too, Cait. But Bud's the one with the policing background. *His* experience is what counts here. That's why I really asked you to come. When I was here earlier, Cait was the one asking all the questions. And now, with all due respect and all that, it seems like you're going to do the same thing again." She almost glared at me.

She had a point. A marketing professor probably wouldn't be the one doing the interrogating if there was an ex-cop in the room. Luckily, Bud came to the rescue.

"I know what you mean, Ellen," he said reassuringly, "and I also know it's *my* opinion you're really interested in. But I told Cait she could be involved, and she's often discussed other cases with me. Besides, she was a real help, reading your notes aloud to me as we drove here," he lied, "so she's as up on the facts as I am. Possibly more so, because I was concentrating on the road. In any case, two brains are always better than one, right, Ellen? You see, while *you* value my professional input, *I* know the value of Cait's amateur approach. It helps me see things from a different point of view."

Ellen nodded grudgingly, and I suspected that Bud was beginning to enjoy painting me as a rank outsider in the world of crime detection.

"So," continued Bud, immediately comfortable in his role as head-of-investigation, "would it be possible to see the coroner's report, the will, and at least a copy of your sister's suicide note?"

The words hung heavily in the air. The clock on the wall tocked away five seconds. I counted. I wondered if Ellen had counted too, because she spoke exactly on the sixth beat.

"I have all that at home, not with me. I remember her note word for word. Do you want me to recite it?"

She sounded like a little girl offering to run through Wordsworth's "Daffodils" for her parents or teachers.

Both Bud and I nodded. It would be useful to know what it had said, even if we couldn't immediately see how it had been written. Ellen cleared her throat and began. "It said, 'Ellen, It's no use, I can't do it anymore. I can't go on. It just won't work. I can't do my job any more. And if I can't do my job perfectly, then there's no point to any of it. I'm sorry. I know you'll miss me. But that's it. I'm done. Love, always, Annette.' And then were three x's. You know, kisses. That's it." She looked at both Bud and myself as if seeking our approval.

"Good job, Ellen," Bud said, "that can't have been easy for you. Those words must hurt." She nodded. "Are you sure it was Annette's handwriting?" he asked, as gently as he could.

"Oh no, she didn't *write* it, Annette never *wrote* anything . . . her handwriting had always been dreadful, so she always typed every-thing." Ellen seemed surprised that Bud would have asked.

"But she signed it, at least?" Bud added.

"Oh yes, she'd signed it," replied Ellen calmly. "Of course she *signed* it."

Bud and I exchanged a glance.

I couldn't help myself—I jumped in. "So are you sure it was Annette's signature?" I asked.

"Well I was . . . and then I wasn't," was Ellen's less than illuminat-ing response.

"So you mean . . . ?" I didn't dare continue.

"Oh . . . right . . . yes." Ellen seemed to sense my confusion. "At first I thought it *was* Annette's signature, but then I realized a while later that of course it *couldn't* have been, because there's no way she'd have killed herself, so there's no reason why she'd have signed a suicide note. So it can't be Annette's signature, you see."

Any minute now I'd be rushing outside for a cigarette—however much it might annoy Bud. There's only so much that nicotine gum can help you handle.

"So it looked like her signature, but you're now sure it wasn't?" I quizzed.

"Yes. No. It can't be." Ellen seemed to be done.

I was beginning to lose the will to live.

"Okay, so, one more thing then," added Bud, "could you dig out an example of your sister's signature that you know is definitely hers? Then we can compare them all." Ellen nodded.

I managed to give Bud a quick kick. Luckily, he worked out what it meant.

"We do have a few more questions, but I promised Cait she could talk to you about them. You don't mind, do you?"

Ellen now seemed quite relaxed with the idea that I would have an involvement in the case too, so I dove right in. Smiling.

"Your notes say that Raj Pinder, who is now the vintner at your winery, used to be the vintner at SoulVine Wines, right?" Ellen nodded. "Raj now owns half your vineyard—that Annette willed her half of the business to him—and that you're *pleased* that she did that, is that right?" Again, Ellen nodded. "So, did you know about Annette's intentions before she died? Had you discussed that with her at all?"

Ellen smiled, "Oh silly me," she began. "I guess I didn't put *that* in the notes. I'm sorry, it's just that everyone here knows what happened. A week before Annette died, she changed her will. She left her half of the vineyard to Raj, instead of to me. We only all found out when the will was read, and that was weeks later. So, no, I wasn't expecting it. No one was."

Ellen seemed calm as she announced that she'd been robbed of what she must have always assumed was her birthright. Bud couldn't hide his surprise at Ellen's delivery of this explanation.

I could see his hand begin to move towards his now perfectly combed hair and I shook my head and made eyes at him. He sat on his hand.

"I'm sorry, Ellen," he said, sympathetically. "That must have come as a shock for you. I guess you expected that the whole business would be yours?"

"Well, of course I did. Mom and Poppa built it from nothing! They imported the vines, they planted it all. And then it was me and Annette who got the real benefits of the crops, and we were able to make wonderful wines because of Annette's gift. And, yes, I did think it would all be mine. But Raj is a good and kind man, and he's an excellent vintner. He hasn't got as good a nose as Annette had, but he took silver behind her golds for the three years he was with SoulVine Wines, so he's not only the best in the area, but he's just about the best in North America. I'm glad to have him. Without *him* joining the business, I'd have had to find a vintner from overseas, or use someone from Canada or the USA who isn't as good as Raj. I'm so lucky that Annette thought of it. When Raj found out about it, he left SoulVine Wines *immediately*. He couldn't work for anyone other than the company in which he's a fifty-fifty owner and we get along really well. He has a wonderful vision for the business. I think that Mt Dewdney has a fabulous future ahead of it, and Raj and I will enjoy running it together."

"Ellen," said Bud in a commiserating tone, "do you think that Annette might have planned the whole thing? That she was depressed, set things up for you in a way that would be good for the business, but had just . . . had enough?" To be fair, he had a point.

Ellen stood up and clenched her fists as she answered, "No! Annette wouldn't have! She would never have killed herself! Oh Bud—I thought *you* believed me. You, of *all* people!"

"It's okay"—I used my calming voice—"Bud's just playing devil's advocate, right, Bud?" I glared at him.

"Yes, yes, Cait's right," he lied. "I have to be sure before I go digging about. And, obviously, you're quite certain. So that's good. Well . . . not *good*. You know what I mean . . ." he stammered. He stood up and announced, "I'm sorry. I hope you don't think we're rude, Ellen, but Cait hasn't quite kicked the smoking thing yet, and I know she'll be hoping to have a quick puff before we hop into that taxi outside to leave for dinner. We'll just head outside to the smoking porch at the side of the house for a few minutes, if that's alright?"

Now it was my turn to look at Bud as though he was having some sort of life-threatening episode, but, never one to turn down the chance to have a smoke without him nagging me to stub out, I was out of my seat as quickly as possible.

"You should speak to Lizzie Jackson about that," called Ellen as I headed toward the front door. "She's helped Serendipity Soul give up, *and* she got Marcel du Bois to kick the habit, which, given who *he* is and how attached he was to his cigarettes, and I mean that literally, is quite something. So maybe she has *some* redeeming qualities."

"Thanks, I'll bear that in mind." I replied to Ellen's backhanded compliment to Lizzie Jackson as politely as I could, while pulling open the front door and heading off to the smoking porch as fast as my feet could take me, leaving Bud trailing behind.

Even before I got there I was lighting up. "So," I inhaled as I spoke, "interesting, right? A *changed* will, a *typed* suicide note with a possible *fake* signature. It all points to murder."

"No, Cait, it's a *real* suicide note, signed by Annette, but read by a sister who can't forgive herself for not seeing her own sibling's anguish. If Annette had been planning to kill herself, she might well have had the foresight to make sure that the next best vintner for the job would be bound to take it because he'd be part-owner. Besides," he added somewhat grumpily, "look, there's no way anyone could get up to this garage, where Ellen found her, without those nosey neighbors at the bottom of the hill seeing them approach. It's *definitely* a suicide, I'm even more certain now."

"And I'm even more certain that it was murder," I replied, cockily puffing toward Bud.

"*Why?*" he cried. "What are you hearing or seeing that I'm not?"

"Who stood to gain by her death, Bud? Ask yourself that. Not Ellen, she's lost control of the family business. But this Raj character does. In Ellen's notes, he's almost the only one about whom she didn't write a bad word. I reckon he's trying to worm his way into her affections, and that he's succeeding. It sounds like he's as good as running things now—it's all about 'his vision.' I don't get the impression Ellen would argue against him if he said black was white. It's a pretty good motive, Bud, you have to admit. He sounds dodgy to me."

Bud was tapping his foot. "Dodgy, eh? Is that another of your 'technical terms?'" he sighed. "Finished that thing yet?" he asked crossly.

"Hey, you're the one who used my 'filthy habit' to give us a chance to vent about Ellen. Don't you go venting at me instead!"

"Sorry," he said sheepishly.

"Me too," I said, puffing hard.

Ellen emerged from the house and made her way to the waiting taxi. I ground the remains of my tiny cigarette into the sparklingly-clean ashtray that stood on the plastic table tucked beneath the roof of the porch.

"Time to go?" I asked, knowing the answer.

"Time to go," replied Bud. "You'd better be sharp tonight, Cait. You know how much I value your skills, and we'll need them all. You can read people against the notes that Ellen has given us and you can use your wonderful photographic memory to conjure up the events of the evening for us to discuss at leisure afterwards. *And* you can make me proud to be the man who's bringing the best looking woman in the world to the party." He smiled.

"Thanks, Bud. That's kind of you."

"No, it's not 'kind' of me, I really mean it," he replied abruptly.

"Oh, but my hair . . ."

"Oh, for goodness sake, shut up about your damned hair. It looks great! Just learn to accept a compliment, Cait."

"I can't help it. I haven't had a lot of experience at receiving them."

"Well, get used to it, or I'll stop giving them to you."

I was beaten, and knew it. I sighed.

"Okay. Thanks for the hair comment. Let's just hope it stays where I've put it," I sulked.

Bud lost it. "Oh, good grief," he tutted and began to walk away.

"Don't go, Bud. I'll be good." I added, "Let's try and have a good time, even though we're sort of working. I *am* looking forward to the food, after all. Is that bad of me?"

Bud didn't answer. Instead, he opened the door of the taxi, I wriggled my way inside, he followed, and we all set off for what was to turn out to be a very eventful evening. And *not* in a good way.

Gamay Noir

THE "COCKTAILS AND CANAPÉS" LAUNCH event for the Moveable Feast wasn't quite what I'd expected. For some reason, I'd imagined an elegantly attired gathering bubbling along wittily, in something akin to the great hall of an historic English manor house. What I got was a small, almost rag-tag group of people rattling around under the beautiful but yawning wood-beamed glass atrium of a very modern building in downtown Kelowna. To be fair, the organizers had installed drapes to contain about half the room, and had provided dim lighting instead of overhead fluorescent, but our voices floated up to the glass that arced above us, then bounced back. Most people tried to talk in hushed tones, as though in a cathedral.

I declined a cocktail in favor of a glass of fruity gamay noir, one of Ellen's, of course, which had a good body, but wouldn't be too heavy to drink for an entire evening. And the canapés were exquisite: tiny little martini glasses filled with cold, savory soups—the strawberry and basil was particularly wonderful; tender local meats, marinated in tongue-tingling herbs or rubbed with nose-tickling spices, presented on pretty bamboo skewers; little pastry packages full of flavor that burst in my mouth with cheesy, fishy, or mushroomy delights. Oh, it was wonderful. I was sorry that I had to give my attention to the folks Ellen was keen to introduce to Bud and me.

When I felt I'd taken the edge off my appetite a little, and had managed to grab a second glass of wine, Sammy Soul was high on the list of people I wanted to meet, but for personal reasons rather than murderous ones. He'd supplied parts of the soundtrack to my teen years with the string of hits from his San Francisco-sound band, Soul Rockers. His wailing guitar riffs had sounded wonderfully raw and dangerous to a young girl listening to her transistor radio under the sheets long after bedtime, in 1970s Swansea. I'd have recognized him even without Ellen's notes, because he hadn't changed a bit— except now he was in his seventies, was completely bald, had filled out somewhat, and was more ruddy in his complexion. Otherwise, it seemed that Sammy Soul had decided to ignore the ageing process and was still dressed in tight snakeskin jeans, with a magenta silk shirt—straining at its buttons—and more earrings than you would think is possible for the human ear to carry. The earring thing was helped by the fact that, as with most older men, his lobes had lengthened. It seemed he'd taken this as a sign to add even more gold hoops. My heart sank when I saw him: my youthful idol, now a pastiche of himself.

After Ellen had introduced us, I reached out to shake his hand. When he replied with a peace sign and drawled "Yeah, man," in a slightly nasal voice, higher-pitched than I'd imagined, my heart sank even further. And then, when he slapped Bud on the arm and added, "Ex-cop. Wow, man. Lost your wife? Downer," I could have groaned out loud. Could this sad, pathetic figure, clinging to past glories, have wanted to kill Annette Newman? First I'd have to find a motive, and, surprise, surprise, his wife all but handed me one on a plate.

"Hey, meet the missus," said Sammy Soul as he waved in the general direction of a woman's back. "Hey guys, this is Suzie, my Soul-Mate . . . ha, ha!"

I saw the back of a short, slim but curvaceous, beautifully coiffed long-haired blonde, wearing an immaculately cut, bronzy pantsuit, and leopard-skin Louboutin heels. Elegantly holding a martini glass, her perfectly manicured left hand was bedecked with umpteen carats of bling and sported long, curving nails encrusted with diamanté.

When Suzie Soul turned, what I saw was a shock: the woman was in her sixties—you can always tell because of the neck—and had the cat-like features that scream *bad plastic surgery*. She was caked in layers of carefully applied but woefully obvious makeup, and, as if to add insult to injury, her lips had been plumped to alarming proportions and were the color of dried blood. I tried to hide my shock as she flashed a perfect porcelain smile at me and extended her other equally decorated hand in my direction. As she allowed me to shake her fingertips she was looking at Bud—*or should I say eating him alive with her eyes?* I bristled.

Bud beamed.

"Hi. Always happy to meet friends of Ellen's," she purred in gravelly tones. "I didn't catch y'rrrr name," she drawled provocatively, directly at Bud.

"That's 'cos I didn't throw it, Babe," replied Sammy Soul, laughing too loudly at his own joke. "He's an ex-cop, would you believe, Babe? Doesn't look like any cops *I* know. And, jeez, there've been a few over the years," he added.

"So pleased to meet you, uh . . . ?" As she waited for Bud to respond with his name, she actually ran her tongue along the edge of her upper teeth.

Bud, ever polite, took her extended hand and said, "Bud. Bud Anderson." Was he blushing? Good grief, men can be pathetic—and predictable!

"And what brings you to these parts, Bud?" She was tilting her head by now. She'd have been playing with her hair too, if Bud hadn't still been hanging on to her free hand. She was in full-on flirting mode. I gritted my teeth. "Have you come to arrest Sammy for making his *oh-so delicious* cannabis wine?" she added coquettishly. "Oh, *please* don't, Bud. He *is* my husband, you know. And it's *lovely* wine, whatever that bitch Annette might have said about it."

I was on full alert. So no one ever had a bad word to say about

Annette, eh? Well, here was one woman who did. She spat out the word *bitch* with true hatred. And he husband *was* already making cannabis wine? Very interesting.

"No, no," replied Bud, looking like a deer in headlights. "I'm retired now, you know. Quite retired."

"His wife got shot, Babe. Shot dead. That's how he met Ellen. They're, like, 'death buddies' or something."

I judged that Suzie Soul was more disappointed that Bud had finally relinquished his grasp on her talons than sad that he'd lost his wife. She made a pouty face, then proved me right. "Oh Bud," she sighed, "I'm *so* sorry. So you're *single* now?"

"No, he's not. He's with me," I inserted abruptly.

Bud looked surprised.

Sammy Soul smiled and said, "Oh yeah, Babe, he's with her," as though this thought was occurring to him for the first time.

His wife looked me up and down, slowly and unkindly, tried to curl one of her unnatural lips, and said coolly, "Oh *really*? I wonder *why* . . ." Then she turned on her nine-hundred-dollar heels and walked away throwing the words "See you boys later—especially *you*, Bud Anderson" in our direction, with a wink, a nod, and a shrug of one shoulder.

I wondered if Bud could see the steam coming out of my ears. His smile suggested he couldn't.

"Hasn't changed a bit in thirty-six years, my Suzie. That's how long we've been together," said Sammy Soul, smiling like the village idiot. He was clearly besotted. Though how he'd put up with her for that long, I didn't know. He became even more pathetic in my eyes, for letting himself be walked all over by that . . .

"I'm sure she hasn't," Bud remarked cryptically, which cut across my less than charitable thoughts. He smiled at me when he said it, which helped. "And that's a fantastic marriage to have had, in your business," he added.

"Sure is," Sammy replied, still beaming. "Married her when she was in her twenties, just before we had Serendipity, our beautiful, magical girl. But, hey, you know man, she's not just the mother of my child, she's a forgiving woman, and I'm a forgiving man," observed Sammy, his eyes gazing into the nothingness ahead of him. "Forgiveness is important, right, man? You gotta forgive to be forgiven, you know? *Gotta* forgive. I'd forgive that woman anything . . ."

"And I bet you have, many times," I said. Aloud.

Bud glared at me. Sammy just nodded. He looked resigned.

"Sure have, man, sure have. Man—I'd even forgive her icing someone, if it was, like, to save my hide, or something." He seemed to be in his own little world, then it was as though a light came on and he snapped back to our shared reality. "Not that she would, cop-guy, not that she *would*. Ha, ha! Hey, gotta go. *Gotta* see my man Grant over there," he said, waving at nothing in particular but ambling off in the direction of a short, very thin man wearing a burgundy-colored Nehru jacket.

I wanted to take my chance to have a few private words with Bud, but he was quicker off the mark than me.

"What do you think?" he whispered.

"She should have spent more money on a better plastic surgeon?" I replied somewhat wickedly.

Bud shoved me and looked shocked, "Oh stop it, you devil. Be *serious*!" Then he broke into a smile. "Oh, Cait—you do make me laugh." And he did.

He leaned toward me as though to plant a kiss on my cheek, but Ellen's imminent return meant I pulled away and hissed "Stop it," then giggled like a schoolgirl.

Ellen was beaming, maybe a little too brightly, when she rejoined us. "They're a real couple of characters, eh?" she said, nodding her head in the general direction of the Souls. "Do you think one of *them* did it?" Her eyes gleamed conspiratorially in the dim lights.

I thought about the way Ellen had described Sammy and Suzie Soul in her notes. She'd been spot-on with her physical descriptions—though rather more kind than I had been about Suzie—and I was beginning to think she wasn't far off the mark when it came to her assessments of their characters, too.

"They could have done it together, you know," she continued, her zeal unabated. "Annette said she didn't trust Sammy when he was negotiating for Marechal Foch grapes from us. That he was manipulative, and bossy." I had a hard time picturing the chilled out Sammy Soul as either.

"You sell grapes to SoulVine Wines?" I was puzzled.

"Oh yes," replied Ellen, as though it were the most natural thing in the world. "Mom and Poppa started by just growing grapes to sell to other people, which is why we have some of the more unusual varieties, like Foch—we have malbec and zweigelt too—then, eventually, they began to make Anen Wines. Some years we have more than we need of several varieties, so we'll sell them off to other wineries for them to use. Of course, we keep everything we want for ourselves first, though *some* people would like us to be actively growing on their part, like SoulVine Wines. Sammy argued that we could apportion part of our crop to him each year even before we knew what the yield and quality were going to be. Annette said no, Anen would always come first. That's why he's playing around with all these crazy ideas like cannabis wine, and wine in guitar-shaped bottles. It's nuts. It's all just *marketing* stuff. You know, the sort of thing *you* do." Ellen made it sound as though it was *my* fault that Sammy Soul was jeopardizing the purity of winemaking. It seemed that choosing the fake role of a marketing professor was going to bring me in for some hearty criticism. *Who knew!?*

Ellen was pulling at my wrist. "I know Raj can't have had anything to do with Annette's death, but I do so want you to meet him." She turned and looked toward the other side of the room. "Damn, that stupid Serendipity is talking to him now," she observed." Oh well, never mind, let's butt in—he won't mind," and we were off, with Bud following meekly behind, and me trying to not spill my drink.

"Raj, this is Bud and his partner, Cait. Bud, Cait—Raj Pinder. *My* partner," she grinned. "Oh," she added, as if an afterthought, "and this is Serendipity—you just met her parents, Sammy and Suzie."

We all nodded and said, "Hi."

Both Raj Pinder and Serendipity Soul were slim and well formed, towered over me, which immediately made me feel short, and very wide. They made a handsome couple. And couple they were, I was immediately certain about that. Their body language, the way they related to each other, literally screamed *lovers* at me, but from what I had gathered from Ellen's notes, they weren't known to be an item. Or at least Ellen didn't believe them to be so.

Raj Pinder had finely chiseled features, latte-colored, even-toned skin and well-styled ink-black hair, with a few strands of pure white threaded through it here and there, as befitted a man of about forty. He wore his expensive suit and snowy open-necked shirt very well indeed. And he spoke with the twang you only develop if you've grown up in the north of England.

"Hello Bud and Cait," he said, his voice strong, yet soft. "Pleased to meet you. As Ellen said"—he nodded first at Ellen, then Serendipity— "this is Serendipity Soul, a very talented chef and someone I enjoyed working with for several years. In fact," and here he patted his annoyingly flat midriff, the way slim people do when they think they've gained an ounce, "I'm only just now losing all them pounds she made me gain, feeding me at her restaurant every day." They smiled at each other. *Couldn't anyone else see that this was a couple?*

Serendipity couldn't have differed more from her parents, both physically and, it seemed, in terms of personality: she was tall— maybe five-ten—had long, flowing, lustrous black hair, dark eyes, and a pale complexion that suited her perfectly. A rose-tinted lip-stain and a hint of mascara were all she needed to look stunning, yet fresh. She was clearly a woman in control of herself, obviously felt totally comfortable in her own body and her surroundings, and had a calm, unflappable demeanor that I suspected would stand her in good stead in the heat and noise of a busy kitchen. *Hmm . . .*

"A pleasure." She shook my hand with hers—short nails, perfectly clean, a strong grip, quite a low voice. *Nice.*

"Is that a Welsh accent I detect there, Cait?" asked Raj Pinder affably.

"Yes, it is," I replied, smiling. "Swansea. And you?"

"Aye, well, there's no hiding mine, is there? Bradford."

"Do you miss Bradford?" I asked. Well, people always ask me if I miss Swansea, so I thought I'd get in first.

Raj smiled broadly, his teeth very white and even. "No, to be honest, I don't. But then, how could you compare this place with Bradford? I mean, don't get me wrong, Bradford's not a bad place, in fact, it's got a lot going for it. But not like the Okanagan. It's like a little bit of heaven here. When I first came to Canada to visit me Mum's cousin and help out with his blueberry harvest in the Lower Mainland, I couldn't get over how big and open and far apart everything were. Same for you, were it?"

Raj was very engaging. I smiled, thinking back to my arrival in Vancouver.

"Yes, you're right. I still grapple with it. The cities here are like tiny dots on the map. And isn't it amazing how even some suburban streets just end in wilderness? The emptiness is magnificent. But then, the UK has almost twice the population of Canada, with less than three percent of the land mass, so I guess we're bound to feel differently in our new home. There really *is* that much more space. I love it."

"Aye, me too. It's grand." He looked wistfully into the distance.

"Do you get back to the UK much?" I asked. That's the other one people always bring up.

Raj shrugged. "I try to get there a couple of times a year. You know, family and all that. Don't want to miss the little 'uns growing up. And you?"

"No, no family there anymore. But Wales will always be my 'home,' even if no one's keeping the actual home fires burning for me. Blood is blood, after all."

"Aye, that it is, lass," Raj grinned.

I was disappointed. Having come to the soiree thinking that Raj Pinder was the one man with a strong motive to kill Annette, I found myself warming to him almost immediately. Surely this pleasant, urbane, and apparently talented, man couldn't have murdered Annette Newman. I pulled myself together: some of the most murderous people in history have *looked* innocent. You really cannot judge a person by their outward appearance, by how they present and project themselves. You have to observe them, know and understand what you're seeing, analyze it and then dig deeper than their skin or their costume. I decided to do just that.

Raj had a good reason to kill Annette—to get his hands on half of the Mt Dewdney Family Estate Winery—and I needed to follow up on my initial instincts. However pleasant he might seem.

"So how's it working out for you, Raj, suddenly owning half a winery?" I asked. Quite out of the blue it seemed, judging by everyone's expression. I'd been thinking, not listening to the small talk they were all exchanging.

Raj seemed to not know what to say, so Ellen answered for him. "He's loving it, aren't you, Raj. We have such fun, *don't* we." Her comments weren't questions, they were statements.

"We certainly do, Ellen," he replied. His tone made me think of Laurel and Hardy.

"Raj is in even earlier than I am," Ellen added brightly. "Then he scoots off to the gym to keep himself in shape in the afternoon, don't you. That's what he says—'I'm scooting off to the gym now, Ellen.'"

"I certainly do, Ellen. I certainly do." Again, Laurel and Hardy.

I tried again. "I suppose it was a surprise to hear about your inheritance?"

"That it were, Cait, aye. Maybe Ellen has told you how it all happened?" Both Bud and I nodded, with appropriate expressions on our faces. "Very sad," he added. "Annette were a wonderful woman. Full of life. Extremely talented, and worked hard at it too. I admired her efforts, and envied her skills. She beat me every time, you know . . ."

"Except once," interrupted Serendipity. "That tasting competition in Sonoma, just a month or so before she . . ." The poor woman realized she'd talked herself into an awkward corner.

"Yes, yes, just that once." Raj jumped in and rescued her. "But, other than that, well—she had one of the best noses in the industry. Such a loss. Her death came as a shock to all of us, of course." He smiled sympathetically toward Ellen, who dropped her eyes. "And then there were the will. No messing, you could have knocked me down with a feather. And that's the truth. I told Ellen at the time she should contest it. I mean, Annette's balance of mind, and all that. Not that I'm not grateful for the chance, of course, because it's not often that a vintner gets to part-own an 'estate vineyard,' where the winery owns all the vineyards that grow all its grapes. Ellen and Annette's parents were such visionaries. They bought just the right pieces of land, in all the right places, to be able to grow the very best of the different types of grapes that give us . . . well, just about the widest choice in the area. It's an honor. A great chance to do something . . . *meaningful*." He chose his word carefully, and gave it a reverent emphasis. "I owe it to Annette's memory, and the memory of her parents who started the vineyard and the winemaking, to make sure that I do the *very* best I can."

Raj's comments made me think again about how dashed Ellen's plans for the future must have been upon hearing her sister's wishes. Bad enough to lose her sister, but then to lose half the family business too? Now it wasn't Ellen's *family* business any more. Annette had handed something that should have rightfully passed to her sister, to a stranger—an outsider, a relative newcomer to the area. After all, what's three years or so in a place? Not much. True, Raj had almost as good a nose as Annette's, and maybe she'd honestly thought that the business wouldn't have survived as well without him. But, still, it was a hell of a bold move to make. I realized I'd have to try to get to understand Annette a lot better than I did, or I'd never know why she changed her will. I was certain that changing it had *something* to do with her death.

"Of course you'll do your best." Ellen was speaking to Raj very earnestly. "I know you will. You're a good, good man, Raj Pinder. And I know, now, that she did the right thing," she continued, addressing the whole group, "though at the time, it puzzled me a great deal. Annette knew that Raj would be good for the business, and so he is. The best *possible* person for the job. But it really was a shock, coming right after her death . . . which is a silly thing to say, because that's when wills *are* read, but you know what I mean. I don't think I handled the meeting at the lawyers' offices too well, and I'll always be sorry for that, Raj," she added. I wondered what she meant.

"What do you mean?" I asked, sensibly enough. Bud glared at me again.

"Oh, it were all very understandable," said Raj gently. "Of course, Ellen hadn't come to terms with Annette's death, and then she had to face this other shock, so soon afterwards. You lost it a bit for a while there, didn't you Ellen?" Ellen nodded, and cast her eyes downward once again. "But it were all summat and nowt. Right? Storm in a teacup, luv," he said, his Yorkshire accent thickening by the second. "And, when you calmed down, you were just a darlin'. Worried about how I'd manage to tell Sammy that I'd have to resign, weren't you?" Ellen nodded, still looking at Serendipity's toes. "And she comes right back to SoulVine Wines with me and tells him herself, didn't she? Said he'd have to understand that I couldn't be working for him for a moment longer, and that she were there to help me gather up me bits and pieces and get out of there that very minute. Well, that took the wind out of his sails, right enough. And there I were, at Ellen's place, before the day were out." He smiled, as did Ellen.

"We were sorry to see you go," said Serendipity quietly.

I bet you were! I managed to think it, not say it.

"But it's great to see you already achieving so much," she added.

"What are you doing?" I wondered, aloud this time.

Once again Ellen answered on Raj's behalf. "Raj was with us for the last winter season and we both think, no, we both *know*, that Raj has created a winner for us. Obviously, we won't *really* know for certain for some time, because it won't go into competition for years yet, but the signs are excellent. Excellent."

"Thanks," Raj answered. "I've called it 'Annette.' It's a pinot noir ice wine, and it's going to be *fabulous*. Dark berries, honey, caramel . . . it'll be a great hit, I'm sure. One hundred cases of magic, in honor of Annette."

"And at a hundred dollars a bottle, it'll be a good way to raise funds for the scholarship I've set up in her name at the university. Oh Cait, I forgot, that's where you teach, right?" said Ellen.

I shook my head and shrugged, puzzled. "I'm sorry, do you mean the University of Vancouver?"

"Yes," she replied, "VORC, at UVan. My alma mater." She grinned.

I was in the dark about what "VORC" stood for. Before I could ask, Bud butted in. Maybe he felt a bit left out.

"Sorry, what's VORC, Ellen?" he sounded interested, which was good.

"It's the Viticulture and Oenology Research Centre. Surely *you've* heard of it, Cait? I know they do a lot of work on brand building with your business school there."

Oh dear, I felt that I was about to be "hoist by my own petard." Again. Frankly, a saying that means "to be blown up by a bomb you have planted yourself" was just about spot-on, because I only had myself to blame. *Damn and blast!*

"Oh, maybe I've heard something about it, Ellen," I lied, "but there's a good number of us teaching at the school and we don't all get involved with each of the inter-departmental programs that exist. Probably my colleagues who specialize in consumer branding are involved. I'm more business-to-business, myself."

"Oh, really?" chimed in Serendipity. "I wonder if I could pick your brains later on. I'm developing a range of peanut-free sauces for catering companies, not direct to the consumer you know, and I don't really know what I'm looking for in terms of advice and so forth. A general chat through the whole field would be real useful, if you could spare the time?" She smiled a warm, hopeful smile.

"Of course," I said cheerily. "But not at one of the events. It would spoil the food." I forced a chuckle. *Oh dear God, how deep is this hole I'm digging for myself?*

Bud looked alarmed, and chivalrously threw himself in front of the train that was hurtling toward me. "Oh, come on now guys, let's leave all this shop-talk and enjoy the food, eh? That's what we're here for after all, right?" His eyes were scanning for a server bearing canapés somewhere in the vicinity. He spotted one. "Oh, hey, over here," he called, rather too loudly. "I wonder if we could have some of those . . ." he peered at the tray, ". . . those . . . things. They look great!"

He plucked from the tray a black porcelain Chinese rice spoon, laden with a mound of tiny, white pearls, topped with a delicate grating of something red and a sliver of something green. He poked it into his mouth. A loud "mmm" emerged from his closed lips.

"It's snail caviar, marinated in fresh, local herbs," the server announced. "It's sometimes referred to as 'pearls of Aphrodite' because of its aphrodisiac powers—you know, like oysters," she added, failing to hide a smile as Bud tried not to show *his* disgust and embarrassment. "It's supposed to taste quite mushroomy," she said disdainfully. She bent her head closer to Bud and me. "It didn't taste like that to me when I tried it earlier on, though. Tasted like dirt. Enjoy!" she called, as she took the tray to her next victims, and the three of us who'd taken a spoon but hadn't yet eaten looked at Bud for guidance. Serendipity had declined a spoon. *I wondered why.*

"She's right," said Bud. "Dirt. But not *bad* dirt. It's not gritty. It's just not—well, I didn't taste mushrooms. But you should try it. Especially you, Cait. I know how you love this gourmet food, right? And I'm guessing that snail eggs are *real* expensive, so this might be your only chance."

He might as well have stuck out his tongue and shouted, "Dare you."

Despite the fact that my last close encounter with snails had involved the sudden death of an old boss of mine, I popped the spoon into my mouth, let the eggs slip onto my tongue and squished them, like "ordinary" caviar. They were lovely: soft and yielding, each tiny little globe popped with a burst of woodlands, not quite a truffle and not quite mushroom flavor. I also noted hints of basil, tarragon, and cilantro. I knew what Bud and the server meant by *dirt*, but I quite liked it. It was certainly an experience I'd never had before. Though one serving was probably enough.

"It's delicious—go ahead," I said, aware that all eyes were on me. Ellen and Raj popped their spoons into their mouths, and I watched their expressions.

"Yuk—not nice!" Ellen pulled a face.

Raj took a little more time and, when his mouth was empty said, "Sorry," to Serendipity, "not my cup of tea. But I'm sure lots of folk will like it."

Bud and I exchanged puzzled glances.

"It's one of the three canapés I contributed tonight," explained Serendipity. "Sorry it wasn't to everyone's taste. I thought I'd try something new and different. But maybe snail caviar is a bit *too* different, even for this foodie crowd."

"Oh, *I'm* not a foodie person, Serendipity," said Bud quickly, trying to get himself out of a bind, "so please don't concern yourself about *my* proletarian palate. Cait liked it, and Cait knows her food. You should listen to her."

Serendipity smiled. "Please don't panic, Bud. We chefs have to be able to take criticism, you know, otherwise we'll never grow and learn. Good chefs don't force food on people that they really don't like. I need to know how far I can go without pushing people *over* the edge. But if you're not a foodie, this weekend may not be quite the place for you. I know that Ellen's planning traditional breakfasts at her place in the mornings, and I think that's just super. Pat will do a great job, and I have no doubt he'll be using all the best, freshest local ingredients he can find. Quite a few of us—me, and the Jacksons for certain—will be pushing the boundaries a fair bit." She looked a little concerned, and turned to Ellen. "I thought Bud was one of your foodie friends?"

"Oh no," said Ellen, just at the point in the evening when all the chatter seemed to die at once, and only Ellen's voice could be heard echoing around the entire atrium, "Bud's here to find out who killed Annette, right, Bud? And I'm quite sure the killer's here tonight."

I looked around in panic for another glass of wine, but there wasn't a server in sight. *Typical!*

Eau-de-Vie

IN THE SILENCE THAT FOLLOWED Ellen Newman's blunt accusation, you could almost hear people's heads swivel to look at her. A collection of open mouths and shocked expressions greeted my darting eyes, as I realized that spotting a fresh glass of wine had to take second place to watching everyone's response to her statement. Immediately, I wished that the lighting hadn't been subdued to such a low level by the party's organizers. Some people were just too dimly lit for me to read their expressions. I knew it was vital to observe everything I possibly could because, if Ellen was right and Annette's killer was in the room, the murderer might give themselves away. I also knew that Bud would quiz me about this moment later on.

Abruptly, it seemed as though everyone in the room exhaled at the same time. An embarrassed hub-bub of "Oh my God," and "What does she mean?" and "Let's get another drink," rolled around our little gathering.

Raj Pinder shut his mouth, then opened it again and said, "What do you *mean*, Ellen? Annette wasn't *murdered* . . . she killed herself. I miss her, of course, and no one can understand why she did it, but she *did* do it. You know what the coroner said. What the police said. It couldn't have been clearer. You found her yourself, in the truck. Dead. With that note. Ellen, you don't know what you're *saying*."

People were shaking their heads and whispering. Ellen threw back her shoulders. She grew two inches.

"Raj, I know *exactly* what I'm saying. She wouldn't have killed herself. She was my sister. If she'd been that unhappy, I'd have known. You can't work with someone every day and not know how they're feeling, even if they don't want to talk to you about it. You can sense that something's wrong. And there wasn't anything wrong with her *at all*."

"Oh come on now Ellen." It was Serendipity's turn to speak. She looked quite cross. "That's not true. Everyone knew that Annette had been acting oddly for weeks!"

This was the first I was hearing about Annette acting oddly before her death, so I listened and watched intently.

"No she hadn't," snapped Ellen.

"Okay then," responded Serendipity sharply, "so why did she pull out of four tasting events before she died? Events she'd committed to months before, including a really big one at my restaurant? Why did she miss the all the Moveable Feast functions last year? Why did she change her damned will and force Raj to leave SoulVine Wines? Eh? Answer me that, Ellen. And why, if she was acting so *normally* before she killed herself, did she start haunting the thrift stores downtown and buying up loads of stinky old clothes? None of that was *normal*, Ellen, not for Annette."

"Garbage. All garbage," was Ellen's indignant reply.

"You have to admit, Ellen," Raj said in a more sympathetic tone than Serendipity's, "Annette weren't her usual self those last few weeks. She seemed very short-tempered with everyone, and she kept wandering off, missing meetings at the local vintners' association, and, like Serendipity said, she pulled out of several events. People were depending on her. She were a big draw at tastings. I know for a fact that I didn't value my wins as much because *she* wasn't in the competitions. I mean, it's grand to come first, of course, but not when you only win because you're main competitor in't there."

"Raj is right. Poor Annette was acting irrationally in those last, tragic days. I tried to help her, but she wouldn't talk to me. She wouldn't *connect*. I failed her."

The voice came from behind me. I jumped. *Preacher-like into-nation, Canadian accent, scent of lemon and sandalwood.* I turned, and found myself eye to eye with the short, almost emaciated man wearing a Nehru jacket that Sammy Soul had referred to as "Grant." From Ellen's notes I knew him to be Grant Jackson, owner of the downtown Kelowna Faceting for Life store and restaurant, a devotee of the Sedona-originated dogma, and a man who, according to Ellen, was too pious for his own good.

His wire-rimmed spectacles, soul patch (*oh dear!*), shaved head, and burgundy, high-collared brocade jacket all told me he was keen to portray an image of spiritual studiousness. I wondered what the man himself was like.

"Oh, shut up, Grant," retorted Ellen angrily. "You hardly knew Annette. She avoided you like the plague. All that Faceting stuff you're always pushing, she couldn't stand it, and neither can I." Ellen was clearly determined that everyone should hear her, and she wasn't pulling any punches. I was beginning to wonder just how much she'd had to drink. I also noticed that Bud was suddenly more alert, ready to employ his professional tension-defusing techniques at a moment's notice.

Grant Jackson looked shocked. To be more accurate, he adopted the appearance of shock, because that's how I read him. His expression was anything but natural.

"Hey, Ellen, let's not talk *shop*, eh?" chuckled Bud, aiming to lighten the mood.

Grant chimed in with, "Come now, Ellen. You're blocking me. Connect. Facet and Face It." *Catchy mantra.*

"*Now* might not be the time, Grant." Another voice entered the fray from behind me. *Calming tones, patchouli oil.*

"It's *always* the time, Lizzie," Grant replied firmly, "it's *always* the place. Faceting *is* Life. Life *is* Faceting. It can help us when we're up, or when we're down. We should all seek to connect every day. Facet and Face It."

As Bud and I managed a quick eye-roll in each other's direction, he gave me a quick wink, which assured me he was on top of the whole situation. I mentally referenced Ellen's notes: Lizzie Jackson, Grant's second wife, five years his senior; a transplant from Phoenix, less pious than her husband, but a Faceting person too. She's a hypnotherapist, waves crystals about the place when she says she's "healing" people, and looks like she's wearing clothes she's patched for years. They met at some sort of Faceting camp about five years ago, in Sedona.

I looked at the woman Ellen had described. Taller, and with a good deal more meat on her bones than her husband to say she wasn't wearing the best put-together outfit I'd ever seen, it was true (lots of royal blue crushed velvet, with a yellow scarf, and several crystal necklaces), but Ellen's get-up wasn't much to write home about either. Lizzie Jackson's long white hair was trying to break free from some type of bun arrangement at the back of her head, and she stared at us all through heavily horn-rimmed, totally round spectacles that gave her the air of a constantly surprised owl. *Very theatrical.*

"Grant, Ellen's clearly not well. I can sense it. Her chi is not flowing properly. Let her alone. Here, Ellen, take this, it'll help you communicate more effectively." She pushed a small, turquoise stone into Ellen's hand.

"Oh, she's communicating just *fine*," slurred Suzie Soul as she tottered towards our growing group. "She let her sister fight all her battles for her when she was alive, and now she's got her own cop to back her up, right Ellen?" All of Suzie's earlier coquettishness had dissolved, and we were in the presence of a cat with her claws out. Partially for Bud, it seemed. "You're a lush, Ellen Newman. Put your glass down and go home to your sorry, pathetic little life. And take your damned cop with you." Suzie Soul ranted on.

Bud had stepped forward, ready to keep the peace and to stop the situation from getting more than testy when Raj Pinder surprisingly took matters into his own hands.

"I think we should all calm down," he suggested firmly. "There's nowt here to be getting hot under the collar about. Come *on*." He was almost pleading. "We're here to start a weekend of celebrating all that's good about the area: its food, its wine—*and* its people. We're all old friends here. If *we* can't get along, who can?"

"And what would you know about us all being *old friends*, Raj?" spat Suzie. "Didn't wanna be no friend of mine when you had the chance, didya!"

I sensed a slippery slope, with Suzie half way down. Bud looked alarmed, but clearly decided to give ground to the woman's husband.

"Suzie, Babe, you gotta let it go." Sammy Soul had followed his unsteady wife across the room.

It seemed as though everyone was drifting toward our immediate circle—which was handy for me, because it meant I could see them much better. Quite often, a hostile environment is a wonderful way to see people at their most honest. I was quite enjoying it all. From an academic point of view, of course.

"Let it *go*?" Suzie squawked toward her husband.

"Yes, Babe. Let it go. He didn't wanna be your lover, and that's that. I don't *get* it, but that's that." He'd reached his wife's side and put his arm around her shoulders.

Bud watched them intently. Could he sense a nasty domestic incident in the making? If so, he was ready.

The folks who'd started to move toward our group did so with more purpose: clearly it was where the action was. And what action. It was pretty obvious that Sammy's comments had surprised and shocked everyone as much as Ellen's had. I suspected that anyone with two brain cells had pegged Suzie as a man-eater, but it didn't look as though they'd considered that Sammy knew as much as he did about her habits.

"Yeah . . . well . . ." Suzie's anger seemed to be subsiding as Sammy rubbed her back, then, rallying, she shot back at Raj, "just as well your replacement's up to the job, right, Vince?"

All eyes turned toward the man I quickly identified as Vince Chen, the new vintner at SoulVine Wines and, apparently, its owner's lover. He looked horrified, as did most of the other people in the room. Except Sammy Soul.

"Come on now, Babe, don't embarrass the poor guy. Let him be."

I was beginning to get a clearer understanding of what Sammy had meant earlier on when he'd said he would forgive Suzie anything. It looked like he did mean literally *anything*.

The atmosphere was electric. In Raj Pinder's home county, Yorkshire, they have a saying I like, and often quote: "There's nowt so queer as folk." It's true. Nothing, absolutely *nothing*, is as strange or unpredictable as human behavior. As a psychologist, I've studied human beings for years, trying to understand why they do what they do. I've narrowed that field by focusing on why criminals do what *they* do. If I've learned one thing in all that time, it's that we don't really know why *some* people do *some* of the things that they do. I wondered what would happen next.

"Desserts and eau-de-vie!" The dramatic cry came from the far side of the room. Everyone turned. Two of the servers had pulled back velvet curtains which had been hiding a table laden with platters of sweet morsels. A barman was showily pouring clear liquid from a frosted bottle into the top of a long chute made of ice that was bedecked with glimmering lights. It was quite the moment, and it produced a gasp, which the barman assumed was for him. He beamed.

"Come on, Babe, you've had enough, we're going home," muttered Sammy Soul as he directed Suzie toward the exit. She was playing with her hair and giggling as they left. Any tension between them had dissipated.

"Oh doesn't it look wonderful!" exclaimed Ellen, surprising me with her reaction, and she dragged Raj Pinder toward the display.

It seemed that the evening's dramas had passed. As everyone else headed to the table, I grabbed Bud's sleeve. We hung back.

"It's turning out to be quite an evening," whispered Bud.

"You're not kidding," I replied quietly. "I could see you were on full alert."

Bud smiled. "Yes, too many years of trying to de-escalate arguments before they turn into fights, I guess. Not that that's a bad thing. But all my training wasn't really needed tonight. I wasn't the only sensible one in the place."

I nodded, though I could spot a few folk I wouldn't have labeled as "sensible" myself. "Lots of motives flying about," I added.

"Okay, I'll give you that," smiled Bud. "We've also discovered that Annette was acting oddly for weeks before she died, which you might expect if she were to go on to kill herself. I'm not hearing anything that makes me more likely to think she was murdered, and I haven't met anyone I can figure as a killer. However odd they might be."

"Odd, yes, but acting within the normal parameters of their personalities, I'd say. No one seems to be under any particular strain."

"What about Vince Chen? I'd say *he's* pretty stressed," Bud nodded and rolled his eyes in the direction of the subject of Suzie's affections, who was hovering between the door and the dessert table looking more than a little awkward. "And what about those two?" He nodded in the direction of a couple to whom we hadn't yet been introduced. "They both look pretty nervous. Angry, even. What's up with them?"

"Let's find out," I said. I left Bud's side and casually moved myself to within earshot of the couple who were quite literally hissing at each other. Words were pouring out of them angrily and rapidly.

"You *said* we were okay to stay until ten," stage-whispered the man, clenching his martini glass a little too tightly.

"If you'd *listened*, you'd have known that I said I wanted to be home by *nine*," the woman replied angrily, pushing a silk wrap roughly off her shoulder. "I don't like him being in the house on his own at night."

"For God's sake, Sheri, he's *seventeen*. He's going to be leaving home to go to university next year. He's just *fine* in the house on his own. I mean, it's not like he's going to throw a wild party or anything. He doesn't even have any friends."

"Don't worry about that! It's him not having a *father* that *you* should worry about! You need to visit more often, Rob. A boy needs his father. He never sees you. You haven't been here since February, and even then you only managed a couple of days' skiing with him."

"Skiing? *Skiing?*" The man sounded incensed. "He didn't *ski*, Sheri. He just sulked about the chalet playing those damned video games of his. The only skiing he does is on a flat-screen TV. He wouldn't know a free-ride board from a free-style one if they were in front of him, and that's not normal for a teenager in these parts, right on the doorstep of Big White. I blame *you*. Like tonight. You're not letting him grow up, Sheri. You treat him as though he's a child."

"He *is* a child, Rob. My child. *Ours*. If you were here more often you'd know how vulnerable he is . . ." The woman stopped as she realized we were drawing close. She smiled, too brightly.

"Oh hello," she beamed, and, with the confidence of an experienced mixer, she held out a small, perfectly manicured hand, damp with sweat. She was red in the face, and perspiration gleamed on her forehead. I suspected she was having "a moment or two of her own personal summer," as my Mum used to say whenever she suffered a hot flash. "I'm Sheri, Sheri MacMillan, and this is Rob, my husband. Pleased to meet you. Lovely evening, eh?"

We all smiled and hands were shaken.

"Hi! I'm Bud and this is Cait. We're Ellen's weekend guests, from the Lower Mainland," replied Bud with almost alarming good cheer. "It's turned out to be quite the party," he added, combining understatement and keen observation in one phrase.

"Um, yes, I suppose it has," she replied hesitantly, nervously smoothing her too-tight cardinal red gown.

73

"Ha! Sure has," was her husband's blustering reaction. His expensive suit didn't quite cover his spreading midriff. "For a small place, it's all really going on here: murder, intrigue, illicit affairs, open marriages. We think we've got it made in a sprawling city like Calgary, but you've got to come to a place like this to realize it's all happening right under your nose."

"Oh Rob," Sheri cooed, clearly using a tone reserved for company, "don't say it like that, dear. I'm sure if you only got to know everyone, you'd see that it's really a lovely place." As an aside to Bud and myself, she added, "Rob has *such* a lot of responsibilities at his office in Calgary, he can't be here as much as he'd like. Isn't that right, Rob?"

"Sure," replied her husband, taking a large swig from the glass he was clenching. It was quite clear to me, from his tone and body language, that not only did he *not* see himself spending more time in Kelowna, he wasn't even too keen on being in the company of his wife at that very moment.

"It's all about the life-work balance," said Bud, which was about as un-Bud-like a sentiment as I'd ever heard him express. Bud was *always* your classic workaholic. I tried to keep my face rigid to hide my shock. My top lip stuck to my teeth, so I took a sip from my almost empty glass.

"Hey, can I get you another? I'm getting one for myself," offered Rob, clearly pleased to have found an easy route.

His wife looked livid as she said, "I thought we were going to hit the road, Rob," in fake-calm tones.

It was too late. Rob was merrily heading for the bar, and she was obviously going to have to wait.

Ever the master of managing the awkward moment, I asked, "Have you lived here long?"

It seemed an innocuous question, the sort that a visitor *would* ask of a resident, even though I happened to know the answer.

Unfortunately, it had an effect on Sheri I hadn't seen coming—she burst into tears and started scrabbling around in her purse, sobbing. In fact, it looked as though she were actually talking to her purse, not me, which might explain why she said what she did. "Oh please don't. *Don't* ask how long I've been here. I've been here *too* long, that's how long. I want to leave, I want to move to Calgary with him. But I can't because of Colin. He's doing so well at school now, I don't want to move him. It hasn't been easy for him, you know, because he never seems to fit in with people very well. But now—oh, he's finally getting good grades. I can't do that to him, can I? It's not fair. We've moved so many times before with Rob's work. I can't move him again. But, if I stay here, I'm going to lose Rob. And I do love him, you know . . ."

What an extraordinary evening, and what a weird bunch of people, I thought. Judging by Bud's expression, he was thinking much the same sort of thing. What on earth had led this woman to speak to someone she'd met moments earlier in such an open and intimate manner? It was very odd. And trust me, being a criminal psychologist, I know odd when I see it.

Finally, she found the paper tissue she'd been hunting for and wiped her eyes and nose—just in time for her husband's arrival with a much-needed fresh glass of wine for me, which I took and half dispatched with one gulp.

"There," Sheri said, as she tucked the tissue back into her purse and looked around, seemingly refreshed, "Facet and Face It. Thank you for allowing me to connect with you as I polish my love for another—my son, for whom no sacrifice is too great."

"Oh Jeez, not *more* of that gush!" Rob glared at his wife. "These poor folks have only been in town two minutes, and already you're trying to shove that rubbish down their throats. You're weird. As is that idiot Jackson. *And* his ridiculous wife. Mind you, maybe they're not as stupid as all that—at least they're building a business on the back of it all. *You're* just spending my money on it. Packets of tea, special water, goddam stupid crystals everywhere . . ." It sounded as though he could have gone on for some time about the ways in which Sheri was spending his money on her discipleship of Faceting.

It seemed equally clear that Sheri's moment of connecting with Bud and me had passed, and that she and her husband were about to launch into another round of backbiting. The fight or flight instinct is well named: as the adrenalin increases with stress and pumps through our veins, we humans revert to base-animal status and apply all our decision-making abilities to making the best possible choice for survival—do I stay and fight it out, or do I run away and live to fight another day? It seemed that both Rob and Sheri were going to stay and fight—a decision I suspected they'd both made many, many times before, but one which Rob generally avoided having to make by not visiting Kelowna very often. In him the flight instinct was stronger, in her it was fight . . . largely, as she'd revealed, because she was fighting for both herself and her son.

I could sense that Bud's instinct was to leave them to it. I was leaning in that direction myself, but I was wondering *how* we could make our escape politely, since it was difficult to get a word in edgeways.

"Come and try this plum eau-de-vie—it's exceptionally good," were the words that saved us. Ellen Newman had returned to rescue us, and not a moment too soon. "Hey, you two lovebirds, I'm taking my guests away." I was glad to have an excuse to run. Rob and Sheri MacMillan had been stopped in their tracks by Ellen's innocent, if inappropriate, comment which allowed us the chance to escape.

Completely oblivious to how far off the mark she'd been with her interpretation of why the husband and wife were just inches apart, Ellen steered Bud toward the ice sculpture that was the current center of attention. It was an impressive structure: a swooping funnel made of ice delivered the liquid, poured into its top by the flamboyant barman, to a large bowl at its base, where a female server was scooping the now chilled fluid into small glasses with a long-handled, silver ladle.

"Is that still the plum?" asked Ellen.

The barman didn't take his eyes off his task, but nodded his head. "Yes, nearly finished the bottle though, and then it'll be apricot."

I grasped my remaining gamay noir longingly. I'm not one for sweet liqueurs, usually, and the thought of either plum or apricot-flavored alcohol set my teeth on edge.

"Oh quick," exclaimed Ellen, "you must try the plum, it's delicious, especially with the salted chocolate squares at the end of the table."

Now she was talking my language: dark chocolate, embedded with crystals of sea salt. Yum!

Ellen was quite right—my tastebuds thanked her for encouraging me to try something I really hadn't thought would taste good. *Live and learn, Cait.* As I sipped and chewed, Bud joined me, grimacing.

"*Way* too sweet for me," he replied, trying to smile.

"Isn't it wonderful?" enthused Ellen, and I had to agree with her.

"Absolutely. And those folks seem to be loving it too," I commented. This was my chance to get Ellen to introduce us to the man and woman I guessed, through a process of elimination, must be the Wisers of Anen Close.

Ellen turned and looked in the direction I was indicating. She smiled a half smile. "Oh, he's probably criticizing the fruit flavors. That's Gordy Wiser and his wife Marlene. He was a fruit farmer for his whole life, then, about five years ago, he managed to drag his property out of the Agricultural Land Reserve and sell it to a developer. He couldn't cope any more, and none of his kids wanted to replant the orchards after fire had swept across them, so they sold up and bought one of the houses Annette and I had built on *our* old family property. There he and Marlene will probably stay until—well, until they can't cope with *that* anymore, I guess. They're both well into their eighties now, and neither of them shows any sign of slowing down. Six children they raised, you know. *Six*. And all of them adopted."

As the couple approached, Ellen bubbled to them, "Come and meet Bud and Cait."

"So you're the folks with that shiny silver truck?" asked Gordy Wiser, rubbing his chin thoughtfully. *Ah-ha—the Curtain-Twitcher of Anen Close.*

Bud was immediately engaged. "She's mine alright. This is her first Big Trip. Took a bit of a beating from the bugs, though."

"Yep, that'll happen on the Coquihalla Highway," replied Gordy Wiser sagely. "What was the road like? Bad?" Gordy struck me as a "glass half empty" kind of guy.

"No, not too bad. Lots of ploughings at the summit, but almost nothing as we swung down into the valley," replied Bud, back to being Bud-like.

"Yep, snow's all but gone here, except the mounds in the parking lots," observed Gordy. "Don't mean there won't be more, though."

"Hopefully not before we get over the top, around lunchtime on Monday. They said it would hold off until at least then," replied Bud.

"Oh, don't trust those forecasters." The old man shook his head. "They don't know their arses from their elbows," he observed dryly.

"Language, Gordy," chastised Marlene Wiser. She uttered the phrase with such ease that it was clear she was used to encouraging her husband to watch what he said. I suspected she'd honed her skills on her brood of children.

"Well, it's true," the man added, rolling his eyes.

"Gordy always thinks he knows best," said Marlene, with such an indulgent tone that I wouldn't have been surprised if she'd patted him on the head.

She looked by far the older of the two, who were a spare and short couple. Her face was incised with those incredibly deep wrinkles that some people develop from a largely outdoor existence, a life well and truly lived—not as a spectator, but as a complete participant. Her body was small and slim, and gave the appearance of litheness despite her age. Her hair was like white candy-floss. Her husband was more bowed than she, but less wrinkled, with a narrow fringe of white hair around a bald pate. Despite his apparent negative attitude toward most things, he had a twinkle in his eye whenever he looked at his wife.

"That's only because I *do* know best," replied Gordy, "like I know that the apricots they used for this drink came from that orchard down on the Naramata Bench where I wouldn't have planted them in a month of Sundays. They're facing north too much. He should have planted them full-on facing east. They'd get the sun on 'em first thing in the morning that way."

"So you used to grow apricots, Gordy?" asked Bud.

"Sure did. And better than these. Apples too. Best in the whole valley. See, if I still had my land . . ."

Marlene seemed a little testy as she snapped, "Well, you don't Gordy Wiser, and we all know why. So let's not go there, dear. These nice people are here to enjoy themselves, not to listen to you talking about how it was all so much better back in the day." She turned to Bud and me. "You *are* here to enjoy yourselves, right? Not to solve a murder that didn't happen." She turned to Ellen. "You know very well that your sister killed herself, Ellen, and that's that. That's an end to it." She turned back to us. "We loved Annette dearly, you know, Cait. With all the children gone, and her just up the hill there, we saw a good deal of her, didn't we, dear?"

Gordy nodded. "She was a good girl, that Annette. Always had time for us. Even had time for me. And I know I'm not an easy man to spend time with."

"Exactly," replied Marlene enigmatically. "She'd pop by with all sorts of treats for us. She very rarely just drove up to her house without stopping, right? She'd hop out of her little car to collect her mail from the mailbox at the foot of the hill, then she'd drop by."

Again, Gordy nodded, sadly. "Except for those last few weeks. Seemed to be distant. Didn't bring me my bonbons then, did she, eh? Didn't even bother to collect her mail every day."

Marlene nodded. "True. She did seem to avoid us for a while there, toward the end. And listen, Ellen," Marlene turned her attention to our weekend hostess who was, by now, swaying more than a little, "I, for one, know that no one else was involved. No one could have approached her house without passing ours, and nobody did. *Nobody*. No people, no vehicles. You know very well, Ellen, that one of us is bound to look out of the window if we hear anything—anything at all, and neither of us did. Not *all* that evening. Not *once*. Well, not after Annette *herself* drove up to the house, that is. And then *you*, the next morning. Nobody *between* the two of you. I'm not a good sleeper, and I'd have been woken by anyone driving, or even walking, up, whatever the time. It *can't* have been murder. I'm sorry, dear, but you're just going to have to work harder at coming to terms with it. She might have been your sister, but you two were always as different as chalk and cheese, so she obviously hid something from you—something that made her so deeply unhappy that she chose to take her own life. People hide things. People lie. Often they think they're doing it for the good of those they love. So you'd better get used to it, dear—your sister lied to you. She killed herself." She used a very matter-of-fact tone, which seemed to subdue Ellen so much that her swaying became quite pronounced.

Marlene wasn't finished. She turned to Bud, patted him on the arm, and said, "You know, young man, I think your time here would be much better spent enjoying the glories of the meals we're all about to enjoy, rather than trying to help this poor woman find a murderer who doesn't exist. Tell her to stop being silly and to face facts. *No one* came up that hill between the two of you sisters. Oh my dear me . . . !"

Bud was lucky to catch Ellen before she fell. As it was, only his glass, and hers, hit the floor, rather than Ellen herself.

"Oh oops, I'm so sorry!" Ellen looked embarrassed as she pulled herself together. "I'm fine, I'm fine . . ." she rambled, as servers approached to pick up the shards of glass, mop up the spilled drinks, and wipe down Ellen's badly stained shirt and skirt.

Bud made eye contact with me as he himself was patted dry, and he nodded his head toward the exit. I nodded back.

"I think maybe we should be going," I said as firmly as possible to the flapping Ellen.

"Would you like us to drop Ellen at her apartment?" asked a suddenly close Grant Jackson. "I'm driving. I haven't been drinking," he added sanctimoniously.

"*No!*" cried Ellen. "I'm fine. Just *everybody* leave me alone. I can manage by myself. I'm quite used to it—managing by myself. However wonderful you might all think Annette was, and however perfect you all might think she was for the business, it was always *me* who ran it. *Me* who balanced the books, *me* who knew what we could and couldn't afford. *Me* who had to do all the dirty work, making sure all the machinery and equipment was fixed, and everything worked out in the fields when we couldn't afford mechanics or engineers. *Me* who had to make sure we both had a roof over our heads for years before we were a success. *I* looked after *her*, not the other way around. And now she's gone, I've got no one to look after. No one to make a success for . . ."

Raj Pinder approached, looking worried and confused. As he murmured to Bud, "Bit too much?" he tipped his hand up in the universally recognized sign for "drink."

Bud nodded.

"Leave it to me," he whispered to Bud, then, to Ellen, he said, "Right-o, Ellen, me dear. I'm going to get you into a taxi and home to that apartment of yours before you know it. Just pop your arm around me shoulder . . . oh, right-o then, me waist, and off we go."

Ellen looked pathetic as she tottered toward the exit, supported by Raj, but she managed a weak smile and a quiet, "See you in the morning," as she left.

"Time for us to go too, I think," said Bud.

"Look forward to seeing you at breakfast," I said to the Wisers. A thought suddenly occurred to me. "Would you two like to share a cab with us? We'll be going right past your door, as you know."

They both smiled. "What, and miss all the fun of talking about Ellen, and the Souls, and of course you two, when you've gone? Oh, you must be kidding!" laughed Marlene.

I felt my eyebrow shoot up my forehead. I wasn't used to such honesty.

The woman smiled again, and this time she patted my arm. "Oh, go ahead, don't panic, there's nothing very interesting to say about you two . . . but the others? Just you go on, and we'll be fine. There was a rumor earlier on that they've got a rhubarb eau de vie next, and Gordy and I know our rhubarb, don't we dear?" Gordy nodded. "I used to grow a lot of it in my day, and I've made my fair share of rhubarb jam, and rhubarb wine too. Ah yes, happy times. I'd like to see what the professionals do with it. Go on, off with you young things now."

Bud and I waved as we left, then sat in silence during the taxi ride back to the B&B. I was reveling in being referred to as half of a young couple. Bud's expression was tough to read, which, given what I do for a living, was unusual.

"Penny for them?" I said, as we stood at the front door of Anen House, watching the taxi wind its way back down the hill.

"I tell you what, Cait," Bud replied thoughtfully, "given what's running about in my head right now, you'd have to pay a lot more than a *penny* for my thoughts. *What a night!* I wasn't expecting that. Well, okay, I don't know quite *what* I was expecting, but it certainly wasn't *that!*"

I looked at my watch. "It's not eleven o'clock yet, Bud. How do you fancy a bit of a chat? You know, pool our thoughts? Run through the suspects, and so forth?"

Bud wandered to one of the plastic chairs that surrounded the little table on the smoking porch and sat down, heavily.

"Are you going to smoke before we go in?" he asked distractedly.

"Sure, I'll join you there," I replied, digging around in my purse for my ciggies. I lit up and puffed away. *Lovely.* The only improvement would have been more chocolate.

"It's all wrong, Cait," Bud said. "With everything we've learned so far, I just cannot bring myself to believe that Annette's death was anything other than a suicide. I can't. You *have* to agree. Surely you must see it my way now?"

I thought carefully about what to say next. I, too, had been mulling over the events of the evening: what I'd seen, heard, and read among people at the cocktail party. And I knew what I had to do.

"Okay, Bud. I'll shut up about it entirely until I see the paperwork that you asked Ellen to rustle up for us. I won't press my case, but I will continue to dig around. When I've seen those papers, then we'll discuss how to progress with matters."

Bud stroked his chin. I lit another cigarette.

My comments seemed to satisfy Bud, who turned to glare at my glowing cigarette. "You're going to finish that, are you?" he asked acidly.

"My addiction, my body, my time," I replied. Immediately I'd said it, I was angry with myself.

Bud leapt up from the little chair and exploded, "This is *not* the weekend I'd planned, or hoped for, Cait, *not at all*. It was supposed to be fun. Okay, a bit of prying, a bit of helping Ellen to come to terms with some tough stuff. But these people . . . they're . . . they're all *off*! Everyone's dysfunctional. Everything is off-kilter. That place was a powder keg tonight. Nothing's *right*!"

Wow. He's usually the calm one, and I'm the one running on emotional, gut response.

"Are you coming in now?"

I stubbed out my smoke. "Yep, coming with you, right now." I trotted after him.

As we stopped between our doorways, Bud turned to me and held me close. "Look, let's get some sleep, and we'll talk in the morning," he whispered, kissing my forehead.

"See you before breakfast?" I asked, hoping he'd rally and say yes.

"What time is breakfast again?" he asked. He sounded exhausted.

"Pat said it starts at eight, so I guess we should be down and ready to mingle by seven forty-five, don't you think?"

"Sounds about right," he replied. "I can't see me being ready for much of anything before that. So I'll see you here, at seven forty-five. Okay?"

"Of course," I said, as he closed his door.

Bottled Water

AFTER I'D LEFT BUD ON the landing, I shut my door behind me, and went into the spacious, sparkling bathroom to take off my makeup. It's not my usual habit, but I try to make an effort when I'm sleeping on pillowcases that someone else will have to launder. Besides, staring at myself in the brightly lit bathroom mirror allowed for a few moments of self-reflection—figuratively and literally. The former can sometimes be uplifting; the latter, not so much. I might not mind the idea of having an interesting landscape etched on my face late in life, like Marlene Wiser, but I'm not enjoying the journey toward it one little bit.

Comparatively fresh-faced, I clicked off the lights in the bathroom and the bedroom to get a better view of the moon that poked out from behind a cloud in the black sky and caught the ripples on the lake. It was delightfully tranquil. I just stood and drank it all in for a few moments, which allowed me to calm down, and to decide that sulking and being cross weren't going to get me anywhere. I wasn't really tired—so I might as well be positive, and get on with analyzing the evening's events.

I stepped away from the distracting view beyond my window and sat at the little desk to one side of the room. All the furniture at Anen House was old: you got the impression that each piece had been lovingly polished for many years. I wondered if these were all original Newman belongings, which immediately brought me back to reality. Did Annette Newman kill herself, or was she murdered? And if she was murdered, who did it, and why?

Okay, Cait—get organized.

I pulled a notepad out of my suitcase, and immediately wished

I'd brought my laptop. I didn't know why I hadn't, unless I'd been focusing on being with Bud and indulging in food and wine, rather than looking into a possible homicide. I suspected that was it—I, too, had been looking forward to a fun weekend.

I sat down, found a pen and my specs, and drew a line down the middle of the page. I wrote on one side, "Murder," and on the other, "Suicide." It's always sensible to take stock, before analyzing. Across the top of both headings I wrote, "Asphyxia, due to carbon monoxide poisoning, created by inhaling truck exhaust fumes," as this applied to both theories of how this cause and manner of death might have arisen.

On the MURDER side of the page I listed everything I could think of related to the murder theory:

1. Method: Psychologically, no way she'd have killed herself *this* way
   - Difficult to stage such a murder
   - How did murderer get her into the truck?
   - Drugs or wine to induce unconsciousness?
   - What about lifting her when unconscious—strength needed
   - Would there be any way to get her to sit there otherwise?
   - Would Annette really type a suicide note? Was it a fake?
   - NB: 20–30 per cent of suicides leave notes—how many are typed?
   - Check autopsy for record of contusions, lacerations, puncture wounds
   - Check autopsy for any signs of smothering prior to final asphyxia
   - Murderer had to get to and from scene unseen
   - Seems like no one *could* have done it!
2. Motives: Knew about cannabis wine? Sammy & Suzie Soul
   - Raj Pinder wanted to get half of Mt Dewdney business (did he know about her will?)

I was stuck. Stumped. There didn't seem to be any more reasons for anyone wanting to kill Annette. I pretended I was Bud and raked my hand through my hair. It didn't help.

I scribbled, "Must find out more about Annette herself. Where's all her stuff? Is it here at Anen House? Build a VICTIM profile!"

Then on the SUICIDE side of the sheet I wrote:

1. Method: Classic suicide scenario—carbon monoxide, empty wine bottle for courage, note
   • Classic female suicide method—passive, restful
   • NB: need to see coroners' autopsy report—esp. Toxicology/drugs?
   • Handwriting poor, so typing note was natural?
   • Easy to arrange physically, borrowed truck: why?
2. Motives: None known, but note says "can't do my job perfectly"—why not?
   • Acting oddly for weeks? (Raj, Serendipity, Wisers say "Yes," Ellen says "No")
   • Missing meetings—why?
   • Canceled tastings—why?
   • Missed Moveable Feast events—why?
   • Bought old clothes at thrift stores—why?
   • Avoided the Wisers—why?
   • Changed her will—why? What did it say, *exactly*? NB: unlikely to get to lawyer at Easter, so have to find out other ways
   • NB: coroner would seek psychological motives—also family doctor input—autopsy

It was clear I needed to see that autopsy report, had to find out more about Annette's will, and much more about Annette herself. Overall, what was becoming obvious was the need to not be swayed by the weight of evidence. Even though there was only the one reason why I felt Annette hadn't killed herself, it still, to my psychologist's mind, carried more weight than all of the unanswered questions about Annette's odd behavior.

I put the notes to one side, and made sure I was sitting comfortably. I screwed up my eyes to the point where everything starts to get blurry and began to hum. I've read dozens of books about memory, and I try to keep up to date on what neuroscientists are discovering about the way that our human brains work. There still isn't a single body of work or a clear set of theories that help me understand *why* I can do what I can do. So I'll just keep doing it, even if no one understands it—or, even if they say it can't be done.

With this method I can see again whatever scene I choose to see. I can be back at the place I was, and take a long, hard look around. I can't visually stop events in their tracks, as though I've pushed the *pause* button, but I can keep looping back to re-examine a moment. I can do this for any of my senses . . . so long as I experienced it in the first place.

One thing the experts do at least agree upon: we humans encode, or remember, much more of what's going on around us than we think we do. To prevent our brains from drowning in a sea of stimuli, we select those things we choose to perceive and ignore those things we don't feel the need to notice at the time. It's called selective perception. We've all done it: we obliterate the sound of a clock ticking in a room; we don't notice the airplanes overhead when we live under a flight-path; we stop noticing the music in the background at the supermarket. It's natural. It's what allows us to function. For me, while I might ignore certain inputs when they are happening, I can go back and experience the whole thing once more—which can be very handy when you're helping with a crime, as Bud quickly discovered when he first saw me perform.

I took myself back to the moment when Ellen exclaimed that

someone had killed Annette, and that she was quite sure the killer was in the room.

Okay—get blurry, Cait, and hummmmm . . .

I'm standing so close to Bud that I can catch his aroma—Eternity aftershave balm. The wineglass I'm holding is the same temperature as my body, the roundness of its bowl resting comfortably in my left hand, and in my right hand is the still-chilled china spoon from which I've just eaten the snail caviar. Its taste is lingering in my mouth. *It's pleasant. Unusual. Earthy.* Beside me stands Ellen, across from Bud. She's almost spilling her drink as she gestures. She's breathing heavily as she speaks. *Her face is set in an expression of . . . satisfaction. Odd. She's gloating. She's showing off.* She speaks. Just as she does, the sounds that have been echoing in the room die down. It takes only a second. Her voice rings against the glass above our heads. She's speaking more loudly than when she was talking within our group. *She's making an announcement.* Even though the other noise in the room has stopped, she still keeps her voice at a high level. *She wants people to hear her—the silence that befalls the room is a lucky break for her.* "Bud's here to find out who killed Annette, right Bud? And I'm quite sure the killer's here tonight." She tosses her head in triumph. Her breaths are shorter now, *she's exuberant.* Her eyes are shining.

At the end of her first sentence, there's a sound from Raj. He's facing me, standing beside Serendipity. They are blocking my view of the rest of the room. A definite "Oh" from him as he sucks in his breath. *His face says . . . surprise. Surprise at the idea that Annette was killed, or surprise that Ellen knows? It makes a big difference. Look closely, Cait, read him. No, I can't tell what he's surprised about. When Ellen speaks again, does his expression change? Yes. Now he looks disbelieving.* His mouth is forming a silent "No," there's a shadow of a shake to his head. Okay. Raj's micro-expressions are the key. *He's really surprised at first, then his disbelief is colored by something. I can see the expression in his eyes change. Got it! It's pity. He's feeling pity for Ellen as she speaks her second sentence. Interesting.*

Now I look at Serendipity: Ellen's first sentence brings an expression of surprise and horror to her face. She clenches her glass more tightly, she leans back from Ellen a little. She's literally taken aback. But she's not just leaning away from Ellen, she's leaning toward Raj. At Ellen's second utterance, she glances sideways, rapidly, at Raj, then back to Ellen. *Is she seeking a cue from him, and is that just because these two are a couple? Or is it because she suspects Raj? Her eyes flash a momentary rounded stare: she's frightened about something, a thought that's slipped into her head, and maybe it pertains to Raj. But, at the same time, her grip on her glass relaxes. Odd. She's releasing tension by looking at Raj. She's receiving comfort just by seeing him. They're obviously very close. I believe she's comforted by the expression she sees on his face. She's relieved that he doesn't believe what Ellen is saying. Interesting.*

Now I must look outside our direct circle, into the dim room beyond. Closest to us, and therefore the best lit, are the MacMillans. *This is before I have met them face to face: what are my initial impressions?* They're standing apart from the rest of the guests, and they're very close together. They're standing side-on to me, about twenty feet away. I cannot hear anything they are saying before Ellen's exclamation, but just as Ellen opens her mouth, Sheri MacMillan's expression is clear: she's upset. Nostrils flared, lips squeezed tight, corners of her mouth turned down, chin puckered, brows drawn together: *hurt, and angry.* Her eyes are downcast, her face is toward me as she turns away from her husband. Her shoulders are down, her head's down, *she's down: she's lost one of their skirmishes.* Rob MacMillan, standing opposite her, is a picture of cruel dismissal and anger: sneering upper lip, one nostril flared, staring eyes, glaring at his wife. *He's won. He hates her. He sees her as nothing. I know that look, Angus used to look at me like that just before he would raise* his arm to hit me. *That's the expression I learned to flinch from, all those years ago, in that loveless, destructive phase of my life—in those months before he lay dead on the floor one morning, and the police dragged me into a car, protesting my innocence, which I continued to do until they had to agree with me. It's a truly terrible look. And she knows it too—I feel sympathy for Sheri. But I mustn't. I must focus. Now's not the time to think about Angus. He's dead. He's gone. I'm here, doing this. I push the thoughts of him from my mind.*

As Ellen speaks, what do they do? How do their expressions change? He whips his head to look at Ellen. His dismissive expression doesn't change immediately: *he doesn't like Ellen.* As she speaks, his face shifts subtly to show that he's now expecting her to say something that's not worth hearing, and, as she finishes, his eyelids become hooded and he rolls his eyes. *He's thinking she's a stupid woman.* On the other hand, Sheri's snaps up and she gives her attention to Ellen. She looks frightened. *Is that a hangover of an emotion she feels for her husband? No. She clasps her drink to her body: she's frightened for herself, but not because she thinks her husband might strike her, I can tell that because, as one hand recoils toward her breast, her other reaches toward Rob. She's seeking his protection. She's frightened that what Ellen has said will somehow harm her.* She looks away from Ellen and her husband, toward the other people in the room. Now I can't see her face, but her shoulders hunch, and I wonder if she's trying to do what I'm trying to do—*see if there's a killer in the room.*

The folks she's looking at are the Souls, the Wisers, the Jacksons, Vince Chen, and another man and two women I never got to meet. I can't see the three unknown people at all—they all have their backs to me before Ellen speaks, and only turn their heads as they realize that something is being said. I can only see the sides of their faces, and then very dimly.

By the time Raj speaks, his pity for Ellen has subsided, and now his entire body is telling me that he's totally amazed that

Ellen has just said what she's said. His body is rigid, his neck is taught, he's confused, almost angry. He's frowning as he speaks, his eyes show disbelief that Ellen could have spoken that way. As he speaks I glance at Ellen. She's looking . . . triumphant. *Wow! She's almost gloating at Raj's amazement. Very odd.* Now she straightens herself up, like a warrior going to do battle, and tosses her hair in the most feminine motion I've seen her yet make. Her eyes are ablaze.

As she speaks to Raj, assuring him that she knows what she's talking about, her nostrils are flared, her eyes glittering in the dim light. *Her manner is shocking to Raj, I can see the change in his eyes. He's more confused.*

Now Serendipity speaks. She takes a half-step toward Ellen, and her manner matches Raj's original stance: *she's angry.* She's telling Ellen off when she speaks to her. *Her face says . . . exasperation.* When she says that Annette had been acting oddly for weeks, her shoulders settle a little, *she's being dismissive.*

At Ellen's rebuff, she doesn't falter. As she's listing the different examples of Annette's odd behavior she's counting them off on her fingers, angrily waving her hands in front of Ellen. Because she's taller than Ellen her hands are right in front of Ellen's eyes. They follow Serendipity's fingers, until Serendipity makes her final point and throws up both hands. *Yes, she's frustrated, angry.*

Now it's Ellen's turn to be dismissive. As she says the word "garbage," she tosses her head again, juts out her chin, and her lips form a sneer. *She's rubbishing Serendipity. Garbage.*

Now Raj steps in, literally trying to move between Ellen and Serendipity, who have moved close to each other. His tone is soothing, more gentle than before. His eyes are pleading with Ellen, to see his point of view. To accept what he and Serendipity are saying. His hands are raised in supplication. *He's trying to ratchet down the tension, while still making his point.*

Then the Jacksons butt in, and I'm not seeing any specific reactions to Ellen's point about Annette's death anymore.

The next thing to happen is that Suzie Soul detaches herself from the group and makes her way, unsteadily, across the forty feet or so between our groups, waving her glass and shouting as she approaches. She's clearly drunk, her face is a sneering mask, her lipstick smeared, she's holding her glass tightly, she's spilling her drink. She's walking in an almost straight line, but crossing one foot in front of the other as she progresses, surprisingly quickly. She's long ago mastered the alcohol and towering heels combination, but she's swaying. No one is paying her any attention except her husband, who is looking panic-stricken as he follows her into the light. His arms are flailing. He's trying to grab her, but she's keeping ahead of him and pulling her arms and shoulders away from his grasp. As she speaks, all eyes turn to her. Or do they? *No, Raj doesn't take his eyes off Ellen. He still looks aghast.*

Suzie Soul waves her glass toward Ellen and shouts, "You're a lush, Ellen Newman. Put your glass down and go home to your sorry, pathetic little life." Suzie's over-full lips seem to be sneering, her nose seems to be wrinkled and her teeth are certainly on display. *It's hard to tell what's due to plastic surgery and what's a real expression. One thing I can see is that she's lost pretty much every micro-expression a face can usually have. They've been nipped, tucked, sliced, and filled away. But her eyes speak volumes: she's not focusing on Ellen, due to the drink, but she's full of hate. Why would Suzie hate Ellen so much?*

Now I must consider Ellen's reaction to this. When it happened, I turned back to look at her as quickly as I could, now I do it again, and I can see what is the last glimmer of disdain on her face. *But Ellen replaces disdain with dismay very quickly. Interesting.*

As she reaches us, Suzie continues with, "And take your damned cop with you." She's looking at Bud as she says this. He looks very surprised, and leans away from the woman. Suzie is now almost showing her top gum, so curled is her upper lip—*I think it would be completely curled if it were still capable of such a movement.* She's pointing toward Bud with an angry hand, her decorated, false fingernails glinting. She's pushed past Serendipity, who, although much taller, has given ground between herself and Raj to this woman on a mission. As she enters our circle, we all lean back from Suzie a little, all except Ellen, who moves toward her, in an almost threatening way. It is at this moment that Sammy Soul reaches his wife's arm and grasps it.

Now all the attention in the room has completely shifted toward the Souls. It's impossible for me to see any expressions other than those that relate to this latest outburst, so there's nothing more I can see that's of use.

I sighed, stood up from the desk, and reached for the little bottle of water that stood on the nightstand. I unscrewed the top and drank the whole thing in one hit. I felt dissatisfied. What had I learned? Well, a few things were of interest. I'd file them away to tell Bud in the morning, but I wasn't sure I'd spotted the reactions of a murderer. *Oh, damn and blast it!*

Maybe a good night's sleep and a fresh start in the morning would help. I was quite convinced, as I snuggled into the comforting, downy bedding, that *someone* had killed Annette, but I knew, in my heart of hearts, that I was probably getting farther away from proving it than I had been when we'd arrived. *Hey, you only got here a few hours ago. Give yourself a break, and get some sleep,* I told myself sternly. And sleep I did—but I had terrible dreams about Angus, which was a very bad thing.

Strong Irish Breakfast Tea

WHEN I WOKE THE NEXT morning I felt dreadful. The first thing I was aware of was that I'd obviously been crying in my sleep. My eyes were sore and puffy, my head was stuffed up, and I was feeling anything but fresh. A sweaty, restless night had brought me to this. As I examined the damage in the bathroom mirror, fleeting images from my dreams haunted me. I hadn't had a night when I'd dreamed of Angus, with all the pain that involved, for months. Not since Bud and I had decided to give our relationship a go. And I hadn't missed those dreams.

As usual, after such a night, I wasn't feeling positive or chipper. The clock told me it was six thirty, so I showered, did the best I could with my makeup, blow-dried my hair, then pulled it into its everyday ponytail. I struggled into the stretch khaki pants I'd bought in a moment of delight at having lost five pounds—which I'd obviously regained, judging by the snugness with which they were fitting. The multi-colored stripy shirt I teamed them with covered most of my lumps and bumps. I was as ready as I was going to be. I wasn't looking forward to a gourmet Irish breakfast in the company of a bunch of murder suspects. I glanced at the underwhelming list of motives for murder that I'd written the night before. Now almost everything in me was telling me that my initial instinct had been wrong: that she'd probably killed herself after all. *I hate being wrong.*

It's funny how time flies when you're getting yourself ready to face the day. I was surprised to see that it was already seven thirty I was due to meet Bud in fifteen minutes. There was a knock on my door.

"It's me, Cait." Bud spoke just loudly enough for me to hear. "Can I come in?"

I opened the door and smiled. "Of course you can."

Bud looked me up and down, a concerned expression furrowing his brow. "Bad night?" he asked gently.

"Is it that obvious?" I thought I'd done a pretty good job of making myself look presentable.

"Only to me—no one else would know," replied Bud, trying to backtrack.

I shook my head. "It's okay, I know what you mean," I sighed. I felt completely deflated.

"I didn't sleep that well myself," Bud added, trying to be sympathetic. *He's not very good at it.* "Comfortable bed, sure, but uncomfortable thoughts. I'm beginning to think that coming here was a bad idea."

"Why so?" I sat on the edge of the bed, and Bud plopped himself, into the chair at the desk.

Bud considered for a moment, then said grimly, "You *know* I believe that Annette killed herself?" I nodded. "Well, I don't think that Ellen can accept it, so she's pulled me into her world to prove that her sister really *did* kill herself. I don't think Ellen really believes it was murder. I don't see how she *can*. I think that the only real help I can give her is to tell her it was clearly a suicide, and that she has to somehow accept all the evidence and move on."

"I agree," I said.

Bud looked surprised. "You think Annette really *did* kill herself? That a woman with a keen sense of smell *would* have done it that way, after all?" He spoke as though he suspected some sort of ruse on my part.

"I've been working it through, Bud," I said with resignation, "and I think it's a distinct possibility. Annette, for some reason we don't know, loathed herself so much that she chose *that* method.

She drank a whole bottle of wine, taped up the truck windows, and sat there breathing in the fumes until she lost consciousness and died. I don't know why she wouldn't have chosen to take a simple overdose, but there it is. We might have to accept that we'll never know why, the same way Ellen will have to accept it. It would be a hell of a lot easier for us, don't you think?"

"Sure . . ." Bud replied thoughtfully. "Right, then, let's go and see what this Pat Corrigan has for us by way of an Irish breakfast. I can't believe it, but I'm starving. You okay?"

It was as though a weight had been lifted from the two of us.

"Yes," I said, smiling, *really* meaning that I felt a million times better than when he'd walked into my room. "Yes," I said, smiling. I felt a million times better than when he'd walked into my room ten minutes earlier.

Bud kissed me on the cheek as he gallantly ushered me onto the landing. It was a happy couple that descended the As we came down, the Wisers entered the front door, which was being held open by a scowling Lauren Corrigan.

Good mornings were exchanged as Lauren relieved the Wisers of their outerwear. The sun was glinting on the lake below, and the sky was already a cloudless bright blue. Even so, the Wisers seemed to be bundled up in clothing that suggested they might be off to tackle the north face of the Eiger. They took off rugged walking boots and layers of cotton, fleece, and waterproofs, and one backpack each. It seemed a little over the top for simply walking up the hairpin road.

"Have you two come straight here from your house?" I asked, curiously.

The both laughed. "Oh, heaven's no," replied Marlene Wiser, still grinning, as she handed a second scarf to Lauren. "We thought we'd better work up an appetite, so we came around the back way."

"The back way?" asked Bud. Now he was curious too.

"This house is on top of a hill, right?" replied Gordy. Bud and I nodded. "If you continue around the bend in Lakeshore Road down there for about five minutes, rather than coming into the Close, you come to a trail that'll take you up around the base of the hill to its backside—I don't mean it *that* way, Marlene"—he grinned at his wife wickedly—"and then you can follow the trail up to the top of the hill. It takes a while, because the terrain is rocky and loose underfoot, and the old apple cart track's crumbled away long since. We're used to it. It's a grand walk."

"Apple cart track?" Bud was holding a discarded backpack.

"Ah yes," replied Gordy. "Behind the hill, on its *backside*," and here he grinned again like a naughty schoolboy, "there is a natural depression, not quite a cave, but a big gouge out of the side of the hill. Fred Newman, that's Ellen and Annette's father, was always a man for making the best of things, as you can see from this house. Built it with his own hands, he did. He fashioned a structure that covered this bite out of the hill that he'd found, and he used it as an apple store. In fact, that's how I came to know him. When he needed less storage because he was growing more grapes than apples, I rented the space from him. We'd haul our apples up in our 'apple cart,' which is what we called the rust bucket pickup we used back then. We'd bring the apples up to the store for the winter then bring them down again to sell. Over the years, since we stopped using it, the little road we'd worked out just got worn away by the weather. Now there's almost nothing left of it. Like the orchards, eh, Marlene?"

"Oh, Gordy, don't start off on *that* again." The woman rolled her eyes as she looked lovingly at her husband. "You're obsessed with those orchards. They're subdivisions now, with a lot of happy people because they have lovely new homes to live in. Come on then, where's this food we're all waiting for?" she asked cheerily, turning toward Lauren Corrigan. "We see all those folks coming up here every day for breakfast, but this'll be our first time, you know."

"Yes, I know," replied Lauren Corrigan grumpily. She didn't have a chance to add more because just then the front door was opened by Rob MacMillan, showily allowing his wife to enter ahead of him. She looked as though she'd had an even worse night than me: her eyes were red-raw, as was her nose. Of course, she *might* have developed a sudden head cold, but I reckoned I recognized the signs of a night of tears.

"Come on, Colin, don't dawdle," she said in motherly tones, looking up at the six-footer who was trailing behind her. Colin MacMillan's thin frame supported a head of red hair that seemed too big for his narrow shoulders to carry. His pock marked skin spoke of battles with acne, and the shortness of his sleeves and jeans suggested a recent spurt of growth. One earbud dangled loosely around his neck, the other was lodged firmly in his right ear. He had an air of terminal boredom about him. "Take your shoes off," his mother instructed him as he crossed the threshold.

"Leave the boy alone," rumbled Rob MacMillan.

I decided to follow the Wisers toward the dining area, rather than engage with the MacMillan family, as I didn't feel up to it. Bud ambled along with me.

Lauren called, "There's pots of tea in the lounge. You can all go in there out of my way for now. Help yourself." Clearly, she was being her usual, hospitable self.

Sure enough, a sideboard was bedecked with cups and saucers, milk jugs, sugar bowls, and two pots of tea—each wearing a natty little knitted jacket.

"Oh—I haven't seen a striped tea cozy like this since I used to have breakfast at my Gran's house," I commented with pleasure.

"I make them," Lauren said, clearly very proud to have her work complimented. "I'm a big knitter."

"Oh, really?" I replied. "My sister, too," I felt glad to find something that might help me connect with the woman. "She lives in Perth, Australia, now. Loves to knit. She can knit anything. Makes her own patterns. Likes circular needles."

Lauren was transformed. Her face was alight with enthusiasm, her voice very different from its usual, bored tones. "Oh, me too. The tea cozies are just little things that I've made to add a bit of a mood for our breakfast guests, but I make a lot of other pieces too. My project pages on Ravelry.com are quite busy."

I worried that Lauren might mistake my sister's hobby for my own. To be honest, I never got the hang of knitting. I was hoping Lauren wouldn't force me to feign interest. Luckily, she rushed off to attend to the needs of the new arrivals.

"Good morning," said Grant Jackson, who had managed to creep up behind me unheard.

"Oh, good morning," I said, forcing a jollity into my voice that I didn't feel, as I turned to face him.

Grant placed his hands together as if in prayer, bowed his head and whispered "Namaste."

I rolled my eyes—inwardly—then braced myself for some sort of pseudo-spiritual onslaught. Sadly, the man lived down to my expectations.

"It's *so* important, Cait, that we polish *each* of our fourteen Critical Facets every day," he intoned with more pious unction than I'd have thought possible. "*Giving* is one of those Facets, which, when it's matched with its thirteen partners, can lead us to a richer, more fulfilling life, in harmony with ourselves, our loved ones and the cosmos. Are you aware of the Faceting for Life movement?" He was looking directly at me.

"Sorry to interrupt, Grant, but I just need a quick word with Cait about something important that's just come up." Bud smiled politely as he took my arm and steered me back toward the staircase.

I flashed him a grateful smile. "Thanks, I thought I was going to get . . ."

Bud stopped me and nodded toward the cell phone in his hand. I could tell there was a text message on it, but I had to push his arm farther away so I could bring the blur into focus.

Screwing up my eyes, I managed to read: "Can't make it. Not feeling good. Go on without me. Get someone to bring you to the vineyard office after breakfast. Ellen."

I looked at Bud. "I'm not really surprised she's not feeling well. She seemed to be very drunk last night."

Lauren was now taking a bear-like fur coat from Sammy Soul, who seemed to have arrived with, of all people, Vince Chen. Suzie Soul was nowhere to be seen. The door opened again and it looked as though a bus had arrived. A group of four, obviously a mother, father, and two daughters, entered, all smiling and rosy cheeked. Mentally referencing Ellen's notes, I took them to be the du Bois family, who owned and operated the C'est la Vie Restaurant down on the waterfront in Kelowna. They hadn't been at the previous evening's festivities, due, I suspected, to the fact that they had a business to run. I was looking forward to the dinner at their place: they were known for their cassoulet and duck confit, two of my favorite dishes.

Rushing in behind them came Serendipity Soul and Raj Pinder. They were followed by the man I'd seen at the party the night before, but whom I hadn't had the chance to meet. Pat Corrigan suddenly appeared from the kitchen, beating the base of a large copper pot with a metal spoon. Everyone stopped chattering and gave him their attention as he walked to the staircase and gained some height by standing on the bottom stair.

"Welcome, one and all, to Anen House Bed and Breakfast. Ellen can't be here, which is a shame, but she sends her best, and she'll be with us all for lunch. My beautiful and talented wife, Lauren, and I welcome you, and wish you a hearty breakfast. Some of you here are great chefs, some of you are gourmets, and some are gourmands aspiring to *become* gourmets . . ." laughter rippled around the room,

"... so I hope that my humble spread tickles your fancy and pleases your palate. Now, you all know that we Irish are famous for our sayings, and there's many I could choose from at a time like this..." another ripple of laughter, "... but I'll keep it simple and I'll offer but one small prayer on behalf of us all: 'May you enjoy the four greatest blessings: honest work to occupy you, a hearty appetite to sustain you, a good woman—or man—to love you, and a wink from the God above.' Now—let's eat!" Once again Pat beat a rhythm on the pot with his spoon, and he ran off to fling open the huge serving hatch at the back of the dining room.

I couldn't have been happier: Bud was beside me, and in front of me were hot plates holding Pat's award-winning sausages—three different types—bacon, eggs, mushrooms, black pudding, white pudding, potatoes cooked three different ways, baked beans in sauce, and fried tomatoes, all just begging me to dig in.

Having piled up my plate, I finally plopped myself down at the table, delighted to see the big basket of Irish soda bread, salted and creamed butter curls, and homemade jams at the center of each table. Trying to chew slowly, I paid attention to my tablemates. I was dismayed to realize that it was young Colin MacMillan next to me, and one of the two du Bois girls across from him. *Damn and blast—two teens, what could be worse?*

"Enjoying it, are you? Isn't it all lovely?" I asked, between mouthfuls. It was probably the wrong thing to say to the two teens. Unsurprisingly, my question drew no response, but at least I got a muffled "Mmm" from Bud.

"Is that a *Welsh* accent?" asked Colin MacMillan a few moments later.

"Yes, I'm Welsh," I replied, relieved to break the silence at the table, but not sure what to say next.

"*Doctor Who* is made by BBC Wales," announced Colin. "Are you a *Doctor Who* fan?"

I smiled. "Yes, I am, as it happens. I even met Russell T Davies once or twice, many years ago. Are you a fan too?"

Colin nodded energetically, and seemed to be *very* impressed that I'd met the man who must have been his idol. "Annette Newman and I used to talk about The Doctor a lot. She liked *Doctor Who* too. This was her house, you know."

"Yes, I know. By the way, I'm Cait and this is Bud. Did you know Annette well?" I asked Colin.

"You liked her, right Colin?" offered the young girl sitting next to Colin brightly. It seemed that, like me, she was trying to engage Colin. I suspected she quite liked him, but he had no inkling she was interested. "I'm Poppy du Bois, by the way," she added.

Colin nodded. "Yeah. She was pretty cool. She used to talk to me. Lots. I was sad when she died. She liked *Star Trek* too, and *Star Wars*, and *Stargate Atlantis*, and she said she wished she had more time to get into more stuff like that. She had lots of cool books about history. We talked about different things. We even went to see *Avatar* together. My Mom thought it was weird, but it was cool."

"So, you like mythologies?" I ventured.

"Yeah," smiled Colin. "She gave me a hardback copy of *The Lord of the Rings* for my birthday one year, and she told me I had to read it all and then we could talk about it. It's really good, though I didn't like *The Hobbit* as much, it's more like a kid's book."

I was enjoying the chance to finally gain a little insight into the real Annette Newman.

"When she killed herself, my Dad said she deserved it," added Colin, taking both Bud and me by surprise. He looked around the room as he spoke, careful to keep his voice so low that no one at the tables nearby could hear his voice.

"What did he mean by that?" I was puzzled. I, too, lowered my voice.

"Oh, I don't know," replied Colin, "he gets all weird about things, for no reason. He's not cool at all, about anything. He didn't like me coming here to visit. When it was her house, it was different then. All her stuff's gone now. She had some cool stuff."

"Where did it all go?" I wondered, aloud as it turned out.

"Ellen took it all and put it in that store they've got on the hillside. I guess that's what she was doing driving that truck back and forth all those times. She didn't, like, announce it, or anything, but I see lots of things when I'm out on my bike."

"The apple store, around the other side of the hill?" Bud asked quietly, finally engaging in the conversation. Colin nodded, then Bud added, "Gordy Wiser was saying that the track isn't there anymore, there's just a trail. How'd she manage that?"

"Oh, she managed just fine. I guess she just used four-wheel drive. It took her a lot of trips. Did it all on her own. Right after Annette died. Like, *right* after. Then everyone started coming around—helping her fix the place up."

"And you saw her do this?" Bud asked. Bud was almost whispering. Our conversation had developed a very conspiratorial air.

Colin nodded.

"Colin sees lots of things that lots of people do," added Poppy.

"Don't say it like *that*," whined Colin, "you make me sound like a creep. Or a stalker. I'm not. I just get around."

"And you *notice*, don't you, Colin? Because you're interested in people?" I said it lightly, to encourage him to continue.

Colin nodded.

"And did you notice anything odd about Annette before she died? Or about anyone else, afterwards?"

Colin pushed a mushroom around his plate, then looked up and said, "A couple of months before she died, she put her garbage in her car and drove it to a dumpster downtown, which was weird. She usually dropped it at the Wisers' for pick-up. Garbage trucks won't climb this hill. And when she drove home from the office in Ellen's truck that last day, she was talking to someone, on her cellphone. I could tell she was upset because she was waving her hands around and crying."

As Colin spoke, several questions began bumping around in my brain, but instead of asking any of them, I chose to say, "Did it surprise you that Annette killed herself?"

Colin gave it some thought. With a maturity that belied his years, he said quietly, "Yeah, it surprised me. She was the one with hope. Ellen's the one without it. When we talked the day before she died, she was real excited about having found a signed James Sandy snuff box that some guy in Newfoundland was going to sell her. She'd been trying to find it for years. She said it was, like, the 'grail' of her collection. Of anyone's collection. She didn't seem down at all. Not like the day she died."

I took a moment to wrap my head around what Colin MacMillan was saying.

"You talked to Annette the day before she died, and she was excited about buying a *signed* James Sandy snuff box?" Colin nodded. "For her collection of snuff boxes?"

"Yeah, she was interested in all sorts of things, but she *really* liked snuff boxes. She showed me her collection lots of times. I had to wear white gloves to hold them. She knew the history of every box, and she had wonderful books with photos and illustrations. She said it was 'ironic' that she loved snuff boxes, 'cos she used her nose to earn her living and, like, snuff's not good for your nose, except to get you to sneeze. She never used snuff. Just loved the boxes. She had dozens and dozens of boxes, but most of them were silver. She kept them all in a little glass cabinet, over there," he nodded toward the area that was now the lounge. Colin MacMillan looked sad when he turned again to look at me. "I miss Annette. She . . . understood me . . . a bit. You know, my Mom and Dad, they don't really get me . . ."

"I don't think there's a single teenager in the world whose parents *get* them, Colin," I said, trying to be sympathetic. "It's a generational imperative: teens rebel, parents worry and try to impose rules. It's what happens. I bet your parents were the same when they were your age."

Colin rolled his eyes. "*Right.*"

"My parents are the same with me," piped up Poppy. "I mean, the restaurant's okay, and all that, but they still treat me like I'm a little kid. They're always going on about drugs at school and stuff like that."

"Yeah, mine too," agreed Colin, "but Dad drinks all the time when he's here, which isn't very often, and Mom drinks all the time, period. But because we're surrounded by wine, and because, like, every other person here makes their living out of it, or knows someone who does, we're all supposed to not think of booze as a *drug*, it's just something people get all fancy about. Annette thought it was funny, you know, the way people talked about wine. She couldn't understand why people couldn't smell it like she did, or taste it like she did. We laughed about it. She made fun of them all, all the time. But she didn't make fun of Raj. She didn't laugh at him. She liked him. They used to fly off to things together, you know, but not together? Like at the same time, to the same place, to do their tasting thing, but not, you know, *together-together*. That's what she said, anyway. Actually, she said that a lot. Then she stopped going. That's when she did the thing with her garbage. Weird. I miss her. I wonder where all her snuff boxes are? It seems a shame if Ellen just, kinda, dumped them into a box in storage. They were nice."

And worth a lot of money, I'm guessing.

It was at that breakfast table, with a cup of very strong tea in my hand, that I decided to stop being an idiot, and to trust my instincts. Colin MacMillan had just given me three very good possible motives for Annette's murder, some insight into how it might have happened, and one very good reason why she wouldn't have killed herself. I threw my earlier doubts out of the window, and decided I was back on the case.

Now I really needed to see the papers Bud had asked Ellen to get together for us. I had a feeling that somewhere within them I'd find a further clue to the real motive for Annette's murder which would lead me to the culprit. All I'd have to do *then* would be to work out how they'd managed to talk Annette into sitting in a truck until she couldn't breathe any more. Or how someone had managed to get Annette to a state of unconsciousness, then lifted her into the truck, given that there wasn't a single person on my list of possible suspects who looked as though they were capable of lifting more than a small sack of potatoes. I mean, some of those trucks are so high I need a stepladder to get into them myself, and *I'm* not hauling a deadweight. Already the prospect of solving the puzzle was exciting me, and I couldn't wait to get started.

Poor Bud.

Kopi Luwak

AS THE BREAKFAST CROWD BEGAN to rise from their seats and take their leave, shaking Pat and Lauren's hands as they departed, I was anxious to have a chance to compare mental notes with Bud. When I gave him the nod, Bud was up and moving toward the staircase in pretty short order.

As we made our way upstairs, I could hear Colin tell his Mom that he'd like to stay for the luncheon at their home later that day, after all. Her reply gushed with gratitude, and they left with her all but patting him on the head.

It wasn't until I was leaving my bathroom that I realized that Bud and I hadn't made arrangements for someone to drive us to Ellen's office, as she'd suggested. I crossed the landing and knocked on Bud's door, which he opened so quickly I suspected he'd been standing right behind it.

"We didn't organized a lift to Ellen's. I'm sorry, it slipped my mind," was my very reasonable opening gambit. He pulled my arm, and the rest of me, into his room, and shut the door. "We learned a lot about Annette this morning," I added brightly.

"Now you're trying to put lipstick on a pig," he observed wryly. "As far as I can see, the only things we learned about Annette were that, a) for some reason, she once took her garbage downtown, b) the day she died she had a row with someone and was upset, and c) she collected little boxes. The first two point to unusual behavior immediately prior to her suicide, the third . . . well, I guess it just tells us she had a hobby."

"Okay," I replied, trying to slide into the topic graciously, "I see where you're coming from, but I interpret those pieces of information differently. For example, the garbage thing: what was it in her garbage that she didn't want anyone to find?"

"Who would *find* anything in her garbage?" was Bud's sharp retort. "I mean, who would even *look* at her garbage—except the garbage collectors?"

I nodded, but wouldn't be dissuaded. "We don't know, though maybe we can infer that the assiduously attentive Wisers might have hazarded a peek. But *she* obviously thought it was important, so it should be important to *us*. And the argument she had. Who was she arguing with, why was she reduced to tears, and what might it mean in terms of a possible murder?"

"Cait, let it *go*!"

"No, I won't, because what that tells us is that she was upset . . ."

"Exactly," interrupted Bud. "And maybe upset enough to kill herself . . ."

". . . but we don't know *why*, so we should look into it." I was *not* going to be sidetracked. "There's also the collection of snuff boxes. If she had a good, large collection, especially of silver boxes, it could have been very valuable. We need to find out if stealing that collection, which Colin says has disappeared, might have been a motive for murder . . ."

"Oh come on, Cait. Colin's a kid. Just because he hasn't seen the collection since Annette died doesn't mean it's 'disappeared.' It's much more likely that Ellen's put it into storage with the rest of her sister's stuff—though that is an interesting point, in its own right."

I recalled how Bud had pressed Colin about the possibility of Ellen hauling her sister's belongings to the old apple store. "Yes, what was all *that* about?" I asked.

Bud scratched his head. "Well, when you were cooing about the canapés to someone last evening, I asked Ellen about the furniture in this place—you know, it's nice, old stuff?" I nodded. "She told me that she'd kept as many family pieces as she'd needed for setting up the B&B, but that she'd 'got rid of' the rest of Annette's things. I was really asking on *your* behalf, because I know how good you are at building a profile of a victim from their belongings. I thought that, you know, if you could root through Annette's stuff, you'd be able to build a better picture of her."

I pounced. "Ah, so you *do* think she might be a 'victim,' after all!"

Bud tutted. "Last evening I was still prepared to give you some benefit of the doubt, but that was it." He scratched again. "Why wouldn't Ellen just tell me she'd *stored* it all? Why would she lie about that? It makes no sense."

I gave it a moment's thought. "Okay, I'll play devil's advocate here, and suggest it might just be a sign that she can't let go of her sister. You know what I'm like with my parents' ashes, the way they're still sitting in urns on my mantelpiece . . ."

"Yeah, that is a *bit* odd, Cait, you have to admit. I mean, it's been a long time now." Bud shifted from one foot to another as he spoke.

"I know it's been a long time, and I also know that they are where they are *because* I can't let go. I don't actually *want* to let go, and I am fully aware of that fact. It's not unhealthy. It doesn't mean I'm nuts, or even odd. Plus there's nowhere *for* me to put them. They never visited me in Canada, so there's nowhere here that was special to them. I didn't want to leave them behind in Wales, where there'd be no one to tend to a memorial. My sister, Sian, didn't want them with her in Australia, which was fine by me. I think that having them on my mantelpiece is just the right spot for them, for now. And don't let's even go to the place where you heard me talking to them about you: you were supposed to be asleep and it was your fault you heard anything. But we're not talking about me. I'm just using that as an example of how people choose to hang onto things. Maybe Ellen wasn't ready to get rid of Annette's stuff: Colin said she made those trips to the old apple store very soon after her sister's death, so maybe that's how she dealt with the issue of belongings."

"Why would she *lie* about it? She said she'd 'got rid of them.'" Bud repeated.

"What if she thinks you'd see that as an indication that she hasn't come to terms with her sister's death?"

"You're saying that Ellen lied to me, to stop me from thinking that she *really* believes her sister killed herself?"

I nodded.

"I guess it's a possibility," said Bud thoughtfully. "I still think that the right thing to do is to confront her with that."

"Okay, but look, don't forget that now we know there's a *back* way that someone could have got to or from Anen House, without anyone who lives in Anen Close being any the wiser, and that's a big game-changer. One of my major stumbling blocks, on the murder front, was how anyone could have gained access to the scene of the crime. Now I know how that could have happened. All I need to do *next* is work out how someone could have got her to sit in the truck until she was dead—that's where the autopsy will come in handy. How about we get ourselves to Ellen's office, then we'll see if she's got the papers we asked her to hunt out, and I just get one more chance to see if there's anything concrete to go on." I wasn't pleading, but I was using my "pretty please" voice.

Bud smiled. "You can stop the super-cute smiley face, Cait," I did, "and tell me why you've shifted from agreeing with me, earlier on, that Annette probably *did* kill herself, to being back to believing she was murdered."

"I had a moment of weakness this morning," I sighed. "I was feeling pretty low. I doubted my instincts, which I shouldn't do. I thought I had learned that. And now I'm beginning to get a little insight into Annette, I realize we don't know the woman, the woman she *really* was, at all. Initially, you had a pretty thinly drawn picture of her from her sister, no more than a sketch of a perfect woman, whom no one would want to harm. And what have we learned about her so far?

She liked science fiction and fantasy; made fun of people who lacked her own skills; collected expensive snuff boxes and read extensively about history; even chose to spend time mixing, thoughtfully, with the young and the old. She was acting out of character for the last several weeks or so of her life, and she actually spent a lot of time with Raj Pinder, to whom she willed her half of the family business. We haven't even been here a day yet! I think we're doing okay, but we could do better. Surely there are enough odd facts coming to light that it's worth spending just a little more time digging around, before you do your big 'grief buddy' thing with her sister?"

Bud had moved his scratching hand from his head to his chin. *A good sign.* "Okay, I'll give you that," he said, almost grudgingly. "If we're going to go visit Ellen, why don't we just take my truck? I know she said to get ourselves a ride, but maybe everyone with a vehicle has left by now. What do you think?"

I shook my head. "I don't know who's still downstairs and who's gone, but I can see the little parking lot behind the house from my bathroom window, and our rooms are mirrors of each other, so you should be able to see it from yours too." Bud trotted into his bathroom as I spoke. "Are there any cars there?" I asked.

"There's one. A white Prius. Don't know whose it is, but if we're quick, we might be in luck. I guess if she said to get someone to drive us to her office, Ellen must have some sort of plan. She seems quite keen on plans."

"Okay, if you pop down I'll just—you know, run back to my room for a minute—and I'll join you."

"Too much tea?" quipped Bud, as I left his room.

A few minutes later I was refreshed, jacketed, and at the foot of the stairs with Bud and the Jacksons. *Oh joy!*

"The Jacksons have very kindly offered to drop us off at Ellen's office before they head on back to their store," said Bud, smiling a little too brightly.

"Super," I replied through almost gritted teeth. I sighed, but only inwardly, of course. "We appreciate it." *Please let it be a very short journey!*

"You're welcome," Lizzie Jackson replied, as she blinked at me through her owlish spectacles. "We felt a little guilty driving up the hill from our house first thing, but we knew we'd want to be back at the store for a while before the luncheon, so it made sense to not have to walk back down to collect the car. Of course, we don't like to use the car more than we absolutely have to, you know, the environment and so forth." *Here we go . . .*

"It's totally understandable," I added politely, as we all walked around the house to their waiting vehicle. "You've made a very sensible choice of car for the environment," I added watching Grant Jackson unlock the hybrid.

"Yes, it's a good one," he said proudly, "and only a few thousand on the clock when we bought it from Ellen. It's got a good few years in it, this one."

"This used to be Ellen's car?" I asked, desperately trying to keep the subject away from anything to do with Faceting.

"No, it was Annette's. But not the one—you know, that she— not *that* one. That was Ellen's truck. I don't think we could, you know . . ." Grant blushed.

"Drive the vehicle that Annette killed herself in?" I offered. Bud glared at me.

"When we leave this world we leave an imprint, and the imprint of poor Annette's final desperation will always be in that truck, which Ellen insists upon still driving," said Lizzie, with a mixture of sadness and disgust. She gathered up the layers of pale turquoise satin, chiffon, and velvet clothing that she'd donned for breakfast as she grappled with her seat belt. She added, "You see, Annette had a lot of back problems before she died, and, of course, everyone knew she'd backed out of tastings, so I suspected that her sense of smell was awry too, both clear indications that her root chakra was completely unbalanced. I told her to wear red. I even gave her a bloodstone to keep with her. But the ultimate failure of the root chakra is suicide. And I couldn't save her."

Grant Jackson managed to find his wife's hand among her multi-layered clothing and held it gently in his. "*We* failed her, Lizzie. We tried, but we failed. We should have tried harder. I should have recognized the signs when she asked me for help. I did what I thought was right, but I didn't understand what it *meant*. Lizzie's right, guys. Annette was definitely doing things in those last weeks that weren't right for her. She was obviously grappling with something. And I didn't connect with that. She wouldn't *let* us connect, or give, or help her to spiritualize her life in any way. We tried and failed. That won't stop us trying with others, *for* others, right, my dear? Right?" He kissed her hand, or more specifically, the large, green, crystal ring she wore.

I wondered what Bud and I were in for on the journey, but, as Grant pulled out of the parking lot and began to head down the road toward his own house at its base, I didn't have to wonder for long. He was clearly an evangelist for his belief system, and all Bud and I could do was nod politely as he rattled on, and on, *and on*.

"I gather you know nothing about Faceting for Life," he began joyfully, "which isn't unusual, eh Lizzie?"

"That's right, Grant," she replied, equally jolly.

Bud squeezed my hand as a warning.

"This is such an ideal opportunity to tell you a little about it," began Grant. *Oh, just shoot me now!* "But, hey, you'll have more of a chance to learn all about it when you come to our humble restaurant for lunch tomorrow. Briefly, it involves the concept that there are fourteen Critical Facets that we need to attend to each day of our lives, in order to allow ourselves to exist harmoniously with our surroundings. They are: playing, achieving, developing,

creating, loving, connecting, giving, relaxing, organizing, spiritual-
izing, vitalizing, indulging, dreaming, and laughing." As an aside he
added, "I don't expect you to remember them all, of course, but I'm
sure we have a pamphlet somewhere in the car that you can take
with you."

"And what we do is make sure we attend to each Facet, each day,
and give it a good buffing," added Lizzie with enthusiasm. "Facet
and Face It, you see. By ensuring that we make a conscious effort in
each of these fourteen parts of our life, every day, we become at one
with the whole cosmos."

I bit my tongue. I could tell that Bud knew how much I was
dying to speak, and he squeezed my hand even tighter. I couldn't
hold it back any longer.

"So Faceting for Life is a simple lifestyle choice, and you just,
sort of, do it all on your own?" I heard Bud "tut" as he let go of my
hand in disgust.

Both the Jacksons laughed. I wondered if that was all the laughing they'd have to do that day to have buffed that particular Facet.

"Oh no. We're not strong enough to do it as well as we might,
completely without help and guidance. That's what we use 'The
Gem' for."

"What's 'The Gem?'" *Well, I had to ask, right?*

"Oh, that's the place in Sedona where we Facetors can meet,
live for a while, learn from each other, and fortify ourselves with
supplies that help us in the outside world. It's where we met, eh,
Lizzie?" replied Grant, blissfully unaware of the vibes coming from
the back seat. Lizzie nodded at him lovingly.

"Lizzie had been there many times, but it was my first pilgrim-
age." *Oh, come on!* "She was so much more powerful than I, and
I learned a great deal from her. We Faceted together for many
days and, eventually, we both knew that our future path should be
walked together. That's when Lizzie sold up in Phoenix and came to

Canada, and I sold up my little business too, in Vancouver. We set up the store, the restaurant, and Lizzie's healing practice, right here. Together."

"Oh yes, I've been told that you help people give up smoking, Lizzie. Cait could do with your help on that one, right, Cait?" Bud was getting back at me for breakfast. *Damn and blast!*

Lizzie turned as much as she could in her seat to look toward me. "Oh my dear, I certainly can. I use a blended program of hypnosis, crystal healing, chakra realignment, and aura manipulation. I'm very successful. It only takes seven sessions. When are you leaving? I could fit you in today, if you like?"

I don't think she caught the look on my face.

"Well, we're leaving on Monday, Lizzie, but I'll certainly bear it in mind for our next visit." I tried to sound as enthusiastic as possible.

"It only took five treatments for Serendipity to quit, though she's still due to have her final two, next week. She's been without the poison in her system for almost a month now. I'm so *pleased* for her, she's taken to it so well. I *thought* I'd had a success with Marcel du Bois, though I understand he might be backsliding a little. It all went well to start with, but, being at that restaurant, he's got so many opportunities to have a sly smoke there."

I was puzzled. "But he can't possibly smoke at the restaurant?" As a smoker, I'm only too well aware of all the places you cannot indulge these days.

"Oh, no. But they have a place out back where the smokers all congregate, and they sometimes leave their cigarettes before they've finished them."

I still didn't get it. "And?"

Lizzie seemed a little flustered. "Well, you see, my particular hypnosis element focuses on stopping a person from wanting to light a cigarette, or cigar. If you don't light it, you won't smoke it. I mean, it's bad enough as it is, without smoking someone else's stub."

"*Ew!* True," I exclaimed. Even *I* didn't like the idea of sucking on a butt end that had already been in someone else's mouth, and a filthy ashtray, to boot.

Lizzie ploughed on. "Ellen eats at Marcel's restaurant all the time—it's pretty much underneath her apartment on the waterfront. She mentioned to me that she's seen him pick up the discarded butts and take a drag on them before he stubs them out properly. In fact, his wife, Annie, was telling me at breakfast that he's taken on the duty of 'making sure the ashtrays are emptied' with what she called 'enthusiasm.' I think I'd better have a quiet word with him, and pretty soon at that. Another failure for me, Grant."

"No, no, dear, he's almost there. If he hadn't ducked out of that final session with you, you'd have cracked it for him."

Lizzie looked somewhat pacified. "Yes, just one more and I'd have been able to fully balance his crown chakra, then he'd have been fine."

"Yes, of course," I said, "shame to not finish, really. Probably better to not start, if I can't finish? I don't want to go back to work and start following students around campus waiting for them to discard unstubbed cigarette ends." I tried to add a chuckle, but it all seemed to fall rather flat.

"We're here," announced Grant. We swung off Lakeshore Road and onto an unmade side road that headed straight up the vine-planted hillside to a large, unattractive, corrugated metal structure.

"That's the winery?" I must have sounded surprised. "*The Mt Dewdney Family Estate Winery?* I was expecting—well, not this." I hadn't meant to sound rude but it appeared the Jacksons took my comments in their stride.

Lizzie smiled as she spoke. "The Newmans have kept it basic. Unlike the Souls who've turned their place into some sort of pseudo-Provençal monstrosity. They've got the golf course as well as the vineyards and orchards to buffer themselves from the rest of us, but all that other stuff they've built—the concert hall, the huge clubhouse, and the restaurant, of course. At least the Newman girls keep it simple, and honest. It's just the working winery, with a small shop attached, and a patio for parties and barbeques in the summer. With them, it's always been about the wine. With Sammy Soul, well, you never can tell what his next money-making scheme will be. That man's chakras have probably been totally undermined by all those drugs he took in earlier decades. You'd think *he'd* listen to me, wouldn't you, Grant? I mean, all that stuff he wrote about in his music, you'd think *he'd* understand that I could help him."

Grant nodded as we arrived at the front door of the small, unassuming tasting room and store. It abutted the massive green metal structure that housed the winery.

"Thanks ever so much for the lift," I said, as I rushed to get out of the car.

"Sure thing," called Lizzie, as she handed me a pamphlet about Faceting for Life. "I found it on the floor," she added, smiling.

"Thanks again." I smiled back and waved, hoping they'd take the hint.

"Quick, let's escape," I whispered to Bud.

"Where do we go? Into the store?" he replied, also waving and smiling at the silently receding car. *Creepy how those hybrids do that.*

"I suppose so. Let's try it anyway," I said, and pulled him toward the door.

Inside the small, wooden structure the atmosphere was calm and inviting. It felt homey, somewhere you could linger, and relax. There were no seats, but a high counter ran the entire length of the side wall. Behind it stood a woman in her thirties with cropped chestnut hair and a welcoming expression. She was one of the women I'd missed the chance to meet at the cocktail party.

"Welcome to Mt Dewdney Family Estate Winery," she said. "How can I help you today?"

"We've come to see Ellen," replied Bud. "She's expecting us, but we're not sure where to find her office."

"Ah, are you Bud and Cait?" she replied. We nodded. "Oh great, I'm Bonnie. Ellen said to send you right up to her office."

We dutifully followed her instructions. I didn't look down as I climbed the unenclosed stairway, ignoring the huge metal containers, miles of pipe work, and rows and rows of barrels below us, and I made it to the top without feeling too giddy. But I wasn't looking forward to descending the stairs later when, let's face it, you really *do* have to look down.

"You okay?" asked Bud, concerned. He knows I have a bit of a thing about heights.

I nodded. I was fine. We knocked, then entered Ellen's office.

The room was large, and lined with that dreadful synthetic wood-paneling that was so popular in the 1980s. My first impression was that it was creaking at the seams. Wine bottles—some full, others empty, some labeled, some unmarked—stood in among neatly stacked boxes and crates, with little piles of labels dotted about everywhere. At the center of the stacks was an immaculately well-ordered desk. There sat Ellen, her back to the window that overlooked the serried ranks of vines on the hillsides beyond. She was facing the boxes, angled away from the door. *Odd choice!*

Looking up, she smiled weakly. "Hi," she said quietly.

She rose and nodded toward a laminate shelf that held some pretty complex coffee-making equipment.

"Coffee?" she asked us both. "It's kopi luwak," she added.

"You're *kidding*?" I exclaimed. "Just your everyday coffee then, eh?"

"It's my little indulgence," Ellen replied, looking a bit guilty.

I eagerly accepted the cup Ellen offered. Bud less so.

"It's amazing, isn't it," I said brightly, "that the folks who gather the beans for this coffee are quite happy to go poking around in civet dung just to harvest them?" As I spoke, I wafted the steam upward, then I took tiny sips of the piping hot fluid. It was magnificent: robust yet mellow, earthy but at the same time almost chocolatey, and syrupy, in an intriguing way.

Bud had already placed his emptied cup back onto the desk. "Dung-harvested beans? Ugh!"

"If it makes it any easier to *swallow*," my eyebrow was playing around my face by now, "it's the world's most expensive coffee bean. Running at hundreds of dollars a pound, right, Ellen?"

"Like I said, my indulgence," she said.

"Do you roast it yourself?" I asked.

Ellen glowed. "Every morning, at home. I have an old batch roaster there, from the 1940s, and it does a great job. I just roast enough for the day, though I roasted some extra for you guys this morning."

"Where'd you manage to find an old roaster like that? They can't be easy to come by." I knew they weren't.

"Well, it's funny you should ask, because I actually got it from Grant Jackson. When he sold his antiques business to come here, he brought a bunch of stuff he thought he might find useful, or decorative, you know, for the restaurant. When I saw the coffee roaster on display, just for show, we both agreed I could give it a better home, so he let me have it at a very reasonable price."

"Lucky," I nodded. "Was that the sort of stuff he used to sell, then?" I asked. "Kitchenalia?"

"Oh no, that was *more* luck. Someone had brought it in to him, trying to sell it, just when he'd decided to close down and open the restaurant here. He usually dealt in silver—you know, candlesticks and such like. Apparently he was very good at it, very knowledge-able. Not that you'd think it to look at him—all that jibber-jabber he's into these days."

Bud decided, in my moment of contemplation, to take the bull by the horns and said boldly, "Ellen, were you able to dig up Annette's will, the coroner's file, her note, and another sample of her signature?" *Way to go, Bud!*

Ellen reached into a drawer near her feet and passed two folders, plus a single sheet of paper to Bud. She also handed me a large board that was clearly the artwork for the label for the Annette Pinot Noir Ice Wine: a part of the label was Annette's signature. "That signature was taken from Annette's last birthday card to me. It's definitely hers," she said, grappling with the board. I looked at the board, then placed it carefully back on the desk. Bud handed all the other papers directly to me, then engaged Ellen in a bit of small talk about the office and its contents, as well as the winery below, earnestly leaning on the desk as he did so.

As Bud chattered, I popped on my glasses and read through the paperwork, in my usual manner. At one point I stuck my nose into their conversation. Bud had asked Ellen why she had so many bottles of wine in the room, and then asked how many she had. *I couldn't resist, could I?*

"There are eighty-three bottles, sixty-seven of which are full."

Ellen stared at me.

"It's a thing I can do," I said. "I'm sorry, I shouldn't have interrupted, but sometimes I can't help myself. Okay, back to my reading." A glance at Bud showed me he was displeased. Breaking eye contact with me, he tried to re-engaged Ellen with more fervor, but with no luck this time.

"It seems to me," Ellen said coolly, "that Cait does *all* your reading for you, Bud, which makes perfect sense, given her background."

Bud and I exchanged a glance. A glance which could not have gone unnoticed.

"I 'googled' you," said Ellen, looking at me. "*Why on earth* did you say that you teach marketing, when you're actually quite well known as a criminal psychologist?"

"I panicked," I said, panicking.

"I don't think it was very nice of you to lie to me," continued Ellen, sounding more than a little hurt. "I thought we trusted each other, Bud. I thought that *meant* something."

Bud was blushing too. "I'm sorry," he said. "Cait thought it would be better if she was incognito, so to speak, if she and I were going to be on the lookout for murder suspects. The folks here might all know I'm a retired cop, but, if they thought that Cait was just my 'plus one' they might open up to her, more than they'd open up to me."

"And have they?" asked Ellen, reasonably enough.

"Not so much," I said, not straying too far from the truth. "It seems there isn't that much to open up about."

"I see." She added, "And what about those files? I'd rather you didn't take them out of this office. Would you like some time to read them?" She asked pleasantly enough.

I smiled. "No thanks, all done. Would you like them back?" I pushed them across the desk in her direction.

Ellen looked at the papers, then me, then Bud. "Well, if you were only going to glance at them . . ." She sounded quite disgruntled.

"Sorry, Ellen. I have a few questions, if you don't mind?"

"About what?" she asked, still obviously miffed.

"Let's start with the coroner's file," I began.

"Okay," she said, but added curiously, "How can you have read it all so quickly?"

I hate discussing my special skills with anyone, so I just muttered, "I read fast, but that's beside the point." I continued. "First of all, because this was a clear case of suicide, there was no autopsy, right?" Ellen nodded, and Bud looked a little surprised. I turned to him. "It's apparently quite usual, Bud, in this region. In these times of tight budgets, the coroner works closely with the family and the physicians of the deceased to understand their general state of mental and physical well-being at the time of death, to help decide if an autopsy's needed or not." Bud still looked unconvinced. I sighed. "Come on, Bud, you've been with homicide and the gang squad for so long now. When was it you were last involved with a suicide? Ten, fifteen years ago?"

"I guess it must be about that," he grudgingly agreed.

"Times change, and policies change. Nowadays, if it's clearly a suicide, and there's no reason for the coroner to suspect anything else, there doesn't need to be an autopsy." Bud shrugged. I continued, "The file says your family physician reported that he hadn't seen Annette in over a year, and that he wasn't aware of any medical issues, and that you weren't either. Is that right? Annette was in good health at the time of her death, as far as you knew?" Ellen nodded again. "The file also makes it clear that your sister's body bore no marks of violence, restraint, or trauma. She hadn't been held against her will, beaten, hit, or wounded at all, right?"

"Correct," replied Ellen, sounding apprehensive.

"The coroner's examination confirms that she died of carbon monoxide poisoning, and wasn't moved after death: blood tests prove the CO levels, and rosy lividity on the rump, lower back, and the lower portions of the legs and feet was evident. She *definitely* died in the truck. So, if she *didn't* kill herself, Ellen, how do you think someone convinced her to sit in that truck until she died?"

I'd decided to tackle the toughest question first.

Ellen thought for a moment, then said quietly, "I don't know. She could have been drugged."

"The coroner did a normal toxicology test. They took samples of blood, urine, and vitreous fluid, and discovered alcohol in Annette's blood, but that was it. No drugs, no other toxins."

Ellen pounced. "Well, maybe she was so drunk that she passed out and they carried her to the truck and placed her in it."

"You'd expect to see some marks on the body if that's what happened, Ellen. It's terribly difficult to carry an unconscious person without banging or bumping some part of the body, and she'd have been alive long enough for some bruising to have formed. Besides, it says here that Annette weighed one hundred and sixty pounds. It's no mean feat to lift that weight. You'd either need to be very strong . . ."

". . . or there were *two* people!" Ellen seemed quite excited.

"So now we're looking for a murderous *team*?" Bud asked. I knew he thought I was playing right into his "it was suicide" corner.

"Oh dear," said Ellen, looking confused.

"We come to the coroner's search of Anen House. He found nothing to indicate that there'd been a struggle, nothing out of place or broken. You yourself told him there was nothing missing."

"No, there wasn't. Nothing missing," replied Ellen distractedly.

"That's not all you told him, is it, Ellen?" I added. Bud was on the edge of his seat now.

Ellen shook her head. She must have known what was coming next.

I sat back in my chair and spoke softly. "Ellen, that morning, when you found your sister's body and the coroner interviewed you, you told him that Annette had been acting oddly for weeks, didn't you?" Ellen nodded, her eyes downcast. "You told him that you weren't surprised that she'd killed herself, didn't you?" Again, Ellen nodded. She seemed to be shrinking in her seat as I spoke. "You told him you were in no doubt that the signature on the note was your sister's and that it didn't surprise you that she'd typed it, right?"

Bud was almost wriggling with anticipation next to me.

"You also told the coroner that she *must* have planned to kill herself that way because she'd specifically borrowed your truck that evening."

Ellen broke down and sobbed.

"I don't get it," whispered Bud as Ellen scrabbled around in her desk drawers, trying to find a tissue. "What's that about borrowing Ellen's truck?"

"Annette drove a *hybrid*, Bud. Can you imagine how long it would take to kill yourself with the carbon monoxide coming out of one of those things?"

"Right!" he exclaimed, looking triumphant. He cleared his throat. "Oh dear, come on Ellen. I think you've just got to face it, Annette *meant* to do it. She'd been planning it for weeks. She changed her will, borrowed your truck, prepared the note, drank the wine, and waited. I'm so sorry." He got up and walked around the desk. Ellen rose from her seat, blubbing and shaking as she sobbed. Bud put his safe arms around her. "There, there. It's difficult, I know Ellen. You must see it now. Poor Annette meant to kill herself. It's really *quite* clear." He pulled back to let Ellen take some deep breaths. She looked completely deflated.

"Oh God. Oh Annette, poor Annette," she sobbed. "I wish I'd asked her what was wrong. I knew she was acting weirdly. I knew something wasn't right, but she wouldn't talk to me about it. And then, when she . . . when I found her, it was such a shock. But after-wards, when I thought about it . . . I just couldn't believe it!" she drew a breath, and blew her nose. "Oh Bud, Cait, I'm so *sorry*. So *very* sorry. You're right. I have to come to terms with it. I *must*. If I'd known what she was planning, maybe I could have talked her out of it. If only I'd gone to the house earlier . . ."

"Ellen, you've read that file, like I have," I said in my most sympa-thetic voice. "You know she was dead before midnight, and you got there at eight in the morning. So that's that. An hour here or there wouldn't have made any difference."

"Alright then," replied Ellen angrily, "if I'd gone there the night before. If I'd gone *then*, I could have saved her."

"No, Ellen," I said, more firmly this time, "It wouldn't have made a difference. You told the coroner that Annette specifically asked if she could borrow your truck that night, so she must have had a plan, right?" Ellen nodded. "We know that she was having a bitter argument with someone on her phone as she drove up to the house that evening . . ."

"What?!" exploded Ellen. "What do you mean? What argument? With *who*? Who saw the truck?" The words tumbled out of her, then she stopped and blew her nose.

"It doesn't matter who saw Annette," I said. "All that matters is we know she was having a row with someone, and she was very upset . . ." I tried to continue, but Ellen interrupted me, angrily.

"I bet it was Marlene Wiser, or Gordy. They're always sticking their noses in where they aren't wanted. Typical!" Ellen was clenching her little fists.

She was clearly very angry, and I was just about to tell her that it was Colin who'd seen Annette that evening, not the Wisers, when Bud piped up. "Ellen, it doesn't *matter*. What *does* matter is that you have to try to come to terms with things. You know what we learned about the stages of grieving?" Ellen nodded in Bud's direction. "I suggest you take some time to gather yourself and think through how they apply to you, and Annette's suicide."

I stopped myself from pointing out that psychologists are divided on the topic of stages of grieving, because I thought that, on balance, it probably wasn't the right moment to toss around an academic chestnut.

"I tell you what," suggested Bud, more brightly, "How about Cait and I get Bonnie, downstairs, to organize a tour of the winery for us, while you take some time for yourself. We can either all go to the MacMillans' for lunch together, if you're feeling up to it, or Cait and I will organize getting ourselves to their house alone." Ellen nodded. Bud looked at his watch. "Hey, it's only ten forty-five now, there's lots of time before we have to get there—it's a one o'clock lunch, right?" Again, Ellen nodded. "Okay—that's decided then, right?"

Finally, Ellen looked up, and managed a smile. "Yes, that's a good idea. You go on. I'm *sure* I'll be fine. I mustn't miss the luncheon too. Tell Bonnie to give me a call when you're done, and I'll come down. I'll just calm myself down and tidy up a bit."

We all nodded. Bud and I took our leave of the once-again sobbing Ellen. I tottered down the staircase, concentrating on my feet and willing myself to not fall. I was relieved when I finally made it to solid ground, but I was still a bit shaky.

"Good job up there, Cait. It was tough, but someone had to do it. You made her face facts, by simply stating them. Well done. I'm *proud* of you!" Bud gave me a lovely kiss, which was very nice, but, sadly, undeserved.

When he released me from his strong arms, I made a big show of straightening myself up, then I said, "I really enjoyed that kiss, Bud, but I hope you don't want to take it back when I've said what I'm about to say."

Bud looked apprehensive as he replied, "And that would be . . . ?"

"Well, I rather cherry-picked the bits I wanted to highlight from the coroner's file, to allow Ellen some sense of acceptance."

"But . . . ?"

"Okay, to begin with, Annette weighed one hundred and sixty pounds: if she'd drunk that entire bottle of wine—that empty bottle they found beside her in the truck—even over several hours, she'd have had a blood alcohol level of something over 0.10. Annette's actual blood alcohol level was 0.015, and that's a *lot* lower—the equivalent of drinking a *glass* of wine over about an hour, not a bottle of wine over an evening. *Certainly* not drinking a bottle in the way you might expect a suicidal woman to do it—by the neck, and in big hits. There was no trace of wine spillage on her clothes . . . Bud, just try drinking wine straight out of the bottle, especially if it's a final, defiant act, without getting a drop on you. I'm pretty sure it can't be done."

"And?" Bud could tell I wasn't finished.

"The coroner mentions that he asked Ellen about an empty cabinet in the living room of the deceased, and she said it had contained Annette's snuff box collection, but that Annette had sold it all, a couple of weeks earlier. Ellen was right, there wasn't anything *missing*, but it begs the question, Why did Annette sell her cherished collection?"

"Because she was planning to kill herself?" suggested Bud.

"No, I don't think so. I think she might have sold the collection to be able to afford the James Sandy snuff box that Colin told us she'd found in Newfoundland. As snuff boxes go, if she'd found an original James Sandy, signed, with a good provenance, which is all I can imagine she could have meant when she spoke of the box as her 'grail,' she might well have rid herself of every other box, just to be able to own one perfect specimen. Don't ask how I know all about James Sandy—I read it somewhere. Anyway, there's always been this rumor that there was a signed box made by Sandy toward the very end of his short life, in 1819, from the wood of the bed in which Robbie Burns died. Sandy was a Scottish cripple from Laurencekirk who invented—or at least perfected, depending on which source you believe—a very specific sort of airtight hinge that allowed snuff boxes to be made from wood. His hinge invention led to an entire box-making cottage industry in early nineteenth-century Scotland. If she'd found it, it's a unique piece. It could be worth a lot of money. I mean a *lot*. You'd only need two collectors bent upon owning it to bid each other up, and there you are. Collectors are like that, you see. They begin with it being a hobby, something they enjoy; then they learn more, and gather more objects about them then; then it becomes an increasingly important part of their life, and sometimes it even ends up defining them. Finally, for many, there's that one elusive, exquisite, or perfect piece that they'd give almost anything to own. It's not dissimilar to criminal psychopathy in many respects."

"Oh come on, Cait, you're just guessing now. Signed boxes. Robbie Burns. It's all smoke and mirrors," replied Bud dismissively.

"I understand why you might say that, Bud, but what you don't know is that the coroner also recovered a slip from Annette's purse that showed she'd made a cash deposit of twenty-five thousand dollars into her account the day of her death. That's a lot of cash."

Bud nodded. He started to scratch his chin. "I wonder where she got that sort of cash . . ." he mused.

"As I suggested, Bud, the snuff boxes are gone, the cash has appeared, she told Colin she'd found the 'grail.' I'd place those facts together as a group. While we're at it—the suicide note had a spelling mistake in it." Bud looked suitably curious. "Yes, it was word for word what Ellen told us it was, but whoever typed it, had typed the word 'perfectly' as '*prefectly*.' The words 'Love always' and the signature 'Annette' *were* handwritten. Now, just trust your local, friendly psychologist on this one, Bud: anyone, and I mean *anyone*, however much distress they might be in—and, if we're going with Ellen's theory, this was a pretty carefully planned suicide, not a spur of the moment thing—anyone would *check* their suicide note. They wouldn't allow their last words to not be *exactly* what they meant them to be. I just don't buy it. The more I find out, the less this adds up."

"You're obviously on a roll, Cait, so go on," said Bud, grimly scratching his head.

"Her will. The new one?" Bud nodded. "It says she leaves everything to 'Rajan Michael Pinder,' then it gives his address at SoulVine Wines, and then it adds, get this—'and thereafter to his firstborn child.' Annette basically tried to entail her half of the winery to Raj's first child, after him, when he's gone. Now, I'm no lawyer, but I have a suspicion you can't do that, legally, but, there it is, in her will, and Ellen hasn't contested it. Any of it. The will was one of those pro-forma things you can buy at the store and do yourself. It might be of interest to note, too, that in the whole of *that* typewritten document—which your theory of suicide supposes that Annette typed herself—there's not *one* mistake. And the witnesses?" Bud shrugged. "*The Wisers.* They must have 'forgotten' to mention that they witnessed Annette's new will when we were talking to them, and asking about her behavior in the run-up to her death."

"Still," pressed Bud, "the new will and her death? That will alone points to intent to kill herself. Right?"

"Not if someone forged it, or knew about it," I replied.

"Only Raj Pinder benefits by the will. Do you see *him* as the murderer?" Bud looked puzzled.

"I'm not ruling him out, just because I like him," I replied hesitantly, "but now, whoever is his 'firstborn' stands to do well out of it too."

"He doesn't *have* any kids." Bud sounded cross.

"Well, not that we know of, but he might have, back in the UK, or he might be planning one soon—which would bring the mother, and her family, into the picture."

"What do you mean, 'planning one soon'?"

"Oh come on, Bud. *Raj and Serendipity?* You must have noticed. She's trying to give up smoking, which might mean she's getting ready for kids . . ."

"Raj and Serendipity aren't a couple!" Bud sounded quite certain. "Are they?"

"Oh dear, for a cop, you sometimes don't see the things right in front of you, do you?"

"Oh, *damn*, Cait. It's all so confusing. Why are you doing this to me?"

"I'm not doing it to *you*, Bud! It's not like this is some personal crusade for me. I'm just looking at the information and working out what it means. And, you're right, it *is* confusing. A straightforward suicide shouldn't be, and probably wouldn't be, which is why I'm now more certain than *ever* that it was a murder."

Bud sighed. "Why did you do all that stuff up there, to convince Ellen you thought it was a suicide? I can't wait for the answer to this one . . ." He was almost smiling under the tone of complaint.

"Because Ellen Newman has found out that I'm a criminal psychologist and I don't want her putting that out there on the street. I want her to think we're off the case, that we're just relaxing and enjoying the Moveable Feast, and then we'll go home. I don't want her opening her mouth and putting her foot in it, like she did last night. I *will* find out more. I *will* push this, Bud. *Someone* killed Annette Newman and worked damned hard to make it look like a convincing suicide. Because everyone, and when I say 'everyone' I mean *everyone*, including Ellen at the time, thought it was a suicide, there was no autopsy. Now there'll never be one, because Annette was cremated a week after her death. That's a pretty clever murderer, Bud. We've got a whole lot more leads to follow now than we did this time yesterday, don't you agree?"

"Damn you, Cait. I do." Bud looked worried, but at least he'd stopped messing with his hair. "This doesn't seem cut and dried anymore," he added. "There are too many unanswered questions, and too much weirdness surrounding Annette's death for it to be a simple suicide—though I should warn you that I'm not giving up on the possibility that she *did* kill herself, forced to a place where she saw it as her only move. So, maybe manslaughter, not murder—which doesn't mean a lack of culpability on the part of a possible perpetrator, and it might even constitute a more devilish form of seeing someone dead."

I reached around Bud's neck and gave him a big kiss on the cheek. "Oh, I love it when you use words like 'culpability' and 'perpetrator,' because it means you're coming around to my way of seeing things. Not that I'm *happy* that Annette was killed, but—oh you know what I *mean*, Bud."

"On this occasion, yes, I do," he replied, smiling wearily, "but don't take that for granted, because sometimes I have absolutely no idea what you're up to, or why you're up to it."

"Good!" I said. "That'll keep you on your toes, then."

"True," was Bud's pithy response. I pulled him toward the tasting store to find Bonnie and arrange tour of the winery before it was time to leave for lunch.

The sun was getting higher in the joyous blue sky, and there were a couple of cars pulled up in front of the store. I felt as though the snowy piles we'd seen at the side of the highway just twenty-four hours earlier were a world away. I wished I hadn't a care in the world, and that I could just enjoy a wonderful break in this magical micro-climate for a few days.

I was back on the case though. And now, with Bud on my side, I had no doubt that we'd work out what had happened to Annette Newman, and why.

A Flight of Reds and a Flight of Whites

AS BUD AND I APPROACHED the Mt Dewdney Family Estate Winery tasting room's front door, we had to literally jump out of the way of Colin MacMillan, who was free-wheeling down the hill toward us on his bicycle, happily screaming "woo-hoo," and furiously ringing his bell. Despite the fact that it was still early in the year, a trail of dust shot up from his wheels as he passed. Bud and I spent the next couple of minutes brushing its remains from our clothes and, in my case, trying to dislodge it from my lipstick.

Finally making our way into the wine tasting room, Bonnie greeted us with a friendly wave. She said, "He's a devil on that bike, isn't he? Haven't seen him here for an age, now he's back again." She returned her attention to a well-dressed young couple who were paying for a case of wine.

Bonnie whispered, "Back in a minute!" as she passed us to help them to their car.

Bud looked at his watch. "It's gone eleven now, do you want a trip around the winery, or do you fancy a tasting?"

"Let's see how long a trip takes," I replied. Bud nodded.

Bonnie bustled back into the room. Keeping an eye on another older couple who were standing at the bar sipping from their tasting glasses, she said, "So, good meeting with Ellen? How's she doing? Didn't look very good when she arrived. Raj hasn't shown up at all, but he'd be the one I'd expect to see with a sore head."

"Well, Raj was at the breakfast at Anen House," I offered, "but I don't know where he went after that. Does he come here every day? Does he have his own office here—or does he share with Ellen?" Picturing the desk isolated amid the boxes upstairs, I couldn't imagine where he'd fit into Ellen's space.

"Oh no, not every day, because he's often away, at weekends and that, so then he'll take the odd weekday off to compensate—not that he has to punch a clock or anything. I mean, he owns half the place. He's got his own office, downstairs, in back of the winery. Of course," she drew conspiratorially close, "Ellen and Annette used to share the office upstairs, but Raj said he'd prefer his own space. I don't think Ellen liked that." Bonnie's voice dropped so low that she almost mouthed her last comment.

"Oh, why's that?" I asked. Bonnie was obviously dying to tell us everything she knew—or *thought* she knew.

"Well," she said, checking to make sure the tasters were still sipping, "I think Ellen's a bit over-protective of Raj. Always making sure she knows where he is, and what he's doing. She fusses around him like I don't know what. I don't think he's keen on it, but he's polite. Always. Such a gentleman. And that funny accent? Oh, he says some *real* cute things sometimes. And he's pretty easy on the eye too, eh?" She winked at me as she nudged my arm.

Bud cleared his throat. "Ellen's a good deal older than Raj, right?"

Bonnie rolled her eyes in my direction and said, "Ah, bless him!" nodding at Bud. I smiled and shook my head. Sometimes it was hard to believe that Bud had been a cop as long as he had.

"But enough chitchat," said Bonnie, turning toward the bar. "Fancy something to taste?"

"We wondered if we might have time for a tour of the winery?" ventured Bud.

"Well, the next organized tour is at noon," said Bonnie, looking up at the clock on the wall. "It takes about an hour, and you end up here for a tasting."

"Oh dear, we need to be at the MacMillans' by one," I replied. "Could *you* tell us something about the wines and let us have a tasting here, now?"

"Oh, *absolutely*!" Bonnie was delighted. She handed us each a laminated card. "Why don't you two have a look at the wine list while I help this lady and gentlemen? Then we'll get you sorted out, okay?" Bud and I nodded our agreement.

We spent a few moments reading. *Everything* sounded delicious.

"So how do you want to do this?" asked Bonnie upon her return. "We usually serve three or four wines for tasting, but, you *are* friends of Ellen, and I don't think that either of you are driving, right?" We nodded. "Okay then, how about a Full Flight of Five? Each."

"Can I do all red?" I couldn't imagine she'd say no.

"Oh yes, whatever you want—some red, some white, all red, all white—it's up to the customer. By the way, this is on us. Ellen's orders."

"In that case, if Cait's going to do all red, I'll do all white . . . then we can always taste each other's if we want." Bud smiled cheerily as he spoke.

"You think I'm going to *share*?" I couldn't believe he'd even think I'd share my reds. We turned our attention to the ten glasses Bonnie lined up in front of us. I have to say, it looked like a *lot* of wine! Although each of the glasses held only a small amount, it was the overall vision that was a bit daunting.

"You'll want to go from light to full for red," Bonnie announced, "and from dry to sweet for whites. Both work from your left to your right. If you look at the list it'll tell you what you're drinking: this is the Luxe Full Flight of Five. It's at the very top of the sheet. The tasting notes are there. Now, is there anything else I can do, or shall I just hover and listen in, like I usually do?" Bonnie grinned wickedly—clearly a woman who enjoyed every aspect of her work.

"Oh yes, please stick around," I replied, "I'm sure we'll have a lot of questions. But I can see you're needed by those guys, so we'll see you in a minute." Bonnie moved away to help the potential buyers, who seemed to be trying to work out how to split a case of twelve bottles between five different wines.

I read the wine tasting notes, noting the author's initials beside each one, and found that the taste descriptions with "AN" next to them were better at hitting the mark for me than those with an "RP." I guessed that my palate was more in tune with Annette's than Raj's. Carefully sniffing and swirling as I went, I dutifully took one sip, washed it around my mouth and swallowed, then took the first true tasting sip of each wine. I worked from one wine to the next. Finally, as I'd suspected, it was the most robust of the wines that really caught my tastebuds and set them alight: described as having "aromas of blackberry, cherry, plum, and dark chocolate with raspberry, blackberry, coffee, layering soft smoky notes on the palate," the Anen Nightshades really was "a full-bodied red wine that displays soft tannins and a lengthy finish." I *loved* it! I could imagine sipping it with a steak, or with strong cheeses or, frankly, just all on its own.

Bonnie was smiling at me. "You're enjoying that, right?" she quipped. "More?" she asked, as she offered the bottle of the final wine.

"Just a drop, thanks." I returned her smile. "You should try this one, Bud. I have a feeling we might be taking some of this back home."

"Go on, then, I'd better see what I'm in for," and he waited as Bonnie poured some Anen Nightshades for him too. I watched as Bud swirled, sniffed, sipped, sipped again, sucked . . . and smiled. "Okay, I get it. Pretty wonderful."

We nodded.

"It was the wine that won most golds for Annette," said Bonnie sadly. "It's a blended wine. That's what she was really known for. There aren't a lot of folks around here who grow Marechal Foch, but we do, and she came up with this wonderful way of making it work with just the right balance of gamay noir, merlot, and another unusual one we grow called michurinetz, which is a Russian varietal. It's the out-of-the-ordinary varietals that give this winery the edge. The Newmans had vision. A lot of folks said they were crazy, of course, but I think they just planted different things to see what would work and what wouldn't. They chose all the best terroirs for the right varietals. Genius, really. I'm so glad that folks enjoy it."

"I'm pleased to see that you enjoy being part of it. Have you been here long, Bonnie?" I asked.

"About five years, now," Bonnie replied wistfully. "Raj is very good, and he's always fun to have about the place, but it's not the same since Annette—you know . . ." She trailed off, as most people seem to when they don't really want to acknowledge the death of someone close.

"Were you surprised that Annette killed herself?" Someone had to ask, so it might as well be me.

Bonnie paused, as if to organize her thoughts, then said with feeling, "I wouldn't have believed it of her. Not for a minute. And *then*? *When* she—did it? Well, it made no sense to me at all. She'd been a bit off for a while, but she was so *happy*. Bursting with it, she was. Like she had some sort of a secret maybe a plan, that excited her, but nothing she talked about. You could see it in her eyes, though. Dashing here and there she was, like a bird in spring—never still. Moving stuff from her office to her house, from her house to her office. Always hauling things about. Action. All go. Maybe she was just getting everything in order before she . . . *you know*. I had to take a couple of days off I was so knocked by it. And Ellen just fell apart, took her weeks to come back. Not until they'd read that will. And then she comes right back in, that very day, with Raj in tow, if you please. All over him, like gin on an olive. He's good at keeping her at arm's length, I'll give him that. Must get lots of practice at it, too, if you believe everything you hear. For all the attention he might get, he's never been lucky in love, that one."

It was clear that Bonnie heard quite a lot, and I was anxious to keep her on topic. "What do you mean, Bonnie?" I asked innocently.

Topping up our glasses, Bonnie drew close and became our instant confidante. "Well, a few years back, he was seeing a nice girl,

Jane. Can't remember her last name. She was from somewhere near Terrace. No family. Just one of those wandering types, you know, they work at the ski resorts in the winter and the wineries in the summer? Well, they do around here, anyway. Came to all the do's together for a while, you know. Good-looking girl. One day, she ups and leaves. Very down he was about it. Then there was a young girl, Stacey Willow, over in West Kelowna, killed herself because of him. At least that's what folks said at the time. *Terrible.* Raj said he hardly knew her, but there's some around here think they had *quite* the thing going. Pills. She was alive when they found her, but, you know, they couldn't do anything. Pumped her stomach, everything. She was too far gone."

Bud and I must have registered surprise. Bonnie asserted, "*Yes*, too much of the poison in her system for them to save her. No note. Just did it. They don't always leave notes, right? Kid was only in her twenties. Very sad. Raj didn't bat an eyelid. Said he didn't know what all the fuss was about. He said that it was sad and all, but he didn't know why people were sad for *him*. They'd only ever had a couple of drinks, in a group. No one could think why she'd have done it otherwise. It *must* have been a boy, a man, you know, letting her down."

"When Annette left this place to him, well, her half, anyway, you know, it makes you think, right? Not that they were ever seen together, but they did go away to the same places a lot of times. *Had* to, I guess." She sounded disappointed. "It was their job. Ellen said it was all rubbish. She keeps telling folks who'll listen that the business is better with him, and that Annette did the right thing. I've heard him telling her she should go back to the lawyers and ask them about it again. He just can't seem to settle here. I still think it's all very odd. I wonder what he said, or *did*," she winked, "that got Annette to leave him the business?"

"Do people think that Raj somehow convinced Annette to

change her will, and then he killed her?" I had to follow up on this one. Bud was now listening intently too.

The couple dithering over their wine selection had clearly come to a decision, and Bonnie indicated she'd better attend to them. She left us with a quick remark as she walked away, "Not *my* idea, but Ellen's commented that it's awful that folks say that sort of thing, and then she's off on the warpath!"

"So we're back to Raj, the ladies' man," observed Bud wryly. "We should take another look at him, Cait. He's the only one who really benefitted from Annette's death. I wonder if there's someone here at the RCMP station I could have a word with about the Willow girl. At least we've got a full name." Bud had spotted a chance for him to play to his strengths. "I'm just going to pop outside and make a quick call. Can you hold the fort here? *Without* drinking yourself under the bar?" he added, smiling.

"Absolutely, *ossifer*," I slurred playfully. "The Leith police dismisseth us," I added, grinning. Bud gave a "What are you talking about" expression.

"It's one of those pub things, in the UK," I replied to his unasked question. "You know, if you can say it aloud three times, you're obviously not drunk. Try it when you're outside, it's not as easy as you think. Now leave me alone so I can grill Bonnie." Bud did as he was told, muttering to himself.

"Like some more?" asked Bonnie, offering the bottle again. "Or, how about some of this? With a wild hibiscus in it, as a special treat?" She pulled a bottle out of a wall-hung cooler. It was the Anen Angel sparkling wine that Bud had brought with him to brunch at my house the week before. With it, she brought out a jar containing something dark, red, and alluring. Dropping a somewhat gloopy-looking flower into the bottom of the champagne glass, Bonnie added a little of the syrup in which the flowers were obviously preserved, then filled the glass with the sparkling wine. I watched, delighted, as the bubbles from the wine fizzed through and around the flower, which gradually unfurled in the pink liquid. It was very special.

"The flower tastes like a cross between raspberry and rhubarb," said Bonnie, as I sipped.

"Oh yes, it's delicious," was almost all I could manage. "Do you grow the flowers locally?"

"Well, Sammy Soul is looking into planning permission for some greenhouses so he can take it up in a big way. You need tropical conditions for the hibiscus to thrive, you see. These all come in from Australia. Small producer, high-end, family run. It's a good fit with our business. We sell quite a lot of them. Fun, eh?"

I had to agree.

As I continued sipping, and watching the ever-changing show within my glass, I took my chance to press my earlier query. "Do *you* think that Raj might have had a hand in Annette's death so that he could inherit half the winery?"

Popping the suitably stoppered bottle and the jar of preserved flowers back into the fridge, Bonnie gave her pronouncement. We were finally alone, so she was able to speak freely. "I know you hear these things about people changing their will, then five minutes later they're dead and the person who gets the cash is the one who's killed them. That's all in books, and on those TV shows, right? People don't go around *really* doing that kind of thing. Raj isn't the type. The ones who do it on the TV? You can *always* tell. Not Raj. There are whispers, but he either doesn't know about them, or he chooses to ignore them. It's Ellen. *She's* the one. She's like a terrier about it."

This was all *very* interesting. If there was some sort of miasma of gossip surrounding Raj's inheritance and Annette's death, why on earth was Ellen—who seemed to be quite protective of Raj if nothing else—asking Bud to look into it at all? Why wouldn't she just have let it lie? Stick with the findings of suicide, and not make the sort of scene she had the night before? It made no sense. Well, not with a few glasses of wine inside me it didn't. *Oh dear!* I gave the whole puzzle some more thought. My only real conclusion was that I needed a bathroom, and Bonnie was kind enough to point me in the right direction. When I re-entered the tasting room, refreshed, Bud was there and making the sorts of motions that told me he needed to talk to me outside. I looked at my watch.

"Can you tell Ellen we're ready whenever she is?" I asked Bonnie.

"Sure," she replied, as she happily mopped the rings we'd left on the countertop.

"Is there an area where I can smoke?" I asked, a bit timidly.

Bonnie grinned. "Outside, turn right, keep going, and there are some benches and a big old sand bucket. Will you take this with you?" She held up my unfinished glass of now-pink bubbles. Well, I couldn't say "No," *could* I? I still had the hibiscus to eat!

We thanked Bonnie and we scuttled outside into the now-warm sunshine. I pulled Bud toward the smoking patio, where I tossed my jacket to one side, and scrabbled around in my purse for my cigarettes, lighter, and sunglasses. Once I'd stopped pawing about, dropping things, then picking them up again, and finally settled myself with my face to the sun, I said, "Okay, spill." *I felt quite devil-may-care.*

"I've done pretty well, I think." He smiled. "I called the RCMP station downtown and asked to speak to an old acquaintance of mine, who I knew wouldn't be there. I introduced myself to the young guy at the desk, and we chatted. Anyway, it turns out he knew the Willow girl. Because there was no note, no apparent reason for her killing herself, the parents insisted on an autopsy. Stomach full of pills. She'd ground them up and put them in a milkshake, of all things. Took it home with her from her job at a burger place downtown. Strawberry, in case you're interested. Enough to kill a horse, apparently. Pills, not milkshake. I don't know how much strawberry milkshake it would take to kill a horse." Bud nudged me playfully, then cleared his throat and said, "Sorry, that wasn't really . . . you know. Sorry. I'm not used to wine before lunch."

"I know," I said, puffing. "And what about Raj? Was he connected to her at all?"

"I asked about that. The guy said she'd been dumped by a biker-type she'd been seeing, and that he was the sort who'd do it hard—known to them apparently—but she had no close link to Raj. I stopped then, because he seemed to feel he'd said too much. I didn't get into Annette's case. Thought it best to not push my luck."

I was thinking.

"*Strawberry* milkshake?" I said aloud.

"Yes. *Strawberry*," replied Bud. "Does the flavor matter? I was really only, you know, joking about that." He sounded puzzled.

"It might, if she didn't kill herself," I replied.

Bud stood up, immediately raking his hair in frustration. "Oh, come on, Cait. Stop it. Some girl who may or may not have known Raj Pinder takes a bunch of pills because she's had her heart broken by some pseudo-gang-banger, and *you're* thinking she's another murder victim? Why? What particular bee is buzzing in your bonnet now?"

I didn't answer Bud's testy question directly, because it would have taken too long, and I could see Ellen Newman heading in our direction. Instead, I ate the hibiscus, glugged the last of my drink, stubbed out my cigarette, and said, "Where would any gossip about Raj and this girl have started, if he *didn't* know her? And *why* would it start? Has someone got it in for Raj? Maybe someone hates him so much they're working on a long-term, elaborate plan, with him in the frame for two fake suicides. Or, is he really responsible for the deaths of two women, and, maybe, the disappearance of a third?"

Bud opened his mouth to reply, but he, too, spotted Ellen approaching us.

"Do you need to go back to Anen House to change?" asked

Ellen brightly—surprisingly so for someone we'd left dissolving in tears earlier on. What also took me aback was the fact that she was wearing a different outfit than the one we'd seen her in that morning. She looked rather odd, with puffed out hair, sporting a jade-green skirt-suit with big, '80s-style shoulder pads, and giant, gold-colored plastic earrings. She looked like something out of a down-market version of *Dynasty*.

Our faces must have shown our confusion. *How could they not?*

"You know you're supposed to come dressed in something 'retro,' right? The lunch at the MacMillans' house is a 'retro' lunch." Suddenly, her expression changed and her hand shot to her mouth. "Oh no, don't say I didn't put that in your notes?"

Bud and I both shook our heads.

"Oh dear. Oh dear. Right. Let's think a minute," said Ellen. She did. So did we. "I wonder if I've got anything suitable at home . . ."

Oh *come on*: she was, at most, one hundred and thirty pounds, and I haven't been that weight since I was about twenty-five. She was also about three inches taller than me. She wouldn't be likely to own anything that would fit me.

Ellen looked at her watch, clearly having made a decision. "Right. It's twelve fifteen. If we're quick we can pop over to my apartment downtown, and I know just where I've got some things that'll do, for both of you. No one will worry if we're a few minutes late. Come on!" She turned on her heel, marching toward a big, old, dark gray Ford F250, with a four-person crew-cab and a full canopy. We hauled ourselves into the truck, buckled up, and she was off, crunching along the unmade vineyard trail, until we reached Lakeshore Road, where she skidded around the corner and we raced toward Kelowna.

French Lemonade

I WAS BEGINNING TO GET my head around the layout and the lifestyle of Kelowna. Lakeshore Road was the main drag that took you out of the core and to most of the wineries that had sprung up along the east bank of the lake. On this occasion, the job of Lakeshore Road was to deliver us back into downtown Kelowna itself, where the grid-pattern streets presented a mixture of old housing stock, newer apartments, and a core shopping area full of delightful character, set away from the strip malls that appeared to extend all the way out to the airport. Obviously, Ellen was used to negotiating the lunchtime traffic, as she took right and left turns to avoid major junction snarls.

Within about ten minutes of setting out from her office, all three of us were jumping down from the cab of Ellen's truck, now tucked into a rather tight spot in the underground parkade of her apartment building, which was right on the waterfront.

As Ellen marched toward the elevator, she seemed to be in full *bossy* mode—a role usually appropriated by myself. I felt a bit left out, but I tagged along like a good little guest. Emerging from the elevator, Ellen unlocked the door to an apartment. We trooped in behind her, suddenly slowing as we found ourselves turning sideways to negotiate a very narrow hallway. Ahead was the living room, but every wall we could see was piled high with plastic buckets, neatly stacked in rows, each bearing a description and a date.

"I know *exactly* what to pick out for you, Cait," Ellen cried excitedly as she dropped her purse onto a small desk that stood in front of the window facing the glittering lake.

"Great. Thanks," was all I could muster. I was finding the apartment claustrophobic, and I eyed the stacked bins with suspicion.

"But I should offer you something to drink, first. How about some lovely French lemonade—I've got a bottle here, unopened. I think you'll like it Cait, because it's just like British lemonade— you know, it doesn't have any lime in it, like we always seem to have here. I use it with Pimm's—that's very British, isn't it? Annette introduced me to it, and sometimes, when I sit and think about her, I'll make myself a glass and remember how she enjoyed it. Just a minute . . ." and she dashed beyond a pile of boxes to the kitchen area.

Bud looked at me and mouthed, "Oh my God!" He surveyed the room, peering wide-eyed into the open plan kitchen.

I mouthed "Shh!" back at him, as Ellen reappeared with two glasses of lemonade, which she carefully placed on coasters on the desk.

"There, that'll keep you busy! I'll give some thought to Bud's get-up while I'm digging out yours. I won't be long—make yourselves at home," she called and she disappeared, sideways, back along the corridor toward what I assumed was a bedroom or two.

Bud and I dutifully sipped at our lemonade as we took in our surroundings.

Ellen was, clearly, a hoarder. But, unlike many, she was a very neat hoarder. As I glanced around the boxes, I read the labels: ELLEN AGED 27; MOM & DAD: VACATIONS, 1960S; ELLEN AGED 30; ELLEN AGED 28, and so on. The multi-colored boxes were all clean, not dusty, stacked not just five high, but three deep, which reduced the width of the room, and therefore the view of the lake, to about four feet.

Bud couldn't constrain himself any longer. He, too, was eyeing the stacks of boxes with alarm.

"What the hell . . . ?"

I whispered, "She hoards. It's a compulsion. I understand her a good deal better now. She cannot let go of things. *Anything*, it seems."

"Explain it to me—quickly," hissed Bud. "Is she sick?"

"Okay," I replied quietly, "I'll try. Hoarding is complex. There are many different types of hoarding, stemming from many different psychological roots. I'll give you my take on Ellen. She's not compulsively hoarding what we might see as 'garbage'—you know, she hasn't got filthy old bits and pieces, or piles of old newspapers here, and it certainly doesn't smell of decay. I'm guessing her bathroom is still accessible, and we can see that her kitchen is clean and tidy, though it's stacked with boxes. She hasn't even gone out and compulsively bought fifteen sets of paper napkins or a dozen sets of Christmas lights, in case she 'runs out.' No, Ellen is keeping things from her past, and, it seems, her parents' past, too. Often, hoarding suggests an inability to make decisions. People keep things because they literally cannot make up their mind if it's good or bad to get rid of it, so they hang onto it 'just in case' they might need it one day. It looks to me as though Ellen *has* made a decision, and that's to keep everything that's precious to her about her own history and that of her parents. I'm thinking that it might be the death of her parents that started her on this route. There's often a trigger that is traumatic. It's not surprising she couldn't get rid of Annette's stuff. She can't get rid of *anything*."

"This *cannot* be safe," said Bud, standing as close to the desk and the window as possible. "Not for Ellen and not for the folks who live below—or even above her. What if there was a fire? Do you think I should say something? Are there pills for this sort of thing, or is it not that simple?"

"*Bud*. Hoarding isn't something Ellen necessarily sees as odd. She might see it as completely normal. If you're going to raise it as an issue you'll be opening a can of worms she might not even know exists. It's not something you approach easily. In fact, a cognitive behavioral therapist would probably need to work with her for a long time to tackle this level of obsession and compulsion. Many don't even think that hoarding and obsessive compulsive disorder are on the same condition scale, though, for me, the jury's out. If, as I'm guessing, the loss of loved ones is at its base for Ellen, it might take years. In fact, with Annette's death, it might get worse before there's any chance it'll get better. She *has* lost every member of her family to sudden death, after all."

Bud took my point. "Okay, I won't say a thing," he said, rolling his eyes and holding up his hands in surrender.

"But you know what, Bud," I was relating this new insight into Ellen's psyche to the case of her sister's death, "Ellen hoards, and we know that Annette collected, so maybe they weren't 'chalk and cheese,' as Marlene Wiser described them—maybe they were both grappling with loss in their own ways. What if this means that Ellen possesses other personality and behavioral traits that are often associated with hoarding?"

"And what might they be?" asked Bud nervously.

"Oh dear—it's a long list and we psychologists don't really know the level to which they always, or only sometimes, present. It's complicated."

"I get it! You need multiple degrees and a brain the size of a planet to do what you do, but just give me the Cole's Notes version, okay?"

"Anxiety, depression, neuroticism, self-consciousness, vulnerability, indecisiveness, impulsiveness, and perfectionism. All jumbled up, in different ways, somehow related and intertwined. We're not sure which, if any, of these traits, have a causal relationship with hoarding, we just know they are observed traits. So they might lead to hoarding, or hoarding might lead to them. All we know is that they are related. Like collecting and hoarding: not all collectors become hoarders, but you're unlikely to become a hoarder without first seeing yourself as a collector."

"So am I on the slippery slope with my collection of baseball hats?" Bud looked alarmed.

"Is your collection preventing you from using your home for its purposes? Is it disrupting your life? Is it hurting those around you? Do you only find beauty, fun, or joy in your hat collection, or do you see it in absolutely everything? If it's 'No' to the first three questions and 'Just the hats' to the fourth, you're okay . . . so far," I smiled.

"Here you go—these should work," said Ellen breathlessly as she returned to the postage-stamp of a living room. I envisaged her lifting boxes in a small, confined space. *She must be pretty fit*, I thought.

"Bud—go to the last door at the end of the corridor, you can change there. Cait, you can have the bathroom, it's first on the right." Ellen handed me a bagged hanger, which I unzipped. Inside was a dress and a fluffy petticoat. "It was my Mom's, she made it herself," said Ellen softly. "She was short and . . . about your sort of shape. I hope it fits. What size shoes do you wear?"

"Six and a half," I replied, heading for the bathroom, which was clean, though also stacked with boxes, smaller, all white.

"Oh great, my Mom's size!" yelped Ellen. "I'll just go find the right shoes and purse—YAY!" She seemed absolutely delighted to be doing this.

A few minutes later Bud and I stood looking at each other in disbelief as we compared outfits. He'd got away with it lightly: a red and cream 1950s-style leather jacket, obviously originally worn by a much bigger man, a pair of Ray-Bans, and his own jeans and shoes. He looked quite dashing. But me? The bathroom mirror had told me a part of the story, but Bud's face told me the rest. I was wearing an early 1960s dress, with a buttoned-up bodice (which actually fit—wow!) and three-quarter length sleeves; the full, gathered skirt skimmed my knees and was held out by the petticoats beneath it. White stilettos, a white purse with a gold clasp, and white gloves finished off the outfit. The whole thing wouldn't have been too bad if it hadn't been for the pattern of the fabric: it was light blue, with stripes of yellow roses, surrounded by little white flowers all circling my body. I looked as though I'd been upholstered!

Ellen walked around me, as best she could in the limited space, and said, "You look fabulous! Oh, dear. You remind me of Mom!" She burst into tears.

I sighed. Ellen wasn't the only one who felt like a good cry. All of a sudden, this "retro" lunch was looking like a bad idea.

I rushed to the bathroom to get some tissues. Handing them to Ellen, I asked, "Would you like a glass of water?"

"Thanks," she snuffled. "There are some bottles in the fridge."

I headed to the kitchen, circumnavigated more storage boxes, and pulled open the fridge door. A quick survey of its contents told me that Ellen lived mainly on salads and stir-fries. There couldn't be any other reason for owning so many different types of oil—sesame, cold-pressed virgin olive, peanut, walnut, hazelnut, avocado, and flaxseed—all arranged in dark-glass bottles with handwritten labels beside a dozen small bottles of water. I grabbed one and headed back to the other side of the room.

While we waited for Ellen to stop crying, I tried to cheer her up by observing, "You've done a good job of kitting us out. Thanks. I wonder what Raj and Serendipity will wear. I bet they could wear almost anything and look good. Maybe Serendipity's parents will let them raid their old closets."

"I don't see why you're talking about them like they're a couple," sniffled Ellen.

"Oh come off it. Of course they are!" I realized what I'd said. "Or would that be a bad thing, if they're at competing wineries?" I asked.

Ellen was beginning to calm down a bit. "Not really. Serendipity isn't wine, she's food. I guess if they were competing vintners it might make things a bit awkward. Anyway, I don't think you're right. He doesn't see that much of her."

I was puzzled. "When he scoots off to the gym in the afternoons, he could be visiting her then. She'd be between lunch and dinner at the restaurant at that time of day. They do seem very well matched, physically and in terms of lifestyle."

"I guess," Ellen replied curtly. "Could you guys make your way back to the truck, while I just sort out my makeup?" she asked plaintively. I got the impression from the way she'd been dabbing at her eyes that she wasn't used to wearing mascara, and she was right, she needed to give her face some attention.

"Sure," said Bud, "take your time." Ellen gave Bud the keys for the truck, and the bags containing the clothes we'd arrived in, and we left her to her own devices.

Back at the truck, it wasn't that easy to get into it. I felt ridiculous. Finally, after a few moments of silence, with Bud grinning over his shoulder from the front seat at me, and me *not* grinning back at him, Ellen joined us, started up the engine and we set off for lunch, hurtling around corners, across intersections and back along Lakeshore Road toward the MacMillans' house. I was hoping that other guests at the luncheon would look as idiotic as I felt.

As I battled my petticoats in the back seat, I took off the white gloves I'd been wearing to be able to transfer the essentials from my own purse to the tiny little thing that Ellen had given me. It obviously hadn't been designed to cope with anything more than a lipstick, a hanky, and some change; try as I might, all my bits and pieces weren't going to fit. Finally, I managed to squash in my cellphone, nicotine gum, and my cigarettes and lighter. This *not* being the 1960s, I suspected that could probably live without lipstick for a while.

Harvey Wallbangers and Sangria

WHEN WE ARRIVED AT LAKEVIEW Lodge, a few vehicles were already parked along the roadside and the driveway to what looked like a tiny, one-storey house with gray wood siding and white trim. Bud graciously helped me out of the vehicle (*so that's why men did that—because women wearing those skirts had no idea where their feet were!*) and I tottered over the gravel on my kitten heels toward the front door.

Colin MacMillan was there to greet us, wearing a green velvet smoking jacket, a frilly pink shirt, and gray-green dress pants: the Jon Pertwee version of a *Doctor Who* outfit.

"Ah, ready to 'reverse the polarity of the neutron flow' at a moment's notice, eh?" I quipped, puzzling both Bud and Ellen.

"Absolutely," replied Colin, beaming. "You'll spot Poppy, she's Sarah Jane Smith from the Third Doctor period. I suggested she wear Amy Pond's policewoman outfit, but she said it wasn't 'retro,' so she's gone with Sarah Jane. We don't think many people will get it, but it's 1970s clothing, and *we'll* know, so who cares, eh? By the way, Mom said everyone's to keep their shoes on today, 'cos of, like, the costumes. Some of them are great—like yours." Colin seemed very excited, and clapped a little round of applause at me as he ushered us inside.

As we walked into the MacMillans' house, my concerns about it being too small to host a large luncheon evaporated: the part of the house visible from the street level gave way to a huge edifice. Built on stilts, the house jutted out over the edge of the cliff face, with three floors of space for entertaining, all glass-fronted, facing the lake. A swimming pool, hot tub, and multi-layered decks were set to the side of the house, and the final stairway from the bottom deck led to a wooden jetty at which two boats were moored. Not your average dinghy-type boats, but sleek white things with lots of chrome that glinted in the sun. *What a way to live!*

"Hey, Colin, it's bigger on the inside, like The Doctor's TARDIS," I quipped.

"That's what I said the day we moved in, but *no one* got it," he replied. He smiled, waved, and ambled off.

Bud nodded at Colin's back as he left us. "You seem to have acquired a new puppy," he noted. That's what we call the students who latch onto me and make it their business to follow me about the university. There's usually one in every class, and sometimes a whole string of them. It seems that I specialize in their acquisition. I don't know why.

Having arrived late, the lunch was in full swing. Everyone had clearly taken the retro-dressing theme to heart. Bud headed off to chat to the Wild West era Wisers, while I searched the knots of people to find Raj, whom I'd decided would be my target at the lunch. Finally, I spotted him, dressed as a Beatle, standing beside Serendipity, who was wearing a simple white sleeveless shift dress, with a circlet of white flowers in her hair. She looked clean, and cool, calm, and I was just a little jealous that she looked so perfect.

Luckily, I was saved from having any less charitable thoughts about Serendipity by the bustling arrival of Lizzie Jackson.

"Good to see you. How are you? Long time no see," she grinned. "Hey, you look great. Boy, that dress is just your size, Cait. Wherever did you find it?" She was almost vibrating with excitement.

I smiled politely as I replied, "Ellen rustled it up for me. Apparently it was her mother's. Bud and I didn't know about the dressing up thing, so we were lucky that Ellen had some clothes we could borrow."

Lizzie grimaced and said, "Ah, have you been to Ellen's apartment?" I replied, "Yes. Have you ever visited there?"

She peered through her round glasses with eyes that became just as round. "Hmm," she nodded. "She came to me about four years ago and asked for some advice about it. You know, the hoarding. Said she'd found someone she wanted to 'make space for' in her life and that she knew she'd have to make some *real* space for them too. Back then she was quite open-minded about such things, and we talked a great deal. I even showed her some techniques for meditation and self-hypnosis that I thought might help her."

"Something like wakeful dreaming?" I asked.

Lizzie looked both taken aback and delighted. "Why yes, that sort of thing, but what's a marketing person like you know about my field?"

Damn and blast—I'd forgotten my cover!

"I once helped promote a line of self-help books, and one of them was about mental reorganization," I lied.

"Ah yes, it's an area where folks *can* help themselves much more than they think. Ellen and I had a few sessions together, and she seemed to take to it like a duck to water. Surprisingly, she has a talent for using words to calm. I even thought she might be about to join us in the Faceting fold, but something happened. I don't think that whatever relationship she was hoping for came to anything, and she became, well, as you see her now. Sometimes she's quite scathing about our approach to life. You think she'd have let it go by now. But hey, that was her problem all along."

I nodded. "Is the food good?"

"Oh yes," she replied. "Sheri's totally onboard with our views on food, and she's had help for this." Lizzie nodded in the general direction of the food-service tables as she spoke. "We've loaned her Ray from the restaurant to oversee the food prep, and she's got some local girls to help with the serving and clearing. I think it's a great idea to go back to some of those old favorites we used to enjoy in decades gone by. Of course, I love what Ray does with food at our place nowadays, but, sometimes, it's nice to bump into an old friend on a plate, right?" She laughed as she added, "You should go see. It's quite a spread."

"I will," I replied quickly, seeing a chance to escape, and I waved my farewell as I moved away.

As I wandered across the spacious, high-ceilinged room toward the food, I could see that every finish in the MacMillan home was about as high-end as it gets. On the laden tables I spotted aspic-encased salmon, slices of aubergine topped with tomato and parmesan, prawn cocktails, and even a row of fondue pots: all very retro.

"Hey, have one of these!" Colin appeared in front of me holding a tall glass full of an almost fluorescent orange fluid. A slice of orange and a maraschino cherry speared onto a little pink umbrella was balanced on its edge. "It's called a Harvey Wallbanger, Mom says. Looks horrible, but everyone's drinking them. It's this, or sangria. And that's got fruit actually floating in it." He wrinkled his nose.

As he pushed the glass under my nose, I caught a whiff of Galliano and maraschino cherry, and it all came back to me: one too many of that exact cocktail during a friend's birthday party in Swansea almost thirty years ago. I began to gag. I pushed the glass away as politely as I could. "Could I have sangria instead?" I asked, praying my saliva glands would calm down. "But first, the loo?" Colin pointed me in the right direction. *Keep calm, Cait. Don't go throwing up just because of your perfect memory.*

Locking the loo door behind me, I took some deep breaths and ran cold water over my wrists. I patted my neck with dampened loo paper, and finally managed to think of enough things opposite to vomit inducing to calm my stomach: sea air, freshly cut grass, sunlight dappling through trees onto springy undergrowth. All freeing, cleansing images. It usually works.

Eventually, I managed to calm my gag reflex, and I took a

moment to gather my thoughts. I had to get out there, find Raj, again, and get him to open up to me, a complete stranger. *Easy!* But first, a smoke. I'd have to ask where I could light up.

Peering out around the bathroom door, I spotted our hostess, who was dressed in a chequered, sleeveless dress that I suspected was of late '60s, early '70s vintage. I made a beeline for her, as she fluttered her way between guests.

"Hi Sheri, nice dress," I opened.

"Thanks. Carol Brady did such a good job with all those children, don't you think?"

Ah, the Brady Bunch. *Right.*

"Absolutely," I replied, like a good little guest. "Wonderful spread," I added, meaning it.

"Thanks," replied Sheri. "It's not exactly gourmet, but it is all fresh, local, organic, and peanut-free, because of Colin, of course," she replied, looking over my shoulder at the table traffic. "I just hope there's enough of everything."

"Oh, I'm sure there will be," I replied. There seemed to be enough to feed a small army. "Is Colin allergic to peanuts, then?" I ventured.

"Yes. Always has been. It's not so bad these days, it's much better understood. In fact so many children have the same problem that his school is peanut-free now."

"It must be tough to eat out," I observed.

"Well, it sure used to be, but there are a lot of places now that offer peanut-free choices. SoulVineFineDine, for one, and Faceting for Life, for another. They're both totally peanut-free restaurants. Even Pat, this morning, made sure everything was safe. He's thoughtful like that. Well, with both Serendipity *and* Colin there, he *would* make special effort, of course."

"Serendipity's allergic too?" I replied, trying to sound interested. *Why am I talking about this—I want to know where to smoke!*

"Oh yes, that's why she became interested in food, I believe.

She's doing some very interesting things with peanut-free recipes for catering companies."

"Right. She mentioned something to me last night about a range of sauces she's working on, though I didn't realize they were peanut-free because she has allergies." *Come on Cait—get to the point!*

"Peanut-free, gluten-free, and preservative-free organic sauces. Oh, they're excellent. She had Colin and myself over to do some tastings and even *he* liked them, which is saying something. I worry about him so, you know. He seems to live in his own little world, all those weird fantasy things he likes." She smiled indulgently at the thought of her son.

"Don't worry. It's *normal*. And all it means is that he's interested in history, mythology, and nice, old-fashioned tales of good versus evil, where a hero is needed. A friend of mine at the university has had a very fulfilling career as a professor of comparative mythologies, and he's written lots of research papers about the invention of mythologies in science fiction. Colin will be just fine. He's intelligent, he's articulate, he's observant and he's pretty fit, too, with all that cycling he does. Which isn't something you can say about all seventeen-year-olds these days."

By now, Sheri was looking much brighter. *Thank heavens, now I can make my break for freedom!*

"Speaking of Colin," I added, "I asked him to get me a drink, which I should collect from him. I wonder if there was anywhere I might be allowed to smoke?"

Sheri smiled. "The middle and bottom decks are the smoking ones. It's where you'll find Rob, no doubt, holding court in the sunshine. A friend of his from West Kelowna hitched a ride across the lake with the Souls on their boat. They might still be down at the pier. At least, I'm guessing that's where he is, because I haven't seen him for ages."

Luckily, I spied Raj Pinder near the exit. I managed to grab a glass of sangria, then made eye contact with Bud long enough to make smoking motions to him as I pointed to the decks.

"Just the man," I said, as I caught Raj by the arm and firmly steered him in the direction I wanted to go. He looked surprised, but didn't object as I asked, "Could you spare a few minutes?"

"Okey dokey," he replied, smiling. He followed me as I grasped the handrail of the deck staircase and tried to not look down the cliffside beneath me. "Let me take that," he said, grabbing my drink.

"*Such* a gent," I replied, not taking my eyes off the steps.

"Well, *you're* such a lady," he responded, which might have made me smile if I hadn't been balancing on kitten heels, on wooden steps, on the side of a cliff. Reaching the deck was a relief, and I plopped into a patio chair, reached into my purse and lit a cigarette. It took about three seconds. I glugged my drink, *then* I gave my attention to my escort.

"You alright there, Cait?" he asked. I nodded, puffing. "Only, you don't look too good. Is it the heights that get you?" I nodded, still puffing. "Aye, poor old Annette were much the same. Mind you, she started to come over all queer for no reason at all toward the end. Flat ground or no, she'd get a look about her that said she weren't feeling well. Maybe that's how depression can take you, I dunno."

"You know Raj, you're a lovely chap. I saw the way you looked at Ellen when she said last night that Bud had come to help her look into who might have killed her sister." Raj opened his mouth to speak, but I stopped him. "I just wanted to ask you a couple of questions about Annette." Raj was beginning to look alarmed. Frankly, I didn't care. I just wanted to get on with it.

Putting all niceties aside, I said, "Look, it's obvious to me that you and Serendipity are a couple, right?"

Raj nodded, "Well . . . yes, but *please* don't say owt. Her parents would go *berserk*. Well, her mother would, any road. It's awkward.

You saw her last night. There's nowt can quiet that woman when she wants summat." His Yorkshire accent was oddly calming.

"And what about Annette? Did you and she have a relationship?" I was pretty sure I knew the answer, but I asked anyway.

"What makes you say that?" Raj's expression signaled even more alarm.

"Raj, you're an attractive, single man. You and Annette traveled to a lot of the same places, for several years, had a huge amount in common, and she, too, was single, and not unattractive. It's not beyond the realm of reason to imagine you two getting together, though I'm guessing that the fact that you were competitors in the world of wine might have made it difficult to be open about it." I kept my voice low. I wasn't sure how sound might carry against the cliff.

Raj finally nodded. "Okay, but *please* don't say owt about that, neither." He drew close to me and whispered. "*No one* knows except Serendipity. I told her, but no one else. It weren't nothing big, just a bit of a fling that didn't last long, just two events really, one in California, one in Niagara. And that were it. We couldn't cope with the sneaking about back here and the fact that we couldn't talk about owt we wanted to. I were at Sammy's place back then, of course, and there's stuff as goes on in a winery that you can't talk about to the competition. We agreed, it weren't worth it. We broke it off. About six or seven weeks before she died. And, no, I didn't break her heart. I know that 'cos she and I talked it through."

"Is that why she left you the winery in her will, do you think?" *Plod on with it, Cait. You might not get him alone again. Read him.*

"Oh, Gawd. I never expected that, it were a right surprise. I dunno what she were thinking. Floored me. I told Ellen she should argue her case with the lawyers. But no, she says she won't. I feel terrible about it, but there's nowt I can do. It's a brilliant chance for me, but to get it that way? Terrible. I mean, like I said, it weren't nothing serious. Why would she do it? Lovely girl, *woman*, but *that*?"

The closer I studied him, the more I wondered if Raj Pinder was better at controlling his physical self than most people. I pressed on.

"What about the wording of Annette's will? She tried to entail the share of the business to your 'firstborn,' I understand. Why so?"

Raj sighed. Deeply. "*None* of it makes no sense. I talked to the lawyer about it, the one that Annette sent the will to. He said it all looked perfectly legal, but then he said, in front of me and Ellen like, that, what with Annette killing herself, Ellen could contest the will if she wanted. She might win. He weren't being nasty to me, or owt. He just said that he thought he should mention Ellen's options. He also told me that, if I were to keep the inheritance, then I should draw up some papers later on about that weird clause, 'cos it could mess things up if I had more than one kid in't future."

Raj sounded bemused more than anything else. I had just one more topic I wanted to talk to him about.

"Stacey Willow?" It was all I needed to say.

"Oh Jeez—you too? Bloody Ellen won't shut up about that girl. I hardly knew her. Her older brother and I played the odd game of footie—you know, soccer—and she were in the crowd a couple of times when we all had a drink. *That* were *it*. Ellen's hugging me and saying how sorry she is for me that she's dead. I mean, I don't have owt against the girl, poor thing, and I'm really sorry for her brother, who took it hard. But Ellen? Nuts. Aye, nuts."

"So there was nothing between you and Stacey Willow?"

"Nowt. Never."

I was ninety-nine percent sure he was telling the truth. "Pretty girl?" I asked.

"Oh yes. Very easy on the eye she were," he replied, smiling wistfully. "So why are you poking about in this, anyway?" asked Raj, finally rallying.

"I promised Bud I'd ask a few questions. You're top of the list of suspects for killing Annette, because you're the one who profited from her death," I said bluntly. He deserved the truth. He looked horrified.

"There's folks going about saying I've *killed* Annette?" He seemed nonplussed. "No one's ever said owt to me. Not to me face, any road."

"Well, they wouldn't be likely to, would they, Raj?"

"No, I s'pose not," he replied quietly. "I had no idea."

"No, I can tell you didn't," I said, stubbing out my cigarette. My mind was racing. A few things were beginning to make more sense. Whatever my growing suspicions might be though, I still had to work out how someone could have convinced Annette Newman to sit in the cab of a truck that was gradually filling with exhaust fumes, if she hadn't wanted to do so.

As he stood, Raj looked at me with his dark, soulful eyes and whispered, "I liked Annette. She were good at her job, she worked hard, she were fun, and we had some good times—you know. But, it's the real thing with Serendipity. She's the one, I'm sure of it. We've known each other for years, but we never got together until after I left her Dad's place. Mainly because her mother followed me about all the time when I were there, and it seemed, well, not *right*, to be going about with her daughter. But we can't say *anything* yet. We've got to wait for the right moment. So, you know . . . ?"

"I won't say a word, promise," I replied, and I twisted an invisible key against my closed lips, tossing it with abandon over my shoulder. Had it been real, it would have hit Colin MacMillan in the face.

"Hey, I brought you that drink!" It sounded as though Colin was shouting, so hushed had been the conversation between Raj and myself.

"Hey, thanks, you're very kind," I replied to Colin, waving, unnecessarily, at Raj's back. "I've nearly finished this one. It's very good. Who made it?"

Colin sat beside me, in the seat that the escaping Raj had vacated.

"Mom. She drinks it a lot. It's organic wine, of course, from SoulVine Wines, and all the fruit's organic, and local. She even buys local organic gin to put in it from a place in Pemberton, just along the lake. I guess she thinks that makes it a health drink."

I had a thought. "Colin, you know you said you saw Annette driving home the day she died?" Colin nodded. "What exactly was she doing? You said she was talking to someone on the phone?"

"Yeah, hands free. She always did that. I can show you," he replied. He turned in his seat to face away from me, so I was looking at the left side of his face. He sat upright and adopted a driving pose. Suddenly he started to flail both of his arms, shaking his head and making exaggerated howling motions with his mouth. Next, he wiped away non-existent tears with his right fist, intermittently flailing his right arm away from me, as he placed his left onto the imaginary steering wheel. It was quite a performance.

"Thanks," I said. "You saw her from the driver's side of the truck?" He nodded. "And about how far away were you?"

"Oh, she drove right past me. I was sort of parked, with my bike, just standing there in Anen Close, right next to the sign for the B&B. I don't think she saw me, though. I was only about five feet away. Her window was open, that's how I know she was shouting. Oh—and I just remembered something she shouted . . ."

I was all ears. "And what was that?"

"'So—you've never loved me, then—why should I help *you*?' That's what she shouted."

Very interesting. A lover? An ex-lover? Who needed help?

"Is that good?" Colin was almost panting with excitement and anticipation.

"It might be," I replied slowly.

I smiled and stood up. "I need to go and get something to eat, now before my stomach thinks my throat's been cut."

We walked up the stairs together, and Bud met us at the top.

"I'm glad you're back," he said, smiling enigmatically. "I didn't want you to miss all the fun."

"What fun?" I asked, innocently enough. I peered through the glass wall at the area where the food had been laid out, to see Suzie Soul, in her full Betty Boop regalia, hurling a plate of something at Vince Chen's head. Sammy Soul was trying to hold her back, his Elvis wig askew on top of his bald head, and Serendipity, her little circlet of innocent white flowers now trampled underfoot, was trying to grab her father. Sheri MacMillan and Marlene Wiser both darted toward the airborne plate to try to prevent it from reaching its target. They failed. In the corner, Ellen Newman was sucking her thumbnail and smirking, holding Raj's arm as he tried to pull away from her, toward Serendipity. The whole scene was even more wonderful because I could just hear the Beach Boy's "Good Vibrations" above the crashing of the crockery.

"What on earth is going on?" I asked, not really needing to.

"It seems that, after last night's embarrassment, Vince told Suzie he'd had enough, and she doesn't agree with him," smiled Bud. I nodded. "Maybe he thought he'd get away with it easier if he told her in public. Poor guy."

"Yes, poor guy," I replied. "Do you think there'll be any food left when she's finished? I haven't eaten anything yet, and I'm hungry."

Suzie Soul suddenly flung her arms around her husband's neck and kissed him, while he was trying to haul her away from yet another party.

Bud and I walked into the room to see if there was anything left worth eating, just as Ellen tapped her glass with a spoon. I expected some sort of toast, but, no, Ellen had one more lunchtime surprise up her sleeve for us, it seemed.

"Listen up, folks," she shouted. "I know that last night was quite eventful, and today's turning out to have its own very special moments, but there's something I must say. I had a bit too much to drink last night, and I said some things about the death of my sister that I very much regret. I know many of you have now met Bud, and Cait of course, and Bud's put his considerable experience as a police officer to work. He's looked into matters, and has convinced me that my poor, dear sister, Annette, really *did* intend to take her own life. Now I hope that puts paid to any speculation that might have been running around the city, or the industry. I know it's difficult, but I must accept it. I'm working on that. I feel better now that I've talked it through with Bud, so, thank you, Bud, and, of course, thank you Cait." Then she raised her glass toward the two of us and drank.

Bud's mouth was open, but I'd managed to clamp mine shut. Our surprise was mirrored around the room. The body language I observed was screaming, "At least she's come to her senses," mixed with "Maybe she's had too much to drink again?" *All very telling.*

Bud shut his mouth and headed to the bar. "Coming, Cait?" he called over his shoulder.

"Right behind you!" I called back. I followed him as fast as my little kitten heels allowed.

For about twenty minutes, no one talked to us, and we barely spoke to each other, except to mutter about the food. We had decided, after a quick drink, that it was best to graze. The atmosphere was—difficult, despite Sheri MacMillan's best efforts.

By about three o'clock, most people had already drifted away, and I said to Bud, "Have we got a plan? What are we doing when we leave here? Which, by the way, I think should be soon. We've got a dinner at SoulVineFineDine at eight, after all." I looked at the bowl of sherry trifle I was holding and decided I'd have just one more spoonful before setting it aside. Though I knew I'd have to wrestle with my conscience to put down a bowl that was anything other than completely empty.

Bud looked around, "Caitlin Morgan, I want nothing more than to have some time alone with you. Do you think we could arrange that? We need to *talk*, Cait. I found out some interesting stuff about the Wisers from Ray and Gloria, over there." He nodded toward Bonnie, and the man and woman who I *still* hadn't managed to meet.

I referenced Ellen's notes for Bud. "Ah, that's who they are: Ray Murciano, chef at Faceting for Life Restaurant—originally from Florida, a Cuban-American, now a Canadian. He built a reputation for his Cuban cuisine when he worked in South Beach, Miami—now building another one for his work with organic produce and the Hundred Mile approach. Gloria Thompson—a Kelowna born and bred flake, according to Ellen. Most of her notes were a pretty scathing physical description. That said, she does seem to be on the overpowering end of the dress code, but, hey, look at me! She works at the Faceting for Life store. Ray wasn't here when Annette died, because he hadn't arrived from the States at that time and, conveniently, Gloria was away on an extended stay at 'The Gem' in Sedona. They're both out of the frame as far as Annette's murder is concerned. I am guessing they might both be back in it for Stacey Willow."

"Okay—stop right there, Cait." Bud sounded stern. "Stacey Willow killed herself. That's that. Forget her. She's got nothing to do with Annette. I'll tell you what *has* got something to with Annette..."

But he didn't get the chance to tell me, because at that very moment, Ellen pounced and offered to give us a ride to Anen House. Of course we accepted, and we thanked Sheri and Colin on our way out.

As I tottered back to Ellen's truck, which was now sitting almost alone on the roadside, I had to avoid a pool of yuk on the roadside. Finally, once I'd managed to find all the bits and buckles to secure myself, Ellen took off along Lakeshore Road. It should have taken us about five minutes to get back to the sanctuary of Anen House, and the chance of slipping into some less constraining clothes, but we didn't make it.

Rounding a bend that swung down a steep part of the road toward the turning for Anen Close, we came up behind a small, orange car, its front end smashed against the cliff face of the hill upon which Anen House stood. Smoke rose up from under the hood. Ellen slammed on the brakes.

"It's the Wisers. That's their car," she shouted. "Oh no! Someone call 911!"

At least, I'm pretty sure that's what she said, because at that moment the Wisers' car exploded, hurling rocks and debris at Ellen's windshield. Blinded by the smashing glass, Ellen lost control, and the truck skidded into the roadside ditch, all three of us lurching forward against our seatbelts.

The world seemed to stop. I looked around. Bud seemed okay, and we nodded at each other .

"Are you alright?" Bud asked Ellen. She was clearly shaken, but uninjured, it seemed.

The truck was lying in the ditch at an angle of about twenty degrees, with Bud's door facing the ground. He opened it, but I could see he wouldn't be able to push it far enough to get out that way. I felt for my buckle, popped it, and grabbed the little white purse that had slithered across the seat—my phone was in it. I managed to push open my door, up into the air, and I wiggled up and out.

I finally made it to the ground. "Stay there, I'm going to see if I can help," I shouted at Ellen and Bud.

I heard Bud yelling back, "No," as I ran toward the blazing car.

But there was nothing I could do. It was quite obvious that the two figures in the car were beyond help. The whole thing was ablaze. I just stood there, numb. Fighting back the tears and rage, I felt so totally and utterly *useless*. Then I gave in, and let the emotion wash over me.

I remembered the phone call I'd received about my parents' accident—word for word, pause for pause, sob for sob. I remembered the trip back to Wales from Canada, to make the arrangements; the funeral, the hymn singing, the smell and feel of damp in the church; the crematorium, the softness of the vicar's hand shaking mine. Then there was the reception, the warm sandwiches, the smell of flowers dying in vases. My sister Sian's uncontrollable crying. Our hugs, our shared sense of loss, the smell of the photo albums as we'd sorted through them and divided up the photographs. I don't usually let myself relive it all. *Too painful.* Now, I couldn't stop myself.

Finally, I dragged myself back to reality. Poor Gordy and Marlene. How awful. They were such lovely people, so full of life. I hoped they'd died instantly, before the explosion or the flames, and wondered why they would have had an accident *there*, on a corner they must have driven around so many times over the years. Then I remembered the puddle of yuk on the road I'd side-stepped back at the MacMillans.

Oh Lord—brake fluid!

Tea and Brandy

MY VISUALIZATION OF BRAKE FLUID on the roadside was interrupted by the screeching arrival of Colin MacMillan on his bicycle. He took in the scene from beneath his lime-green cycling helmet, open-mouthed. Turning to me, horror-stricken, he mumbled, "I heard the bang. The explosion. I thought it was *you*." He was clearly distraught.

"No, *we're* all fine," I managed, still crying. "Ellen says it's the Wisers' car?"

Colin nodded. "I'll call 911," he said, pulling his cell phone from his pocket.

"No—I'll do that. Could you see if you can help Ellen out of the truck? I'm too short."

"Sure," he nodded. He picked up his bike, and laid it carefully on the side of the road.

I made the call—*why didn't I stuff a hanky into this damned stupid little purse?*—and Colin managed to get Ellen out of her truck. He helped haul Bud out, too.

The next half-hour was a blur of sirens, paramedics, police, and a creeping sense of the tragedy that we'd witnessed. I told a young officer about the brake fluid I'd seen back at the MacMillans' house, and he noted it, looking concerned. I didn't go into the whole Annette Newman/Stacey Willow thing. Everything seemed to be moving at half speed, me included, and I suspected that the three of us who'd been in the truck were feeling the effects of shock. Luckily, none of us had sustained any injuries, which was something of a miracle, given the broken windshield, if nothing else.

Pat Corrigan arrived on the scene in his car: the sirens had alerted him to the fact that something wasn't right, and he'd driven down from Anen House to see if he could help.

The fire had been doused, the road was cordoned off, and the medics were done with us, as were the police—for the time being—so we were allowed to leave. Colin headed homeward on his trusty metal steed, and Pat drove us back to the B&B, where Lauren was anxiously hovering on the front doorstep.

She ushered us into the house, then settled us in the lounge. I could hear Pat explaining what had happened. It still didn't seem real. We'd only left the MacMillans' lunch about forty-five minutes earlier. It was all so fast. So . . . final.

Lauren brought a pot of tea and three brandies. There wasn't much talk, just a general numbness. We all drank the tea. I drank my brandy first.

"We'll host the wake here, of course," announced Pat, breaking the gloomy mood, "if that's okay with you, Ellen?"

Ellen nodded. She studied her still-full brandy glass.

"Sure we will," agreed Lauren. "No two people were more full of life. It'll be a grand party. A big one. Such long, loving lives. There'll be a lot of folks that'll be wanting a last knees-up with Gordy and Marlene."

It might seem to be an odd way to think of it, but I totally get the Irish thing of wanting to celebrate lives, not cry over death. I think it's a great idea—it's even psychologically sound. The thought of a party reminded me about the dinner we were due to attend at SoulVine Wines that night.

"Do you think the dinner tonight will go ahead?" I asked. *Somebody had to.*

"How about I call the Souls and find out?" suggested Lauren. She certainly came into her own when there was someone to fuss over. Ellen nodded. Lauren left the room.

We were still all sitting there, silently, when she returned. "Well, bad news travels fast. They know all about the Wisers and they're going ahead. Serendipity says that everything'll go to waste otherwise, and Sammy Soul thinks it's the best way to honor two fun-loving people, and I cannot disagree with him."

We all half nodded. Lauren was in her element. "Now listen up, you three. You've all had a terrible shock, so this is what I suggest. Pat, you'll drive Ellen home. It'll be a while before that truck of yours is on the road again, Ellen, so you should get off to your own place, have a long, hot shower, or a bath even, and get yourself ready for the evening. Bud, Cait, you should do the same. Pop up to your rooms, why don't you, and get relaxed. Clean yourselves up, then maybe have a bit of a nap. You don't have to be there until eight, so you've plenty of time. Right. Come on with you all, let's be moving and doing." She clapped her hands, and we all seemed to snap out of our stupor.

She was right, of course. Sitting about wasn't going to help at all, and the thought of a soak in the bath upstairs was very appealing. We all did as we'd been told. Bud and I hugged each other, for a long time, at the top of the stairs, before agreeing we were each headed for our own bath.

"You okay?" he asked, as I turned to go. "*Really* okay?"

I nodded. "I had a bit of a thing back there. About Mum and Dad. It brought it all back."

He pulled me back into his arms again. "I did wonder," he whispered.

I nodded. I pulled back, recalling what Bud had said at the lunch. "What was it that Ray and Gloria told you about the Wisers? Something to do with Annette?"

Bud looked puzzled. His expression changed. "Oh, right. They'd mentioned to Ray and Gloria, when they were having lunch down at Faceting for Life one day, that they'd taken it upon themselves to collect Annette's mail and they'd put it in the old apple store with all her other stuff. Apparently, Colin was right: that's where all her things are, and all her mail, it seems."

I nodded. "And that's it?" I said, somewhat underwhelmed.

Bud nodded. "Okay then, Miss—how about we both go and get cleaned up and sorted out, eh? Give ourselves an hour or two to relax and rejuvenate? At least we have a bath each to use." He smiled, but he looked tired.

"Right-o. See you in a while." We squeezed each other's hands as we separated and went to our own rooms.

Once inside, I stripped off Ellen's mother's dress, and dropped it onto the slipper chair in the corner of my room. I hoped that the sound of the running bathwater, and the warmth of the billowing steam, would begin to ease my sadness. It didn't. I cleaned off the bits of makeup that had mingled with smuts of ash on my face, washed my hair, wrapped it in a fluffy towel and soaked in the deep bathtub for the next ten minutes, trying not to think of anything. *Trying* to not remember.

Puckered fingertips told me it was time to get out of the bath, dry off, and sort out my hair. Then I lay on my bed in my waffled robe staring out at the still glittering lake. *The permanence of nature, the frailty of life.* I shook my head. It was no good, I wasn't going to be able to catch a nap. I looked at the clock: 4:55. I got up, pulled on the pants and shirt I'd planned to wear to breakfast the next day, and padded over to Bud's room.

I knocked. No answer. I opened the door quietly, and there he was, in his waffly robe, sleeping like a child on top of his bed, flat on his back with his hands curled like otter paws. He looked adorable. I didn't want to disturb him. I closed his door as silently as I could, went back to my own room, grabbed a pair of flats and my purse, and tiptoed downstairs, where I headed to the kitchen in search of a Corrigan.

"Hey, you're looking a bit better," said Lauren as she looked up from the bowl in which she was mixing something yellow and creamy.

"I feel it," I replied, smiling. "Thanks for everything. You're *great* in a crisis. A bath was just what I needed, though I'm pretty restless now."

"That'll be the shock," she observed knowingly. "Funny thing, shock. My mother was a nurse. Often talked about shock, she did. And it's come in handy at last."

"I wondered if you could help some more?" I asked.

"Sure thing, what's it to be?" Lauren wiped her hands on her full-body apron.

"There's an old apple store, behind the hill?" Lauren nodded. "Is it locked do you know?" I guessed it was. "Do you have a key?"

"To be sure it is, and we do, though why you'd be wanting to tramp down there I don't know." She walked over to a small cupboard on the wall. Inside were two rows of hooks, six of which had keys hanging on them. She pulled off a single big, iron key, which she handed to me.

"Ellen's stored all of Annette's belongings there, and she said I could take a look at them," I lied.

Lauren shrugged. "Do you know where you're going?" I shook my head. "Go out the back door, past our place, then there's a path that'll take you there. It's only about ten minutes away, and it's quite well done up—you know, a few lightbulbs, power, and so on. Though that old lock might take some work. It's one heck of a key, to be sure. I haven't seen one like that before. Big enough for you?" She laughed. The key was about six inches long, and its shaft seemed to have been welded into a huge old iron doorknob. I wondered how big the lock would be!

"Thanks, Lauren," I said, heading to the back door. "I won't be long. Tell Bud where I've gone, and I'll be back by seven—that'll give me half an hour to sort myself out before I leave. You know, put a bit of slap on the old mug?"

"You Welsh! Always putting yourselves down, you are. You should be more like us Irish and revel in the beauty God gave you!"

"I did when I was your age, Lauren, but just you wait and see how *you* feel about makeup when you're forty-seven, not around thirty. You're young yet—enjoy the collagen while you've got it!" I called back as I left, and I chuckled as I headed out past the double-wide, which looked very homey, and found the path Lauren had described.

The path wasn't wide, but at least I was going down it, not climbing up. Unfortunately, that meant I had to look down the steep incline. I focused on my feet, which was a shame, because it was still such a beautiful day, though there wasn't much warmth left in the sun and a few clouds were starting to bubble up in the west. I really didn't know what I hoped to find at the apple store. While I didn't know what it would look like, it was quite clear that I'd reached it when I got there. It was something like an old log cabin built onto the side of the hill, with a spacious, flat area in front of it, and a wide, if rugged, track leading down the remainder of the hillside. The structure itself had no windows, just one large door, covered with an iron gate. An old iron padlock secured a bolt to a big metal plate that was set off to one side of the doorway. The padlock was massive.

Come on, Cait, don't hang about, I told myself, so I pushed the key into the lock. It turned easily and the lock fell open. I pulled it off, slid back the metal bolt it had been holding, and popped the padlock back onto the U-shaped hook on the end of the bolt for safe-keeping. I pushed the key into my purse and pulled open the heavy gate. It made soft, metallic scraping sounds as it swung open, but there didn't seem to be any problems with the hinges. The wooden door itself wasn't locked, it just had a thumb-lever latch, which was also in good working order. I stepped into the cabin and felt the cool, dry air inside. The place still smelled of apples. *Lovely.*

As the light from the northern sky fell onto the smooth dirt floor ahead of me, I allowed my eyes to adjust to the dimness, then looked around for a light switch. *Stupid!* Just ahead of me a light bulb attached to a simple wire had a little chain hanging down beside it. I pulled the chain, and the bulb lit. I repeated this three times as I walked further into the cave part of the apple store. Ellen's father had been very clever. He'd managed to turn a natural depression in the cliff face into a wonderful storage space about forty feet deep, including the ten feet or so of the cabin, and at least forty feet wide. It was big, airy, and very dry. Ideal for apples. The wooden door swung itself shut, but I patted the heavy key in my purse and looked around.

The scene was reminiscent of what we'd seen at Ellen's apartment—row upon row of stacked plastic storage boxes, each bearing a label. At one end there was a bit of a jumble and some pieces of furniture, so I headed there first.

A small wooden cabinet caught my eye, upon which there sat a plastic box, filled with mail. *Annette's mail, delivered here by the Wisers.* I picked up the box and realized it was standing not on a simple cabinet, but on a wind-up gramophone player. I couldn't resist! Recalling my grandmother's old machine, which I was never allowed to play, I opened the little cupboard door in the front of the cabinet to reveal a stack of hard, black 78 rpm records in tattered paper jackets. I enjoyed feeling their considerable weight in my hands. *Just like Gramma Morgan's!*

I pulled the "Moonlight Sonata" from its cover, and wound the handle. I placed the record on the bed, worked out how to lift and swivel the needle-holding arm, and set the record in motion. As I lay the needle onto the spinning disk, a rasping sound, interspersed with clicks, echoed around the apple store, then the long-dead fingers of Paderewski beckoned me to join him on a magical journey. By the time the needle was bumping around in the center of the disk, I was crying my eyes out. *It's been an emotional day, and Beethoven's nothing if not cathartic,* I told myself.

I scrabbled around in my purse for a hanky. Of course I didn't have one—*note to self, must pack hankies in purse*—so I used my sleeve. Not pleasant, but necessary. I set about finding my specs and began wading through Annette's mail. A lot of it was rubbish—*Why would the Wisers bother bringing that here to store?* Some was clearly from institutions I guessed Ellen was now dealing with on behalf of her dead sister, and there was one very intriguing, boxy package. It had been opened. The sender's address was in Newfoundland, and it had been delivered by courier, not Canada Post. I knew what it was before I looked inside. It had to be the James Sandy snuff box.

My fingers trembled as I opened the end of the package that had already been split apart. Inside the outer box was a fat roll of bubble-wrap, which, uncurled, revealed a green velvet pouch. I could feel the snuff box inside, but I hardly dared open it. Finally, I took the little treasure out of its soft envelope. It sat easily in the palm of my hand and was exquisitely plain, except for the signature which had been, so the story goes„ burned into the wood with a hot iron nail. *James Sandy.*

I opened the lid, which moved easily and showed a hinge and a liner without a single dent or abrasion. It was as close to perfect as a used item could be. I peered into the packaging again, and found a cardboard and plastic wallet. Inside, protected against the elements, was a letter written in spidery copperplate that was difficult to read in the dimness of the apple store. I could at least tell that the signature, James Sandy, was the same as on the snuff box. *Wow! Grail indeed!*

I wondered how much Annette had paid to be the proud owner of a box she'd dreamed about, and I read through the copy of the paperwork that bore the logo of the courier company that had delivered it. Then it dawned on me—someone must have signed for this package. *The courier wouldn't have just left something this valuable on the doorstep.* The date of delivery was two days after Annette had died. The signature on the paperwork was Annette's. *Annette's!* Exactly the same as I'd seen on the suicide note. *Exactly the same* as on her will. *And exactly the same* as the facsimile of Annette's signature that Ellen had shown me on the artwork for the wine label.

How could Annette have signed for a package two days after she was dead?

This is important! I'll talk to Bud about it.

I looked at my watch. Six o'clock. I couldn't dawdle! I picked up the snuff box and put it back into all of its packaging, shoved it and the signed receipt into my purse—*just as well it's as big as it is!*—turned out the light as I went, then pulled open the big wooden door. The metal-barred gate had swung shut, so I pushed it outwards. It wasn't budging. I pushed again. I turned the light nearest the door back on again, and tried to peer out, but I could only fit my nose between the metal bars. I rattled the gate. Nothing. *How on earth has it got stuck?*

"Hello?" I shouted. "Anybody there?" *Don't be stupid, Cait! Of course there's no one there!*

I rooted around in my purse for my cell phone. *I'll call Bud. He'll come and help me.* My cell phone wasn't to be found. I dumped the entire contents of my purse onto the floor of the apple store and spread everything out. It wasn't there.

You stupid woman! It's still in that little white purse you took to lunch!

Damn and blast! What am I going to do now? I've got to get out of here.

"Hello—can anybody hear me?" I shouted as loudly as I could. My voice rang around the canyon, and echoed back to me. It was a very lonely sound.

Apple Juice

MY STOMACH TIGHTENED, MY BREATHING became shallow and rapid. *Don't panic, Cait. Calm down!*

I shouted louder. "Helloooooo! Anyone there?" Once again my voice echoed back at me.

"*I'm* here," came a small voice. I jumped.

"Hello—who is it? I'm in here—in the apple store!" I shouted.

"Yes, I know," said Colin MacMillan calmly, and quite close by. "You've been in there for some time. How did you get in?" he asked as he appeared from the deepening shadows beyond the gate. It seemed to be a very odd question, under the circumstances.

I was a bit nonplussed, but I regained my focus quickly. "Colin. Hello. What are *you* doing here?"

"I was just hanging out, down below, and I heard you shouting," he replied innocently.

I could tell he was lying. "No you weren't. You've been following me, haven't you? That's why you seem to be everywhere *I* am. Colin, it's not *healthy*, you know . . ." I stopped myself. It didn't matter how unhealthy his obsession with me might be, the important thing was that he was there, and he could help.

"*Look, Colin,*"—I adopted my "firm but fair professor" voice—"this gate has somehow shut itself and I can't open it. Can you open it for me from there? It's very important that I get out of here."

"It's locked," he said. "There's a padlock locked onto a bolt. I'd need a key."

Of course! "That's okay—I've got the key here," I said, plucking it from the pile on the floor. I pushed the shaft through the iron bars, but the round knob on the end of the key, which I'd thought charming, if not quirky, now made the object too wide to fit between them. *Damn and blast!*

"It won't fit," Colin observed.

"No kidding!"

"What shall we do now?" he asked. "I don't think there's much chance of me being able to break it off with a rock or anything. I'm not really that strong. Wiry, you know, but not strong." He sounded deflated. "If I were The Doctor on *Doctor Who* I could use my sonic screwdriver," he said, smiling hopefully.

"Well, you're *not* The Doctor, and neither of us *has* a sonic screwdriver, because they *don't exist*!" I shouted back. "Fantasy is all well and good, in its place, but sometimes you just have to face up to reality and deal with it, Colin. The reality is that I need to be somewhere that isn't here. *Now!*"

I wasn't as angry with Colin as I was with myself, but that wasn't what he was getting out of this conversation, and he didn't deserve it. I took a deep breath.

"Colin, I'm sorry. I'm *not* mad at *you*, I'm mad at *me*. Just give me a minute to think." I did. *Well, I took ten seconds because I'm bright and I can think very quickly.* "Have you got a cell phone with you?"

"Of course," he replied, sounding hurt, "but there's no signal here."

"Let me see," I said, then added hastily, "I'm sure you're right . . ."

He was. No reception. So no phone call to Bud.

"Would you be able to run up to Anen House and get Bud?" I asked. I knew he'd be there, and probably still be asleep.

"Sure, but how will *he* open the lock?" he asked plaintively. I thought it might hurt the boy even more if I pointed out that Bud had a good deal more strength than he, and might well be able to smash the lock, so I didn't say it. "He's quite old. Like my Dad, or older even," Colin added, rather unkindly, just as I was having charitable thoughts about *him*.

"That's a little unfair, don't you think? Older can mean wiser, and *can* mean more able, not less able. I think *I'm* getting better the older I get. There's a psychological proposition that many . . . *of we marketers* . . . agree upon that . . ." I stopped, hoping I hadn't blown my cover story.

"You don't have to *lie*, I looked you up," sighed Colin. "You know, you can't *really* pretend to be someone else and hope to get away with it when you use your real name and you're all over the internet, *Doctor* Morgan." He shook his head.

It was my turn to sigh. "Okay. Busted. It was my way of trying to get people to open up about Annette's death without knowing they were talking to a criminal psychologist. I'm sorry, I apologize for lying. Now, can we *please* get me out of here?"

"Sure," he replied. "How?"

I thought about it again. "Colin, can you take a photo of the lock out there with your phone?"

"Sure," he sulked. The flash snapped in the gathering gloom.

"Okay, now hand it through to me." He passed the phone through the bars, and I could see the whole lock and bolt arrangement. It was exactly as I remembered it. "Great photo. If you take that up to Bud, he'll see that there are screws in the wooden panel that's holding the bolt. If he can bring a flat-head screwdriver, and maybe some of that stuff that helps with releasing rusty screws, we could be in business. We won't open the lock, we'll just remove the whole panel. It's not a *sonic* screwdriver, but it was you who gave me the idea, Colin," I added, hoping it would cheer him up.

He brightened a little. "Okay. How about I just ask the Corrigans if they have a spare key?"

I laughed. "Yes, you're quite right, Colin. But I'm pretty sure they don't have one. In the key cupboard there were ten hooks in two rows, four had bunches of keys on them, no one key of which was big enough for this padlock, and on two of the other hooks were this key and one other, single key, that was much smaller. Of course, they might have one elsewhere, so, why not ask—let's adopt a belt *and* braces approach, and do both, okay?"

"Eidetic memory, eh?" asked Colin.

I sighed and nodded.

Colin shrugged. "Several of The Doctor's incarnations have worn both a belt and braces, thereby ensuring a reduced risk of losing their trousers." He giggled. I hoped his levity meant that I'd regained some favor in his eyes.

"Colin—*go*, please! It's important. Quick as you can, right?"

"Sure thing," he said, and off he went. *Ten minutes up, ten minutes waking Bud and finding the bits and pieces, quicker if there's a spare key, and ten minutes back down.* I looked at my watch and then switched on all the bulbs. I decided I'd do something useful with the next half hour—root around in Annette's belongings and hope to find something, anything, that would help me understand what was going on.

It was clear that *someone* had locked me into the apple store, probably when I was floating away on a cloud of Beethoveny loveliness.

Who even knew I was there? Only Lauren Corrigan, and she couldn't have killed Annette because she was in Ireland at the time. I guessed she might have mentioned it to her husband, who was also not in the frame for the same reason as his wife, so what on earth was going on? Maybe the lurking Colin had seen something. I'd have to ask him when he returned. *If* he returned.

I spotted a plastic storage bin marked ANNETTE—BOOKS #1. *That might be interesting.* To get to it I could see I'd have to move two from above it, both of which were marked ANNETTE—KITCHEN CUPBOARD #2. I reached up and shifted the top one. *Whoa— heavy!* Plopping it onto the floor, the lid loosened and I could see that the contents were spices, herbs, packets of seasonings, and a slew of tetra packs of apple juice. *Why would Ellen keep all that?*

I pulled out a couple of the little packages of juice and stuck into one tiny straw that I'd peeled off its side. I sucked. It was pleasantly cool. The taste of apples revitalized my awareness of the smell of the place. It was very pleasant.

Back to business!

What about *Colin? He* obviously knew I was in the store. He'd been following me everywhere. He knew who I was, *and* that I was looking into Annette's death. *He* could have locked me in. He'd admitted seeing Annette on the day of her death. And no one else had verified his story, so he could have been making up the whole thing. Only *Colin* had suggested that Annette had been having an argument with someone. *Only Colin* had mentioned the snuff box. In fact, the more I thought about it, the more the pieces fell into place. Colin liked Annette—he "hung out" with her. Bonnie had said Colin always used to appear around the Mt Dewdney winery during Annette's time there. Clearly, Colin had been following Annette the same way he was following me about the place. He'd probably been even more obsessed with her. Annette had given him gifts, he'd been a visitor at her house . . . on and on—so many links between a fragile, sensitive, unloved teen and an older woman who might not have known that he was infatuated with her.

I pushed a rickety chair against the wall, to give it a bit of help with holding my weight. If I sat down and used my skills, I could do this. I could join the dots.

I took a deep breath, and began.

I hummed, closed my eyes, and took myself to the place where I can allow thoughts to free-form. I began to undertake the "wakeful dreaming" that I'd mentioned to Lizzie Jackson. All I had to do was *think* of each person in turn, and allow them to gather about themselves those things which were "theirs," without my overlaying any sort of judgment upon the process.

Annette's face, the face I only know from a photograph, comes to me first: she's holding a tiny little wooden box in one hand, and a giant garbage bag in the other. She's laughing. She's dressed in rags. Now she's running toward the truck in which she died and floating into the cab.

Ellen? Ellen's scowling, she's crying, she's trying to stuff something large into a storage box, but it won't fit. What is it, Ellen? Ah, it's Annette. Of course. Annette won't fit into the box because it's too full of empty bottles of wine, snuff boxes, wine labels, and a giant scroll, which is obviously Annette's will. Pages and pages of notes about "suspects" are floating in the air around her, fluttering at her feet.

Raj Pinder floats toward me next: he's holding a giant wine bottle and crying. "It's perfect," he says, then he's fighting off Suzie Soul, who's just appeared as a snake with a cat's face (oh dear, that says more about me than her!). She's coiling herself around Raj's legs. He can't escape. She eats him.

Sammy Soul appears with a giant reefer between his lips, puffing away and chewing marijuana leaves at the same time. Serendipity is shouting at him—"Don't eat the leaves!" She's dressed like a picture-book angel, wings and all, and she's flying up to the sky with her father running along the ground trying to catch her. She's scattering a trail of what I know are snail eggs, but they look like tiny little snails, each with Raj Pinder's face.

I conjure up the Jacksons next: Lizzie is wearing a huge, faceted rock around her neck, it's weighing her down, but she's repeating a mantra—"Look into my eyes, my eyes, my eyes"—and smiling. Grant is tiny, like a little scuttling insect, but in almost human form. He's running around on the ground beside Lizzie shouting loudly, but she can't hear him, only I can: "Face It. Face It. You know, you know it. Face it."

Now Grant is chasing Sammy Soul, who hasn't got a reefer any more, but he's scattering cigarettes as he runs, still trying to catch the diaphanous gown of his daughter.

"Don't light it. Don't light it," calls Lizzie to Grant as he picks up one of the now-tiny cigarettes.

Colin, Sheri, and Rob MacMillan appear in a puff of smoke. "Time travel is great," says Colin to his parents, who start screaming at him that they want to go home. He's crying now. His father is wearing boxing gloves and starts to punch himself in the head. His mother is crying too, she's stroking Colin, petting him like she would a cat. Colin's hair grows very long, and he starts to trot toward me. He's panting like a puppy, but the sounds coming out of his mouth are the sounds of Doctor Who's TARDIS as it lands.

"I have to have it." Annette has broken out of the storage box that Ellen is trying to stuff her into. "I have to have it!" She's wearing a gas-mask, and she's running toward Grant who is trying to hide from her giant feet. He grows to her size, and there he is, holding a large candlestick in one hand, a coffee roaster in the other. Annette grabs the candlestick from him and proceeds to bash away at the stacks of plastic bins that are suddenly surrounding her. They start to topple. Everyone is being hit by giant storage bins . . .

I stopped. I pulled myself together. It was a start. What had I learned? *Anything?* What had I *felt?* Immediately I could sense *obsession. Why?* I gave it some thought.

Everyone had an obsession: Annette and her snuff boxes; Colin and The Doctor, and probably Annette, *and* me; Raj and the perfect wine; Serendipity and the perfect food; Sammy Soul and his wife; Suzie Soul and her lovers; Grant and Lizzie Jackson, and their Faceting; Sheri MacMillan and her son; Rob MacMillan and his escape; Gordy Wiser and his orchards; Lauren Corrigan and her knitting; Pat Corrigan and his sausages. Marlene Wiser, poor Marlene, seemed to be the only one who hadn't been caught up with something that was their distraction, or their focus—or maybe adopting six children *was* obsessive?

I allowed my mind to wander back to Colin MacMillan. His sad home life; his other, fantasy world; the kindnesses Annette had shown him; their connection; his obsession. He knew about science; he had access to Annette's home. She'd been acting strangely—*had* she offended him? Would she have known if she had? How would Colin react?

I was questioning, judging. Was I now taking a step too far? Being *too* judgmental? Maybe I was nervous that I'd just sent Colin away, and he might never come back.

Damn, I want a cigarette! Maybe that's why I pictured all those cigarettes?

I got up from the chair and walked over to the contents of my purse, still on the floor in a heap. I gleefully saw that the pile contained a squashed cigarette box, with two smokes in it *and* a limp book of matches. I gathered up the other bits and bobs and put back them where they belonged. I looked around. I couldn't really see any harm in having a smoke. The *door* was wide open, even if the gate was locked. I lit up, and sucked in hard.

The relief was tremendous. Okay, the *rush* was tremendous. *I'm an addict. I admit it.*

Hobbies, obsessions, addictions. A continuum?

I looked at my watch. Thirty minutes had passed. Bud should be arriving at any moment. *If* Colin had actually gone to get him, that was.

I walked back toward the box of books I'd been intending to get to when I'd sidetracked myself. I pulled down the other kitchen box that was on top of it, and finally achieved my goal. Opening the box was a bit of a disappointment. I didn't know what I'd expected to find, but what I saw was a pretty comprehensive collection of books about silver antiques. I picked out one or two, and wandered back to the spot near the gramophone, under a lightbulb. Inside the front cover of one of the books was an inscription: "To one of my best customers, G."

Of course! Grant Jackson! Why hadn't I thought of that before! The candlesticks!

Just then I heard a crunching noise beyond the gate.

"Hello?" It was Colin's voice.

Quick as a flash I was back at the gate. "You're back!" I was relieved.

"Yep," he said.

"Where's Bud?" I asked impatiently.

"He wasn't there," he replied, "but I brought a screwdriver and some WD-40," he added proudly.

"Where on earth is Bud?" I might have sounded a little terse.

"It's a long story, so I'll tell you while I try to undo this, okay?" replied Colin, as though speaking to a child. I wasn't really in any position to argue.

I sighed. "Yes, right, okay. I'm sorry. I'm just a bit . . . you know . . . tense."

"I might be *only seventeen*, but I *am* possessed of a modicum of perception," said Colin loftily.

That's me put in my place! "What's happened to Bud?"

I peered as far as I could out of the gate, but all I could see was Colin's left side. His tongue poked out and he was clearly struggling with the screws. I could smell the oily chemicals of the WD-40 wafting on the cool evening air.

Putting his tongue back where it belonged, Colin spoke calmly. "Ellen came back to Anen House with Pat in his car. She asked Bud to drive her to the winery in *his* truck to collect some ice wine that she'd promised to take to SoulVine Wines for the dinner tonight, 'cos *they* don't make it. They'd left before I got there, because she had to get to Serendipity's restaurant before the other guests showed up. Lauren told Bud you weren't due back at the B&B until seven, so he called your cellphone and left you a message. Pat's a bit tied up right now, but he said he'd drive you over to West Kelowna when you're out of here. He offered to help, but I said I could manage."

I took it all in. Ellen was pretty good at getting people, especially Bud, to help her out. But that's what Bud's like. Damsel in distress and all that.

Well, *I* was a damsel in distress right now, and *I* could have done with his help. *More* than Ellen. But Bud hadn't known that, of course.

"Are you talking to me, or yourself?" asked Colin.

I hadn't been aware I was saying anything aloud. "Myself," I replied.

"Good," he sniped back.

"How's it coming along out there?" I asked.

"Just two more." I could hear the effort in his voice.

I stood as calmly as I could. I *hate* waiting. And it's especially annoying when I'm not in control of the situation, where putting pressure on someone else does anything but help.

I sighed. "What about you and Poppy du Bois then, Colin? I reckon you'd be spending your time much more wisely with her than following the likes of me about the place."

The sounds of Colin's exertion stopped.

"What do you mean *Poppy*? And what do you mean *follow you*?" He sounded quite put out.

"Oh, come on, Colin, you've been following me about. Did you see who locked this gate, when you were skulking around out there?"

"I *wasn't* skulking and I *didn't* see anyone. And what about *Poppy*?"

I smiled. *Ah, so you are interested, after all, eh?*

"I think Poppy quite likes you, Colin. You two have a lot in common: same class at school, similar interests. I guess you spend quite a bit of time together."

Colin was clearly back at work. "Yeah, but she has to help out at the restaurant, you know. Which is pretty cool, I guess. They all work together. Like a proper family. She's okay. She's pretty cool for a girl."

I thought it best not to press the matter. I'd planted at least the germ of a thought that might spur Colin to take up with a girl his own age, rather than obsessing over me and mooning about the place. I didn't want to say anything any more concrete: whoever knew a teen who'd do something if they thought an adult *wanted* them to do it!

"Hey—got it. Last one now!" exclaimed Colin.

"Good job," I offered by way of encouragement. "I'll check that I've left everything in good order here," I added.

"Okay, just a few more turns and it'll be out," Colin called to me.

I darted back into the cavernous apple store and glanced around. I picked up my purse and peered into it. Had I collected *everything* off the floor? I cast my eyes about the place. Yes. Did I have my cigarettes and matches? No, I'd put them down next to the box of mail. As I reached for them, I knocked the plastic box onto the floor. *Damn and blast!* The mail scattered everywhere. I gathered it off the dusty floor and popped it back into the box. I looked around for a flat surface. I spotted a tiny table: that would do. I picked up a couple of photographs that were lying face down on its surface. I could drop them into the box of mail too.

I glanced at them as I placed them on top of the mail. One was the same as the snap that Bud had brought to my house a week earlier, the one that had introduced me to the Newman sisters, but the other one was different. It had obviously been taken a few moments before, or after, the one I'd originally seen. No, *definitely* before. I popped my specs back on, held one photograph in each hand, and studied them. Carefully. Very carefully. I focused on the expressions on the sisters' faces, then on their body language.

In the photo that Bud had shown me, Annette was closest to the camera, smiling happily, her arm around Ellen's shoulders. Ellen was trying to look happy too.

In the other photo, the one I was seeing for the first time, Ellen and Annette were looking at each other, rather than at the camera. Annette's entire body said "happy": her arms were outstretched, upward and toward her sister; her face, even though I could only see a side view, was gleeful; her mouth was open wide in a smile, and her head was thrown back in joy. Ellen, well she'd been caught in an instant of pure disbelief. Her mouth was also open, but in an "o" of shock, not delight; her arms were also raised, but her hands were on their way to grasp her face; her shoulders drooped in defeat, she was curling in on herself.

Wow!

And there was one more significant difference between the photos. This photo showed a side view of the sisters, and I could see that it wasn't only Annette's bra that didn't fit. Her shirt was pulling on her, too.

And that was it. I didn't need any more "wakeful dreaming" to help me work out who had killed Annette Newman, *and* Stacey Willow, *and* poor old Gordy and Marlene Wiser, or why, or how. Everything slid into place like a pattern in a kaleidoscope.

Annette Newman's bra didn't fit—and I knew that a week ago!

Oh, Cait Morgan, you are so stupid!

"It's open!" called Colin proudly. "You can come and push now."

I picked up the photos, stuffed them into my purse, tugged the chains to turn out the lights, and launched myself at the gate. It began to shift. A moment later, I was out, and trying not to panic.

"Can I use your phone to call Bud?" I asked Colin.

"It doesn't *work* here. I think we established that, *right*?" The boy shook his head, despairing of my stupidity as he spoke. "*Eidetic memory?*" He tutted.

I held my forehead.

"You're thinking?" he asked. I nodded. I was also trying to keep calm.

"Right-o, Colin. You've rescued me—thank you so much. Now we have to get back to Anen House, as quickly as we can, then to SoulVine Wines. Let's go. We'll talk on the way." I knew I was barking at him, but it didn't matter. "You lead, and can you use your phone to light the path a bit? It's almost dark."

"Sure can," he replied jauntily.

As we trudged up the hill in the darkness, which was a lot more difficult to do than to wander down it in daylight, I sorted through all the facts in my mind, and I knew I wasn't wrong about it all, which *wasn't* good. We had to get to Bud as fast as possible.

"Once we get up to Pat and his car, how quickly can we get to SoulVine Wines?" I asked, panting.

"This time of day, it's about twenty minutes to half an hour from here by road. It could be longer, depending on the bridge."

That wasn't good. But at least I could phone Bud from the B&B and tell him what was going on. That would help. It *should* help.

"But there *is* a quicker way," said Colin.

"What?" I spoke sharply.

"Our boat. If Pat gives us a ride to my house, we can just zip right across the lake. They're opposite us. It'll only take five, ten minutes."

"What about the other side? Will we need a car there?" I wasn't sure where exactly the dinner was taking place, geographically speaking.

"No!" replied Colin—implying "Don't be so stupid!"—"We just tie up at their jetty and walk up the steps to the restaurant. Didn't you *see* it opposite our house today, when you were there?"

"No, Colin, I guess I just didn't know what I was looking at."

Understatement of the year there, Cait. That's at least two examples, now, of where you just didn't see what you were looking at in the way you should have seen it.

"You'd have a life jacket on the boat I could use?" I asked, now huffing, as well as puffing. It seemed to be a lot steeper than I recalled.

Colin stopped and looked back down the trail at me, smiling, "What, can't you *swim*?" he chuckled.

"No," I said, honestly. "I grew up by the seaside and managed to go my whole life without learning to swim. But you should always wear a life jacket, whether you can swim or not. Right?"

"Yes, *Mom*," sighed Colin. "Are you okay in boats?" he asked after a brief pause.

"No, not really. But I'm sure I can keep it together for ten minutes, so long as that's all it is."

"If Mom let's me drive, it could be five," he said, laughing.

"Colin, your Mom can drive—or your Dad, I don't really care, so long as whoever is in charge gives me a life jacket, hasn't been drinking, and gets us there quickly."

"Well, the not drinking thing is a bit of a challenge," said Colin. "I didn't see much of my Dad today, but when I did, he was knocking back the beers with his mate Dave from West Kelowna. They work together sometimes in Calgary, and when he visits, all they do is drink. And Mom? When I left to foll . . . to ride down to Kelowna, after lunch, she was hitting those cocktails pretty hard and she hadn't stopped when I went back and told her about the accident, or when I left again. I'm of age, I've got all my certificates, and I don't drink, so I really *can* take you there in the boat. If Pat can drive us to it."

Oh damn and blast! Here I am about to put my life in the hands of a kid. A kid who's sad, lonely, and obsessive. But have I got any choice?

I looked up at Colin's back, and at the climb that still stood between me and a place where I could call Bud: the hill still stretched above of us. *Good heavens, I thought we'd be closer. How far have we come?*

I looked back over my shoulder at the path behind us. We'd come a good way. But I shouldn't have looked down, not even along a path. As as I turned back and looked up again, I felt myself sway with giddiness. I missed my footing, my ankle rolled on a rock and I came crashing down onto my knees and side. I put out my arm to break the fall. And broke my wrist. I heard it go. CRACK. Just like that.

And it hurt like hell!

Pinot Noir Ice Wine

"DON'T TOUCH ME! DON'T TRY to help. Just let me get up on my own. I *can* do this!"

I was telling myself I could do it as much as I was telling Colin that I could get to my feet without his help. *I* didn't really believe me, but he seemed convinced. He stood back, held up his cellphone to throw a little more light onto the path for me, and made encouraging noises.

It took a few moments, but I managed it. It was a good job I was wearing pants, because at least they'd saved some of the skin on my knees and thigh. I'd ripped through the left sleeve of my shirt, and the skin on my elbow was pretty badly grazed, which was nothing compared with the greater discomforts of a broken wrist and a turned ankle.

I put my weight back on my damaged side as gently as I could. I found that if I kept the weight on my toe, rather than my heel, it was bearable. I cradled my floppy left wrist in my right hand.

There you go, Cait, left wrist broken—again! That's twice in one year—brilliant! Another six weeks in plaster!

Damn I was angry with myself. I didn't talk, I just gritted my teeth and hobbled up the steep path. Fortunately, Colin MacMillan had more sense than to ask me how I was doing. He lighted my way, as best he could. After what seemed like an age, we finally reached flatter ground. I could see the Corrigans' home ahead of us and beyond that, the lights of Anen House.

I stopped for a moment to catch my breath, but I knew I couldn't give up.

"Does your phone work *here*?" I asked Colin abruptly.

He checked. "Yes, I've got a signal. Can I punch in Bud's number for you?"

I nodded, gave him the number, and took the cellphone from him with my right hand. It rang. And rang. Finally, Bud answered.

"Hello? Hello?"

I could hear laughter, voices, and the clattering of a kitchen.

"Bud, it's Cait. Can you hear me?"

"*Cait?*"

"Yes, *Cait!*" I shouted angrily. "Go somewhere where you can hear me—it's important."

"Okay, okay, keep your hair on," replied Bud jovially. "Hey guys, gotta take this, back in a minute," he called to whoever was nearby.

I stood quietly beneath the star-pricked night sky, blood starting to trickle down my arm, my wrist thumping, my ankle screaming, and I listened to Bud humming as though he were "hold please" music. Usually it was entertaining. *At that moment? Not so much.*

I could feel the blood charging around my veins. I could see my breath puffing in the cool night air.

"Hey, so how's it going?" he finally asked. *Where do I begin?*

"Bud, you know I love you, right?"

"Oh-oh, this can't be good," he observed. *Very perceptive.*

"I can't get there for a little while, Bud. It doesn't matter why. I need you to do something and it's important, and it could be *critical*. Got it?"

"You're with someone and you can't say exactly what you want to say?" asked Bud. *See, perceptive.*

"Correct," I replied.

"Are you in danger? Do I need to come to you?" *He's damn good!*

"No and no. I *will* get there. Between now and then you must *not* leave Serendipity Soul's side. Got it?"

"She's in danger?"

"Possibly *imminent.*"

"Got it. I'll go right back to the kitchen. I'm on my way now. When will you be here, and are you okay?"

"Thanks Bud. I'll be there as soon as I can. I'm fine. Bye. Got to go."

"Got it. I'm on it."

I love it when Bud is Bud.

I could relax a little, but not too much.

"Right, let's get into the house, then Pat can drive us to your boat," I said, handing Colin's phone back to him.

"You can*not* be serious!" he said. "You can't go on the boat like *that*. You can't walk. You can't balance. You won't even be able to get onto it, let alone cope with all the bouncing around."

He was right. *Oh no, time is slipping away.*

"Okay then, change of plan, let's get Pat to drive us over. Come on, let's go!" and I hobbled toward the back door I'd sauntered out of not two hours earlier.

"Pat! Lauren! Need some help, please!" called Colin, racing ahead of me.

As I approached the door, I could see the concerned look on Lauren's face turn to horror when she caught sight of me.

"Oh sweet Mother of Jesus!" she cried as she ran toward me. "Pat! Pat! Call 911!"

"*NO!* Please, no!" I replied, as firmly as I could. "Stop right there—please Lauren. Where's Pat? Pat, you too, come closer, but stop there." They both did as I asked, but they each looked at the other with alarm.

"Lauren, Pat, Colin, I need you all to help me, and by doing that you'll be helping at least one other person—someone who's life might be in danger. I cannot say more than that. Not now. You need to trust me on this one. Lauren, your Mum was a nurse. Did she teach you how to strap up an injured wrist?" Lauren nodded. "Good. Can you go inside and find something that you can use as a bandage for support? I think a large tea towel will do fine for a sling." Again, Lauren nodded, and she was gone.

"Pat, I need you to be ready to leave. You're going to drive me and Colin over to SoulVine Wines. We might not be back for some time, so make sure the kitchen's safe, right?" Pat nodded and headed to the kitchen.

Finally, I turned to my young helper. "Colin, you've already done so much, but I need you to come with me, right? You're not to leave my side. Not for a minute. Okay?"

"Why?" asked Colin.

"I can't tell you that."

"Okay, that's cool," he replied, and shrugged. "Can I help with the bandaging?" he asked.

"Let's go in and see how Lauren's getting on with the supplies," I replied.

Lauren and Pat were brilliant, and Colin was as helpful as he could be. I declined painkillers but allowed Lauren to wipe the grit off my face, as well as strapping up my wrist. Then she very kindly offered to help me in the bathroom.

Because I knew that Bud was on the case across the lake, I *tried* not to mind as much that it took us fifteen minutes to get out of the house, and another half an hour before we reached the grand, gated entrance to the SoulVine Winery and Country Club. *But I did mind. A lot.*

However, if the movement of the car was anything to go by, my poor body just couldn't have coped with bobbing across the lake on a boat. Colin had made a good call on that one. Nevertheless, the time we'd lost was a real concern to me. Every extra moment it had taken me to get there presented an additional moment of danger to Serendipity.

Finally, we crunched along the wide driveway that led from the road toward the clubhouse and restaurant complex. It was huge:

four stories tall in some parts, just one in others. Dozens of windows were brightly lit, and the golden glow pooled on the grass and manicured plantings that surrounded the building. Pat brought the car to a standstill under a two-storey copper awning that sat atop a magnificent pair of gray stone-clad columns. It took all three of them to get me out of the car.

I could feel the swelling really getting a grip on my left wrist and hand, and the throbbing in my ankle was now building into a continuous pain. I'd seen myself in the bathroom mirror at Anen House, and I wasn't a pretty sight. I had no doubt that Bud would go ballistic when he saw me, and then again when he realized the extent of my injuries, but how I looked didn't matter. What mattered was that Bud had stuck to Serendipity like glue, and that Colin never left my side.

As I hobbled through the glazed double doors, I could hear gales of laughter echoing in a distant room. I looked at my watch. It was almost eight thirty. Everyone must have arrived by now. *Good.*

Pat and Lauren's entrance into the private dining room was greeted by a small cheer, Colin's with some puzzlement, especially from his mother, and mine with gasps of astonishment. As I looked around the room I took the time to read every face, carefully—I couldn't afford to make a mistake: Serendipity, Raj, Sheri, Grant, Lizzie, Ray, Gloria, Sammy, Suzie, and Ellen *all* looked completely, *believably*, shocked at the sight of me. Bud looked horrified.

"Oh my God—Cait—what's happened to you?" Bud rushed to my side. I winced. "Don't panic, I won't touch you," he said softly. "What have you done? Broken your wrist? *Again?*"

I nodded. I was *not* going to cry but the relief of being with Bud was pretty overwhelming.

"Is your head okay? No concussion?" I shook my head.

"All in perfect working order," I replied in an undertone. "*Perfect* working order, Bud," I repeated meaningfully.

Bud's eyes showed me that he understood. "We should talk. Or should I call the cops first?" he whispered. I nodded, ever so slightly.

"Can you get them here, tell them I'll be revealing something they'll want to know about the Wisers' 'accident' and then just get them to hover? You know, use your Bud-power on them? Also, can you do it without leaving Serendipity?" I whispered back.

He winked. "I'll sort it." I knew he would.

It was clear that my arrival had rather changed the pace of the evening, and what an evening it should have been. The room was magnificent, by any standards: the chandelier alone must have cost a bomb, and the fact that the light oak-paneled walls glittered with Sammy Soul's collection of framed gold and platinum records just brought the whole thing to a different level. Under any other circumstances I'd have been blown away by the food that was on display: if her presentation was anything to go by, Serendipity Soul was, indeed, a highly talented chef.

She'd used the colors and textures of her dishes artistically, painting picture that would please any palate. Fish, shellfish, meats, vegetables, flowers, fruits, pâtés; lovingly displayed cheeses, fabulous breads, glittering plates, multiple layers. It was all truly breathtaking. But I couldn't have managed to eat one single mouthful of it, and that knowledge was driving me nuts!

Sheri MacMillan was the first to approach me, though I knew that her son was the real draw.

"Why don't you come sit over here?" she suggested, waving an arm toward one of the little tables dotted around the room. "I can give you a hand."

"No, Mom. Cait doesn't need any help, she can manage on her own." Colin sounded terribly grown up; apparently more so to his mother than to me.

"Yes, dear," she replied, looking shocked.

Colin made sure I had a clear path to reach the table, pulled out a chair for me, and turned it at an angle, so it was easier for me to sit. As I settled myself, I could see Bud and Serendipity leave the room through a swing door. I guessed they were headed to the kitchen. I knew I had to buy time.

I allowed everyone to fuss around me. The story was that I'd fallen while out on a walk and that I hadn't wanted to miss the evening and besides, it all looked a lot worse that it really was.

Ellen was particularly attentive. She brought me a plate of food, which looked wonderful, and, at one point, I thought I might even manage to eat a few things from it. Suzie Soul, our hostess for the evening, arrived with a glass of water, *and* a glass of champagne. She even smiled sweetly. Sammy stood beside her and smiled too.

"What do ya think of the room?" asked Sammy, with obvious pride. "Quite a collection. Lotta years on these walls. Lotta years, and a lotta miles. Touring. Recording. My history. Suzie loves this room, don't ya, Babe?"

"It's a really great honor to be here, Sammy," I replied. "That's one of the reasons I didn't want to miss this evening. I knew that whatever you and your family had out here, it would be special."

Having proved I could at least form a sentence, however alarming I might look, Sammy seemed happy to stay and chat. He took the seat next to me.

"You're interesting," he said bluntly.

"How so?" I asked, intrigued.

"A marketer and a cop? Odd. And since you two guys showed up, *man*, everything's gone a bit mad. It's not usually like this here—all drama. It's usually pretty quiet. But since you got here, my Babe's been a bit off, you've had this fall, and then there's the accident, of course. Man, that's a bad vibe. Nice people. Gordy was fifteen years older than me. I hope I've got that much juice when I'm his age."

I looked at Sammy. Fifteen years between him and Gordy Wiser? Gordy had raised six kids, built a business that supported them, educated them, and then had set him and Marlene up for the rest of their lives, all with his bare hands, his knowledge of the soil and the seasons, and the sweat of his brow. Sammy Soul had taken *his* sweat, and *his* hands, and had made a guitar weep like only he could. He'd built all *this*. Such different lives, but they weren't so very different under their skins. Just fifteen years apart, but a whole different generation and lifestyle.

I also looked over at Suzie. She and Marlene couldn't have been more dissimilar and, true, Marlene was possibly old enough to have been her mother, but, again, what a difference. *Chalk and cheese.*

That was what Marlene had said about Annette and Ellen, and it set me thinking about the truth of that observation. As I did, I realized I was crying. I wasn't sobbing, but an unheralded tear was rolling down my cheek. I didn't even bother to reach for my purse— *what would have been the point?*

"Anyone got a hanky I can have, please? Or a paper napkin?" Ellen, Sheri, and Suzie each passed one in my direction. *What's the collective noun for paper tissues? A rustling? A moistening?*

I dabbed at my face silently, and I was relieved to see that no one wanted to make eye contact with me, except Colin, who was right beside me, watching my every move.

I can recall with total clarity what happened next. It was one of the most amazing hours of my life. *Of course* I'll never forget it, I never forget *anything*. But *this* hour? *Stellar!*

I pushed the used tissue into my purse, and turned to find Ellen hovering beside me with yet another glass in her hand.

"It's ours," she gushed. "The pinot noir ice wine. Not the 'Annette,' of course, that's not ready, but this was my sister's most award-winning ice wine. *Please* have some? We're all going to drink a toast to Marlene and Gordy in a minute."

I smiled. I felt I couldn't refuse. I took the glass. It was big, for ice wine, and heavy. My hand was shaking. My head was thumping. The room was warm, stifling: I could smell the seafood on the plate on the table in front of me mixed with Sheri MacMillan's sickly, flowery perfume beside me, and, for some reason, as I took the glass from Ellen, I suddenly fancied some chocolate. And not just any chocolate: Reese's Pieces. Bizarre!

Sammy Soul moved to the center of the room just as Bud and Serendipity re-entered it. Bud threw me a nod and flashed fifteen fingers at me. Okay, somehow I had to busk for fifteen minutes. It looked like Sammy was about to help me out on that front, because he tapped his glass with one of the many rings on his hand and a hush fell over our weird little gathering.

"Hey, though you might think I do a lot of this stuff, I don't, right, Babe?" He grinned at his wife, and she wriggled coquettishly in his general direction. "I kinda let my guitar do the talking for me all those years, but today is different. Special. *Man*, they were cool dudes, right? Gordy and Marlene? Him always moanin', her always fussin'. They loved each other, man. *Loved* each other. All those years together. All those kids. Kids are tough. Except my angel here, of course." There were suitable mutterings around the room.

"Tonight was gonna be my Serendipity's night. The night she did her thing and we all went 'Wow' and she got to be the star. 'Cos that's what she is. A *star*. I know she'd want me to say what I'm gonna say. All *this*," he waved his arm expansively toward the food, "all this, is nothing, compared with the lives we lost today. It's fabulous, my angel, but Marlene and Gordy were fabulous too. They'll be missed. So, hey, come on guys, raise your glasses and let's have a toast. Cait—*stay*, don't get up"—he looked directly at me, as did everyone else—"Now, here's to Gordy and Marlene Wiser."

Everybody raised their glasses, me included, and repeated the toast loudly and with gusto: "Gordy and Marlene Wiser!" We all drank.

"Well, that's mighty nice of you folks, but you could have waited till we got here!" It was Gordy Wiser, standing in the doorway, and next to him was Marlene.

Sheri let out a little scream.

Colin nodded, smiled, and said, "Cool."

Lauren crossed herself, and said, "Jesus, Mary and Joseph, it's a miracle!"

"That it is," agreed her husband.

Sammy dropped his glass.

Suzie swore, loudly.

Ellen gripped the edge of the table she was standing next to.

"How wonderful!" exclaimed Lizzie.

Grant clasped his crystal necklace and began bowing and bobbing.

Raj gasped, "By 'eck!"

Serendipity beamed.

Bud mouthed something unrepeatable, and I felt the room swim, the mists form, and the next thing I knew, my head was hitting the table.

Suddenly I was surrounded. .

"Give her air, give her air!" called Lauren.

"Someone bring *her* a glass of water. I think I need one too!" shouted Sheri.

I sat upright, my head lolling like a baby. I tried to focus on the Wisers, who were rushing toward me.

"What's been going on?" asked Marlene, looking concerned. "We're sorry we're late, we got caught up at C'est la Vie. We only popped in for a quick cup of coffee this afternoon, and we ended up running into some old friends. We haven't even been home to change for dinner. Sorry, Sammy dear, you'll have to take us as we are."

"But you're *dead*," I said, bluntly. *Someone had to.*

"Have you bumped your head, dear?" asked Marlene, peering into my eyes. "I think you should see a doctor."

"Cait's fine," said Bud firmly. "She's right. I . . . *we* saw you, this afternoon. Your car. It crashed, exploded, and burst into flames. At the base of the final bend leading to Anen Close. It went right into the cliff face. It burned. I *saw* you sitting in it." Bud was clearly flabbergasted.

A grim look crossed Marlene's face. "*Our* car?"

Bud nodded. Everyone nodded.

Sheri handed me a glass of water. I took it, and sipped.

"Oh dear. That's bad. Very bad," said Gordy. "We weren't in it. We decided to walk home, change out of our costumes, then walk on all the way down to the waterfront. It was such a lovely day. We thought you all knew. We told Rob."

"You told Rob?" exclaimed his wife. "*When* did you tell him? *Where* did you tell him? I haven't seen him all day, not since Dave arrived with you guys on your boat before lunch." She nodded in the direction of Sammy and Suzie. "Did Dave and Rob come back over to West Kelowna with you on the boat?" she asked. The Souls shrugged and shook their heads.

"Serendipity got us out of there, you know, in a bit of a hurry," muttered Sammy, acquiring himself a fresh drink.

"So where *are* they then?" asked Sheri.

Oh heavens!

"Well that's the thing, dear," replied Marlene, moving toward Sheri. She nodded at her husband, who moved closer to Colin. "We gave our car keys to Rob, in case he needed to move it at all. In case it was in anyone's way. And he said that he and Dave might drive into town, later on. Now, I don't *know* if that's what happened, but if they did . . ."

A strangled "Oh" came from Colin.

"What?" asked Sheri of her son.

Colin shook his head. "It was Dad. *Dad and Dave in the car.* In the Wisers' car. When it blew up."

"No! *Don't be ridiculous!*" Sheri's eyes searched our group for someone who would tell her it couldn't be so. "Rob wouldn't have driven. Not after all that . . . not having drunk so *much*. He's not *that* stupid. It *can't* have been *him*."

"Well, if not him, then who?" asked Marlene Wiser, rubbing Sheri's back. "And where's he got to?"

"Oh, he'll turn up. He *always* turns up, sooner or later." Sheri MacMillan almost sounded sure of herself.

"Mom, stop it! *Stop it*. It was *Dad*. He was *drunk*, like he always is. *It was Dad!*" Colin MacMillan was suddenly seventeen, going on ten. "Mom, Daddy's dead. I saw him, I saw it. He burned. I saw my Daddy burn!" He was red in the face, tears streaming. He was pulling at his hair.

I shook my head. The immense joy we'd all felt at seeing Gordy and Marlene alive in our midst had been sucked out of us by the loss we were seeing unfolding before us. *What a day! I need a cigarette.*

But it was clear that the drama wasn't finished.

With Colin sobbing on Gordy's shoulder, Sheri wailing into Marlene's, Sammy shouting orders to the barman to bring a round of large brandies for everyone, and me wondering if I'd be able to light a cigarette one-handed again, another disturbance grabbed our collective attention.

The door from the kitchen flew open, banging against the wall of the dining room, and we could hear pots tumbling beyond it. Serendipity flung herself into the room, and caught the edge of the tablecloth on the serving table. As she fell to the ground, clutching her throat, the cloth in her hand brought food tumbling onto the floor. Plates smashed, domed lids rang out like mournful bells, food splattered, and we all sat, or stood, paralyzed.

Only Colin moved. He tore himself from Gordy's arms and ran toward Serendipity, screaming "No!" His arm was raised and something glinted in his fist. Something metallic. As he approached the woman's writhing body, her father leapt forward, trying to grab Colin's arm.

"Get away from my angel!" he screamed, and lunged for Colin. But Colin had the advantage of youth on his side, and all that Sammy grabbed was air. As Sammy went down, we all saw Colin, stabbing Serendipity in the thigh, hard.

Suzie screamed, then flew at Colin. She threw herself on him, a frenzied figure made up of snarling teeth and flashing claws. She pulled his hair and beat him with her fists. Sammy picked himself up off the floor and tried to remove his wife. It seemed she was on top of Colin for an age, but it was probably no more than a matter of seconds.

As Sammy finally managed to pull her away, Colin let himself flop, rolling onto the floor beside Serendipity, who was still moaning and holding her throat.

"Call 911," croaked Colin. "Peanuts—Mom—peanuts!"

I suddenly realized what had happened. My wrist and ankle aside, I had to be heard. I stood up, using the table for support.

"Sammy, Suzie—where does Serendipity keep her Epi-Pen? *Quick!* Colin needs it. He just used his own on your daughter. Now he needs one too. *Where* is your daughter's Epi-Pen? Fetch it quick. *Now!*" Neither of them answered. They looked dazed.

"Colin? What's wrong?" Poor Sheri was having one *hell* of an evening. "Are there peanuts? *Where* are there peanuts? I don't understand!"

"Sheri." I addressed the distraught woman directly and calmly. "Serendipity was suffering an allergic reaction to peanuts. Colin recognized the symptoms, and he used *his* Epi-Pen to save her. The contact between him and Serendipity has led to Colin having enough of an exposure for *him* to suffer an allergic reaction himself. That's why we need Serendipity's Epi-Pen, so it can be used to treat Colin."

I turned to the Souls who were both looking a great deal the worse for wear, and still completely confused.

"She's always got one in her pocket," replied Suzie, snapping out of her stupor. "Why didn't she use it herself?"

"Quick, Bud, check Serendipity's pockets," I called, but Bud was already on it.

"Nothing," he said. I was beginning to get a bad feeling about Colin, who was grasping at his throat as he lay on the floor beside the chef he'd just selflessly saved.

"Oh, oh—*I've* got one, I've got a *spare* one!" shouted Sheri, coming to her senses and rising to her feet. "Where's my purse? It's red." Everyone scanned the room.

"Got it!" shouted Bud as he ran to a table diagonally opposite us, grabbed up a large, red-leather purse, dumped its entire contents onto the table, and pulled an Epi-Pen from the heap. He ran toward Colin and stabbed him in the thigh.

Everyone breathed out.

"I'm calling 911," said Bud. *He's good at being in charge.*

Sheri ran to her son's side. The Souls knelt by their daughter. I drank the rest of the ice wine in my glass, and immediately regretted it.

Almost no one noticed the two RCMP officers who stuck their heads into the room, caught Bud's eye, and beckoned him outside.

I sighed. I looked up. Lauren was hovering.

"I wonder, Lauren, could I bother you to give me hand outside, please? I'm going to take this little window of opportunity to go and smoke a cigarette." *God, I needed one!*

She tutted, but smiled. "Sure I will. It's out through that door there, and around the side. Come on with you now."

As I hobbled, she held my good arm, and we made it out quite quickly. I limped toward the large decorative pot that was filled with fine, white sand with a few butts in it, and lit up. As I balanced myself against the edge of the pot I saw it: a long stub of a slightly wet-looking cigarette. I picked it up and sniffed.

Of course! Clever!

That sealed it. If I'd been in *any* doubt at all about the murders, *that* was the final nail in the murderer's coffin. *I had them!* I asked Lauren if I could borrow her cellphone for a moment, to make a long distance call, and she said she didn't mind at all—so long as it was a quick one. I assured her it would be. She agreed to go inside and find me a Ziploc bag and bring it out to me. I knocked the glowing end off the cigarette stub that I'd found, and set it aside for the cops. I puffed as hard as I could on the last thin little cigarette from *my* pack, pulled the number I needed to call from my purse, and made my call—apologizing profusely for disturbing the poor man's sleep. Finally, I stubbed out my cigarette and had a quiet word with myself.

Alright, Cait Morgan. Here we go, then. Time for the show. You'd better be good.

The paramedics would arrive very soon to take Serendipity and Colin, and quite possibly me, to the emergency room, so I didn't have much time.

As I hobbled back inside, with Lauren's help, Bud gave me the nod. Oh bless him, he had absolutely no idea what I was about to do, and yet I could tell he was supporting me totally and completely.

Love you, Bud! Okay—now or never Cait!

Champagne and Cup-a-Soup

"LADIES AND GENTLEMEN," BUD BEGAN loudly. His voice rang out across the small dining room. It was a very commanding voice. *Hey, he had been a commanding police officer in the Force, right?*

"Can I have your attention, please? Everyone, please, sit down. It's just for a few moments while we wait for the ambulances to arrive."

I allowed myself to take in the scene around me.

Bud helped Sheri to lift Colin onto a seat at an unoccupied table. The boy flopped there, pale, panting, and sipping water. His mother's love for him was obvious in every look, touch, and movement.

At the next table sat Serendipity, attended to by both Sammy and Suzie. Raj was perched at her side. I hadn't seen Vince Chen at the dinner, and suspected that dodging crockery at lunchtime had been his cue to exit Kelowna and head for the comparative safety of another winemaking region.

Beyond the two "sick" tables was the "dead" table: Gordy and Marlene sat alone, holding each others' hands, clearly trying to come to terms with all the shocks of the past half hour.

Across the room from the Wisers' table, Lizzie and Grant Jackson were also sitting very close to each other. She was blinking at the goings on through her giant spectacles, he fiddling with the crystal that lay on his breast. Opposite them sat Ray Murciano and Gloria Thompson, the two people the Jacksons employed at their store and restaurant.

Lauren and Pat were at my table, Lauren making sure I had hankies, water, and whatever else I needed, and Ellen came to join us.

Everyone looked surprised when Bud came across the room to help me to my feet.

I cleared my throat.

"Hello everyone. I know you all know me as Bud's 'other half,' but I have to begin by telling you all that I've been here this weekend under false pretences." The folks I'd expected to shoot puzzled looks did so. *Good.*

"Yes, my name's Cait, Cait Morgan, and I am *indeed* a professor at the University of Vancouver, but I'm not a marketing professor, I'm a criminal psychologist. I specialize in profiling victims. And, as those of you who were at the party last evening will know, Ellen invited Bud, who's a retired police officer, to come to Kelowna to look into her sister's death. To be fair to Ellen," I nodded in her direction, "she didn't know that Bud's 'accompanying other' for this weekend visit would be me—well, she knew it would be *me*, Cait, but she didn't know *then* what I do for a living. She was just lucky, I guess, that she actually got two investigators for the price of one." I forced a smile.

I'd expected a buzz around the room, and that's pretty much what I got. *Good.*

"I realize that Bud and I have only spent a very small amount of time with each of you, but we've managed to learn a lot in a short time. Now, with the events of this afternoon and this evening, it's clear that something's amiss here, so it's time for me to speak up. With Bud's support, of course, and with the indulgence of the RCMP, who, you might have noticed, have a presence in the room."

It was clear from the response that several people *hadn't* noticed the cops hovering at the door. To be fair, there *had* been rather a lot going on. There was a lot of shuffling on seats. *Also good.*

"Now, of course, we're all devastated by the tragic deaths of Rob MacMillan and Dave . . . um, his friend and colleague, Dave, this afternoon." As the room muttered, Sheri blew her nose, and Colin looked toward me with red eyes, his face a mask of despair, with a hint of relief. *Interesting.*

"I also know that you might think that the reason for the accident was that the driver had been drinking. When Bud, Ellen, and I left the lunch today, I saw a puddle of brake fluid on the side of the road where the Wisers' car had been parked. I mentioned this to the police"—I raised an eyebrow in Bud's direction, and he nodded at me—"and they have confirmed that the brake fluid line on the car had been tampered with."

Gasps. Open mouths. The Wisers grabbed each others' hands even tighter.

"Oh my God!" cried Sheri.

"Mom, he was drunk anyway," added Colin blackly.

I held up my hands for quiet. I got it. "Obviously the police need to find out who might have done this, and why. I believe I can help them. First of all, we have to wonder if Rob and Dave were the intended victims of this, and I cannot discount the facts that Rob and Dave are friends who sometimes work together in the oil business in Calgary, and that some sort of reason for them to be killed might have followed them here to Kelowna from Alberta. However, I think you'll all agree, *most* people would have expected that the Wisers would be driving that car, heading down the steep curves and bends of Lakeshore Road this afternoon."

Accepting expressions and head nodding all around. *Good.*

"The question is, who would want to kill Marlene and Gordy Wiser? And why?"

This time a round of head shaking, rather than nodding.

"Who *are* the Wisers?" I asked, rhetorically. "Gordy's been a farmer in this area for decades. He and Marlene have raised six children, all adopted, and have secured a future for themselves by the efforts they have made to tame the land and grow fine crops. They are fun-loving, happily married people, who, I think everyone would agree, have their little quirks, as we all do,"—a few smiles, and even the Wisers nodding—"but they are well respected, well known in the community." More nodding. "One of their little quirks is that they like to know what's going on around them. So keeping an eye on things is second nature. Interested neighbors can be very useful." I was trying to err on the side of politeness, but realized I'd have to cross the line at some point. "Though some might see it as nosiness. And nosiness can be dangerous, because a nosey person might see things that others would rather they didn't see. And they might do things that others might wish they hadn't done. The Wisers even went so far as to keep collecting Annette's mail after her death as a way to continue to 'keep an eye on her.'" I let this thought sink in.

"So what might the Wisers have seen or done that might have caused them to become the target of a killer?" I paused. I didn't expect any suggestions. "This is what brought me to a possible link with Annette's death. You all know the circumstances: Ellen found her sister dead, with a note and an empty wine bottle beside her. It's always been accepted as a suicide, and, when I thought in *detail* about the reactions to Ellen's little outburst last night, it became very clear to me that the idea that someone might have *killed* Annette was *completely alien* to most people in the room. That was a most telling discovery. But that's exactly what Bud and I were asked to come here to consider: was Annette Newman murdered? Which brings me to the answer to that question: *yes, she was.*"

The silence that followed was broken by Grant.

"At lunch, Ellen said that Bud had looked into Annette's death and had convinced her it *was* a suicide after all. I'm confused."

"I'm afraid that after Ellen had that epiphany this morning, Bud and I discovered more facts that led us to believe it was murder after all."

"You didn't tell Ellen? You didn't tell *anyone*?" Grant seemed to be speaking on behalf of my entire audience.

"Okay, I understand your confusion, because I, too, was confused for a long time. Right up until this evening, actually: but here it is. I *know* Annette Newman was killed, *and* I know a good deal more. I know who tampered with the Wisers' brakes, and why—*and* who made sure that Serendipity Soul suffered an almost fatal allergic reaction tonight."

"Okay—out with it! You're saying someone *did* that to my angel? Someone *poisoned* her? Tired to *kill* her?" Sammy was on his feet, ready again to fight for his child. Maybe even ready to kill for her. He couldn't have been *less* laid back. All the passion he'd put into his stage presence was still there.

"Serendipity is quite safe now, don't panic," I replied, "and I can hear the sirens coming. It won't be long until she's at the hospital."

"I'm fine, really I'm fine," said Serendipity weakly. "Sammy, sit down. *Dad!*"

It was clear that both Sammy and Suzie were taken aback at the use of this term by their daughter, and it had the desired effect. And the sirens had their effect on me. I had to get a move on.

"If Annette *was* killed, then maybe the attempt on the Wisers' lives had something to do with that. After all, they were close to Annette. They saw her frequently, they each dropped into the other's homes. She brought them little treats, they knew of her hobbies, her interests, her passions, and they had a bird's eye view of all the comings and goings at Anen House, all day, every day. If they knew that much about her life, what might they know about her death? Now, Gordy and Marlene did mention to me that Annette had become distant in the last few weeks of her life, but, somehow they *forgot* to mention that they'd witnessed her new will. Why would they *forget* to mention that?" I peered over at them. "It was quite important, really, wasn't it? Especially since the new will was one of the things that quite a few people in this room used as an example of how Annette must have been getting ready to kill herself."

"It's an odd thing, that: the will that left her part of the winery to *you*, Raj." Now it was Raj's turn to wriggle with discomfort beneath my withering glance. "To you and your 'firstborn child,' that is, which is *very* odd, isn't it, eh? Got any kids, Raj? I mean, you're about forty, you've only been here a few years. Plenty of time for you to have had a kid as old as what, twenty, twenty-two even, back in Yorkshire. Anything to say? You are, as I've already told you, the prime suspect here, given what Annette willed to you. Did the Wisers know something about you that you didn't want them to share? Did you convince them to sign a fake will, thereby gaining access to what you've told me more than once is a unique collection of grape varietals? Did Serendipity begin to suspect? Maybe she wasn't the first girl who needed to be disposed of. Maybe . . ."

Both Raj *and* Sammy leapt to their feet. Serendipity jumped up between them.

"Dad, stop. You stop too, Cait. This isn't fair to Raj." She turned toward the man she clearly loved and said, "No more messing about. This is it, right? Cards on the table?" Raj nodded, and sat. He held his head in his hands, shaking his head.

"Look everyone, Raj and I love each other. We've been together a while, and, whatever *you* might think, Cait Morgan, I *know* he didn't kill Annette. He *really* quite liked Annette. In fact, they'd been together for a little while, back when he was still working here, right?" Sammy looked shocked, Suzie rolled her eyes, and Raj just kept shaking his head. "Raj hasn't got any children. But we might have, in the future."

"Are you two . . . ?" Sammy sounded amazed.

Both Raj and Serendipity nodded. "Yes, Mom, Dad, I'm sorry you're finding out this way but we are, and we always will be, a couple. We've decided. I think we're old enough to know our own minds, and I don't think I really need your permission to do anything I want, right?"

Sammy shook his head, dazed.

"Raj," I said, cutting across the personal dramas of the Souls, "would I be right in saying that, when you and Annette hooked up at a wine event the first time, you weren't as 'careful' as you might have been?" Raj nodded.

"I told you, Ser," he said, looking at the smiling face of Serendipity, "we was drunk. It were just one of them things."

"Raj. I *know*. It's not an issue." She was still calm. She reached out and took his hand.

"But, you see Raj," I continued, "Annette got pregnant. She was pregnant when she died. In fact, it was *because* she was pregnant with your child that she was killed."

I watched. I saw. I carried on.

"Annette's odd behavior was because she was pregnant: even Bonnie said she was 'dashing here and there like a bird in spring.' A *nesting* bird. She lost a tasting event to you, Raj! There's a lot of research that suggests that taste and smell change during pregnancy. She missed meetings, canceled tastings. She was likely suffering from morning sickness, and knew she couldn't hide her changing abilities when it came to her job. She was, literally, clearing out her house and beginning to prepare for a baby in her life. She started to buy larger clothes at thrift stores, and she dumped her garbage herself, probably because it contained items she didn't want anyone, even garbage collectors, to see—maybe pregnancy test kits, even the debris from cleaning up unexpected attacks of vomiting. She didn't want *anyone* to know. She didn't even tell you, Raj, did she?"

Raj was shaking his head sadly. "Is that why she changed her will, then?" he asked plaintively. "'Cos she were having my child? It *would* have been my 'firstborn.'"

I nodded.

"Oh, dear, dear," said Marlene, quietly. "Terrible."

"Yes, terrible," I agreed, "because Annette's killer committed a double homicide: Annette *and* her baby." I let it sink in.

I looked around the people in the room. "And yet *none* of you knew. None of you *guessed*? Not you, Ellen, her loving sister, who saw her every day? Not you, Gordy and Marlene, who said she was acting oddly, and yet agreed to sign a new will? Not you, Raj, who continued to see her constantly in and around the locale and the business? Not *any* of you? Lizzie—you told me Annette was suffering from a bad back, an altered mood, and a changed sense of smell—how could you come up with 'root chakra' and not 'pregnant?' *Amazing*. No one saw what was right under their noses. All the clues were there, and not one of you put them together to work out that she was having a baby. That's largely because you were all, to a greater or lesser extent, fixated on your own obsessions."

People shifted uncomfortably.

"Of course, there was the complication I had to work through about Annette selling her entire collection of snuff boxes, but that related to *her* obsession, and not to the fact that she was pregnant. Grant, you told me that you tried to help Annette, but you let her down?" Grant nodded.

"I did, and maybe even more than I thought, if what you're saying is true," he said, grimly.

"Oh, it's true alright. It's also true, isn't it, that Annette, one of your 'best customers' according to an inscription you wrote in a book on silverware for her, came to you and begged you to sell her snuff box collection—in a hurry. Right?"

He nodded. "We'd worked together building her snuff box collection over many years. That's how I came to get to know Kelowna, driving up here with boxes I'd found for her, when I still had my silver and antiques business in Vancouver. She came to me, a couple of months before she died, and asked if I could go back to my old contacts and sell her whole collection. *Fast*. I told her she could have got a lot more if only she would wait for the right sales to come up, but she said she needed money, and she needed it quickly. I should have pressed her. I should have made her tell me why she needed it. Though," and here he looked puzzled, "I still don't really get it. I mean, okay, she might have been about to have a child, but the winery's doing well. She can't have been short of money."

"She needed the cash to be able to buy her collectors' 'grail.' She told Colin about it, right?" Colin nodded. "Otherwise, like the obsessive collector she was, she kept the whole thing to herself. I'm going to suggest that you sold her collection of silver snuff boxes for around forty thousand dollars, would that be right?"

Grant looked surprised. He nodded. "How'd you know that?" he asked.

Bud's face was telling me he wanted to ask the same question.

"I just spoke to a very nice, if sleepy, man in Newfoundland, by the name of 'Sanderson.' His family name used to be 'Sandy' back when they were in Scotland: such a well-respected name, in certain parts, that it was an honor to be known as a 'son' of the house, hence 'Sanderson.' He confirmed that he sold Annette a signed James Sandy snuff box, made from the wood of the bed in which Robbie Burns died, with a letter in Sandy's own handwriting giving it an impeccable provenance. She paid fifteen thousand dollars—which he assures me was a very fair price—and Annette had deposited another twenty-five grand in her bank account. That's forty."

There was a sharp intake of breath from Ellen, to my right. *Ah!*

I turned toward Ellen. "Yes, you didn't know that the plain wooden box that arrived at Anen House by courier, two days after Annette's death, was worth that much, did you Ellen? Otherwise you might *not* have tossed it into the apple store with all her other mail. All that *stuff* you hang onto, Ellen. All the years you've been filling storage bins, surrounding yourself with the evidence of your inability to let go? It speaks volumes about you. You're a very unusual hoarder: you're neat; you're highly organized; and, unlike many who see the 'value' in everything, which is why they can't get rid of it, you're a hoarder who sees 'value' in nothing. Not in a small, perfectly formed little box. Not in your sister. In fact, the only thing you do see 'value' in, the only thing you see as 'important' is you. *You*, Ellen Newman. You are the center of your world. You are the only one with desires that matter. It is only *your* obsession that counts. *You* are the person in this room with by far the strongest, most driving obsession. *Your* obsession is Raj Pinder, isn't it? It has been since he arrived in Kelowna, four years ago. Which was when you went to Lizzie Jackson and asked for her help to 'make room' in your life for 'someone special.' It was because of your obsession with Raj that you've killed four, probably five people, including your own sister, and have tried to kill again tonight."

There was complete silence. Even the approaching sirens had stopped wailing.

"Don't be ridiculous!" exploded Ellen, jumping to her feet. She drew herself up to her full height and looked down at me. "You're talking rubbish. It was *me* who said Annette had been murdered. Why would I say *that* if I'd murdered her, when everyone said it was a suicide. Why wouldn't I just shut up and get away with it?"

Everyone looked at me, Ellen's question reflected on their faces.

"That is *such* a good question, Ellen, and, you know, that had even *me* confused for quite some time. If you'd managed to stage the perfect murder, because everyone thought it was a suicide, why would you be rattling the cage, asking Bud to come and look into your sister's possible murder?"

"And the answer is?" asked Lizzie, on behalf of the room.

"The answer is because of *Raj*. Again, back to Ellen's obsession. Let me explain."

"Please do," said Sheri, "because I want my boy to be off to the hospital—but *only* when you've explained, right, Colin? I have to *understand* why my Rob is dead, and I don't."

I nodded at Sheri, then at Bud. He understood, and began to move toward the doors.

"This is what happened, and how it happened, and why it happened," I said, suddenly feeling very weary. I took a sip of water. Then one of champagne. *Much better.*

"Ellen and Annette Newman lost their parents, tragically, in a road traffic accident. Ellen stepped up and made sure she and her sister were okay. She, and then her sister, built up a successful and, thanks to Annette's fabulous nose, world-renowned winery. About four years ago Raj Pinder comes to town. He's younger than Ellen, good-looking, and a bit out of the ordinary for a woman like her, whose major brush with the outside world—her years at the University of Vancouver—I'm guessing made her feel a bit left out of things. It's not an unusual story: Ellen Newman fell for Raj Pinder. What *is* unusual is the psychological profile of the woman doing the falling."

I looked down at Ellen, who had plopped back onto her seat. She looked up at me, nostrils flaring, face all pink. She was *seething*.

"I haven't spent a great deal of time with you, Ellen, but I can see traits in you that suggest a borderline personality: you are a woman of extreme emotions. You will *not* be denied, you *will* organize and arrange, you *will* have your way. And if you don't, you *snap*. You *are* clever though, I'll give you that, Ellen. You've balanced your impulsiveness with your intelligence very well. For example, you knew, rationally, that you couldn't invite Raj to your apartment with all those storage boxes in it, so you sought help to work through how to get rid of them: your mental condition wouldn't allow you to simply make a dozen trips to the dump, but it *did* allow for at least trying some hypnotherapy. It didn't work for you, did it? And, because you 'didn't get your way'—in other words, because Lizzie Jackson and her healing powers, and by association Grant and the Faceting for Life dogma, couldn't help you—you didn't just *walk away*, you launched a campaign of vitriol against the Jacksons and their beliefs."

Grant and Lizzie moved in their seats, muttering to each other.

"So, you didn't get Raj. It just didn't happen. Sometimes these things just aren't meant to be. That didn't mean it was over for *you*, Ellen, did it? Raj's life progressed here, yours stagnated—with him as your sole obsession. Suzie, I'm going to suggest that you made your play for Raj pretty soon after his arrival at your winery."

I didn't expect a response, so I was surprised when Suzie shouted, "So what if I did?" at the whole room. "He's cute . . ." She stopped, put her talon-tipped fingers to her mouth, looked at her daughter, and said, "Oh, sorry Serendipity, baby." She looked deflated.

I carried on. "When you threw those vitriolic comments at Ellen last night, Suzie, I was puzzled. Did you hate Ellen so much because you thought that she, and when she was alive, her sister, were going to spoil the nice little business you and Sammy were developing in cannabis wine? Or was there another reason? Having put this all together, I'm suggesting that Ellen and you had words about Raj, and that's where your hatred of her stems from. You'd have made an open play for him, and I think that Ellen wouldn't have been able to resist telling you to back off."

"You're right, she did," Suzie replied. "Who did she think she was? She told me that Raj would rather be with her than me. When he turned me down, flat . . . I was pissed. Sure. But I soon found out he wasn't with her, either. Miserable little cow. Look at her. Who the hell would want *her*? She's all *desiccated*. Eaten away from inside. That's where *real* beauty is born." The irony of these last words, spoken by a woman whose many procedures had so clearly gone a long way toward supporting at least one child of a plastic surgeon through college, was not lost on the majority of the room.

"Thanks for being so—open, Suzie," I said. Suzie sat down again, flicking her hair in triumph as she did so.

"What about Raj's girlfriend, Jane? I'm sorry Raj, I don't know any more about her than that, and that she was a girl who held down seasonal jobs and then just disappeared. Could you tell us a little more?"

Raj rolled his eyes toward Serendipity. She reached out and held his hand. "Aye, she were a nice lass. Like you said, she worked at Big White in't winter, then at a winery in't summer. It weren't nothing serious, just a bit of fun. But she were nice, and pleasant."

"And she just 'disappeared?' Is that right? In what way?"

Raj nodded. "She went out one day on her rollerblades. Loved them, she did. She went really fast. At least, that's what she *said* she were doing. But when I went to her place the next evening to pick her up to go out, all her stuff were gone and *she* were gone too. Didn't leave no note, no rent, just did a runner. Didn't hand in her notice or nothing. And never a word from her since."

"Did you, or her family, or anyone, report her as missing? I can't imagine you were the only person who knew she'd gone."

There was a bit of fidgeting around the room. Clearly more people than Raj had known about this Jane's disappearance and had done—*what*, I wondered?

"Well, I didn't think it were my place. I mean, like I said, it weren't nothing serious. I did phone her aunt in Terrace and told her, and she said I weren't to worry because Jane was always up and leaving places. She'd done it before, and she usually got in touch when she were good and ready. No, I didn't do owt. And it were chaos here, anyway. It were when those fires hit, you know, the really bad ones? We was lucky, over here at SoulVine Wines, but we could see the fires over on this side of the lake, and thousands were out of their homes. What with all the coming and going, and people's houses being burned down, and folks with nowhere to live, I think we was all just a bit involved with that." Raj hung his head.

"Okay, I think that maybe that'll be something for our friends here in the RCMP to look into at some future date. I don't believe that Ellen's carefully panned murder of Annette is where it all started.

I believe there might have been an *un*planned, impulsive crime before that, which showed Ellen that she *could* get away with killing someone. Right, Ellen?" I looked down at the woman sitting beside me, her arms crossed in fury, spots of color on her cheeks.

"Of course, there was poor Stacey Willow, right Ellen?"

"Who's Stacey Willow?" asked Sammy, raising his hand like a schoolboy.

"Let's ask Ellen, eh? What—did you catch sight of Raj, and the sister of one of his soccer buddies, laughing in a crowd one night, maybe in a bar downtown? Was that all it took *that* time? A *hint* of him enjoying himself with someone other than you? Poor Stacey Willow: twenty years old, and drugged to death with pills ground up into a strawberry milkshake. How did you get her to drink it, Ellen? Just befriended her at the end of her shift at the burger bar? Treated her to a milkshake? Popped in the pills, knowing they'd kill her as she slept in the bedroom at her parents' house that she'd had since she was a child. *Since* she was a child? What am I saying? She was *still* a child! Another 'rival' bites the dust, right?"

The enormity of what I was saying was hitting home around the room. I knew I was beginning to run out of steam.

I looked across at Bud, and he winked at me. I smiled back, sighed, and continued.

"Which brings us to Annette. You had no idea that Annette and Raj had been seeing each other when they were away at wine events, did you, Ellen? You really didn't notice what was going on right under your nose. You didn't notice Annette's changing habits, or body. In fact, two photographs that I found of you both in the apple store show the moment that Annette told you she was pregnant, right?"

I didn't expect Ellen to respond, and she didn't.

"In one photograph, the camera has snapped at the moment when Annette is telling you the joyful news, and you are clearly horror-stricken that 'your' Raj has got her pregnant. Your sister, and the man you love, *together*? I'm not surprised you were shocked. I suspect it didn't take you long to decide to get rid of your rival—your sister—and the baby, did it? What, did you beg her to not tell Raj, or anyone else except her big sister, until she'd reached the magic three-month mark? Buying yourself some time, right? *Planning* how to do it. That was clever, Ellen. *Really clever.* How *do* you get someone to write a suicide note, and then actually commit suicide? Because that's what you did."

"I did *not. No one could,*" said Ellen, with a venomous emphasis.

"Oh, but you *did.* It was difficult for me to work out how you did it, because it was so clever. I have to admit that when I saw that the signatures on Annette's will, her suicide note, and the receipt for the courier, signed two days after she was dead, were all the same, I toyed with the idea of forgeries: you could have forged Annette's signature on the suicide note, as you obviously did on the courier receipt, and you could even have supplied a birthday card to yourself, written *by* you, as 'proof' that what I was seeing was, indeed, Annette's hand. What about the will, though? The Wisers had *witnessed* that signature. I wondered if, for some reason, they were in cahoots with you, and they had willingly witnessed a forged will, and so, eventually, they had to be done away with. But, no, the signature on the courier's receipt was the clincher. You didn't know that anyone would ever see that. But then I *got it*: I've been thinking about my relationship with *my* sister, since I began to think about you and Annette, and that's what gave me the answer—you're able to sign *your* sister's name just as I can pretty much sign *my* sister's, and she mine. Same school teachers, same handwriting lessons, same family—it's not odd. The suicide note? It *was* Annette's signature, because Annette *did* type and sign that letter herself. Her letter of *resignation*, right? Not a suicide note at all."

I looked up from Ellen and addressed the room. "For those of you who don't know, Annette wrote: 'Ellen, It's no use, I can't do it anymore. I can't go on. It just won't work. I can't do my job any more. And if I can't do my job perfectly, except she typed *prefectly*, then there's no point to any of it. I'm sorry. I know you'll miss me. But that's it. I'm done. Love, always, Annette.' The letter was telling Ellen that Annette was leaving the *winery*, not *life*. A typo wasn't the end of the world. It wasn't the last thing she'd *ever* write, it was just a loving note to a sister. When you saw that letter, you *knew* you could use it against her. First piece of the puzzle: a handy, dandy suicide note. Sorted. Then you had to get to Anen House without anyone seeing you: the fight that Annette was seen having in *your* truck, the truck she 'borrowed' the day she died? Annette's arms were flailing, she was crying. She was fighting with *you*. You were in the truck with her. Hidden in the back seat. I should know: I've been in it. It's easy to hide in there, you just duck down. When Annette shouted 'So—you've never loved me—why should I help you?' it was *you* she was fighting with. A sister who couldn't hide how she felt about her sibling's pregnancy. I got the wording right, eh, Colin?"

Colin nodded.

"*Colin?*" Ellen sounded shocked.

"Yes, Ellen, it wasn't the *Wisers* who saw Annette in the truck that night, it was *Colin*. He didn't see *you* at all. You were quite safe. But, once Bud and I mentioned that Annette had been seen having a fight, in her truck, you *couldn't* run the risk that you'd been seen. You knew that no one would have seen you *leave* Annette's house. You took the route down the backside of the hill, a route you've known since childhood, and made your way through the vineyards to your car, or should I say *Annette's* car. You left it parked out of sight along the way. You *assumed* it was the nosey Wisers who'd seen you arriving with Annette, and you certainly know your way around vehicles well enough to be able to cut a brake fluid line. Why, when you were ranting last night you even threw it out there that it was you who kept the machinery and the vehicles in working order at the winery in the days when you couldn't afford mechanics. Of course, I knew that the *real* witness had been Colin, not that he'd actually witnessed anything, but at least I knew *he* was safe. Once I'd worked things out, I kept him close by me. Just in case there was some way you'd found out that he was the one who'd seen Annette, and very possibly you, in the truck that evening. Now you're safe, Colin. It's all out in the open."

"You, Ellen? *You* killed my Rob? *You* cut that brake thingy? *Why?*" Sheri was wailing, and clearly having a hard time coming to terms with it all.

"Of course not, she's just rambling," replied Ellen dismissively.

I sighed. Poor Sheri. "Ellen was trying to kill the Wisers, not Rob, and she tried to kill the Wisers because she thought they'd seen her go to her sister's house, fighting with her on the way, the evening that she died. Ellen simply slipped out of the lunch today, snipped the lines, and came back in. She knew that the leaking fluid and the steep hills would take their toll. And they did. It's just that the *wrong* people were in the car at the time. I'm so sorry, Sheri, Colin. Rob wasn't the target, but he and his colleague became two more victims of this woman."

Sheri and Colin hugged each other close. I knew time was getting short.

I pressed on. "How *exactly* did Ellen arrange Annette's death? That was a difficult part of the puzzle to solve, because it seemed physically impossible for Ellen to have drugged Annette, then carried her to the truck. If that wasn't how she'd ensured that her sister sat in the truck long enough to become unconscious, then how on earth had she done it? I worked it out. *You* taught her how to do it, Lizzie."

Lizzie looked horrified. "What do you mean? *I taught her how to kill her sister?* How?"

I sighed. "When you were rattling on about your list of fourteen

Critical Facets in the car, remember?" Lizzie nodded, looking slightly wounded. "You mentioned that you use hypnotherapy techniques in your practice, and you also mentioned that you'd used hypnosis in your 'healing' sessions with Ellen. *Hypnosis.* You even told me at lunch today that Ellen had a real talent for it, right?" Lizzie nodded. "She coldly and calculatingly used that talent on her sister. I can see it now. Annette, distraught after an engineered argument with her big sister; Ellen offering to help her calm down by using some deep breathing and relaxation exercises; the ability to then suggest to Annette, when she's in an almost hypnotic state, that she sit in a comfy seat and sleep, quietly. All Ellen needed to do was make sure that the big, comfy seat she led her sleepwalking sister to was in the truck, and the job was done. Annette simply slept, peacefully, shut in the vehicle, with a hastily attached hosepipe run through an almost closed window, until she'd been poisoned. When her sister was dead, Ellen placed the note and the bottle beside her, taped up the windows of the truck, hooked up the hosepipe 'properly'—then *ripped it all open again.* Ellen's not stupid. These days, when we're all bombarded with forensic detective TV programmes morning, noon and night, she'd know enough about Locard's principle—the theory that there's always an exchange of forensic evidence when there's contact between two things. She knew she had to have a plan that could explain away all of the evidence she was about to create. If any of Ellen's fingerprints were found, they were there because of her rescue attempts."

I looked down at Ellen, who was beginning to lose her color. "You just had to place the duct tape in Annette's hands as you unwound it, to get her prints onto it, and put the bottle into her palm for the same reason. Oh, and that's where you made your one big mistake, Ellen." I looked at the top of her head. She was ignoring me. "Annette had nowhere near enough alcohol in her blood for having drunk a whole bottle of wine. A glass, yes. A glass you'd probably have shared as sisters, as a part of the relaxation process, but not a bottle."

Serendipity interrupted me. "If Annette knew she was pregnant, surely she wouldn't have had a drink at all. I mean—*the baby*."

I nodded. "Yes, I know what you mean. I'm guessing that as a wine taster she knew quite a few female colleagues, who'd carried on with their jobs—if their senses of taste and smell allowed them to—throughout their pregnancies. She'd also have likely been aware of the research that shows that a small amount of alcohol, even on a regular basis, doesn't harm the fetus. It's binge drinking that does the damage. She probably happily sipped a small glass that evening with her sister. That was the extent of your plan, wasn't it, Ellen? A murder set up to look like a suicide."

There were puzzled, and horrified, faces all round.

"Yes, that was the *original* plan, right? *Plan* it to look like a suicide, *execute* it to look like a suicide, back up the *theory* of a suicide, and you'd be home clear. You saw Annette as your rival for Raj's affections: she was between you and the object of your obsession. A quick kill, and she'd be out of the way—no questions asked. Well, very few asked, in any case. Not even an autopsy. Which was perfect, because then no one would find out that she had been pregnant. A finger-tip examination by the coroner wouldn't detect a pregnancy of ten or so weeks, especially given that Annette's body would have been supine for the process. No one need ever know. And that would be it."

I could see that, while people might not like what I was saying, they were beginning to understand how it might be possible.

"But that *wasn't it*, was it? Because what the *very clever* Ellen didn't know was that, despite the fact that she hadn't told anyone about the pregnancy, Annette was getting ready to go public. She'd changed her will. A few weeks after her death, there was the meeting at the lawyers' office, the one where Raj told us 'you lost it for a while?' You had *no idea* about Annette's new will, and your immediate reaction was what we'd all expect: you were mad because you'd been robbed of your rightful inheritance. It wasn't *why* you'd killed Annette, but you expected to get the whole winery nonetheless, as your birthright. That was a very telling meeting: you're quick, Ellen, *very* quick. You suddenly realized what Annette's will meant: Raj would be working alongside you, every day, in every way. This was your *chance*! You pounced, going so far as to physically drag him out of SoulVine Wines and off to your winery—*that very day!* Last night, when you introduced Bud and me to Raj, you introduced him as your 'partner,' the implication being that you're a couple. *Because that's how you see the situation.* Raj wasn't comfortable with the inheritance: he suggested that you contest the will, the *lawyer* suggested that you contest the will. You see, if Annette's mind had been set on suicide when she'd written that will, you'd have had a good argument against her plan to leave her interest to Raj. And Raj didn't let it go, did he? He kept bringing it up. He couldn't help but communicate his discomfort. So you had to do something to help him to feel comfortable in his new role, as your 'partner.'"

Bud cleared his throat and tapped his wrist. I got it.

"When you found out the real identity of your online 'grief buddy,' you formed a plan. As a grieving sister unable to come to terms with her sibling's suicide, you'd invite Bud to investigate. And Bud was all for it. *Clear suicide.* No evidence to the contrary. You'd have had an ex-cop say so, in public. Which is why we all got treated to those two little scenes: the sister in denial at the party, the sister in acceptance at lunch. Very nice. Raj could rest easy, *should* rest easy. It would help him settle into his new role as your partner in business, and then, in your mind, at least, in life."

It was clear from the faces, and the tension, in the room that no one was in any doubt any longer. Raj was shaking his head in disbelief.

"It all might have worked if Bud hadn't spoken to *me* about it. *I* didn't buy it *for one minute* that a woman with such a finely tuned sense of smell would asphyxiate herself with noxious fumes. When I realized your obsession with Raj, worked out that Annette was pregnant, and put that together with what I'd found out about the death of poor Stacey Willow, it all made a warped sort of sense. I knew that Serendipity was in danger too."

Sammy raised his hand again. "Ellen somehow made Serendipity eat peanuts because she found out that Serendipity and Raj have been dating?" He was trying to wrap his head around the whole thing. I guessed he'd have welcomed the return of a few of the millions of brain cells he'd slaughtered through excess over the years.

"Sort of, and *I'm* to blame for that," I said, addressing Serendipity and Raj. "I'm so terribly sorry that I put you in harm's way. I should have been brighter, I should have seen Ellen's fixation for what it was, but I didn't. You see, I mentioned my observations about your obvious love for each other to her, without realizing the implications." I looked at the beautifully matched, if terribly distressed, couple and repeated, "I'm *so* sorry."

"*How* did she make Serendipity eat peanuts?" asked Sammy still puzzled. "I don't get it. Serendipity's always so careful."

"She didn't eat peanuts," I replied. "In Ellen's fridge yesterday I saw lots of cooking and salad dressings, one of which was peanut oil. When I was outside, grabbing a quick smoke, I spotted a cigarette stub that looked wet. In fact, it was a little *oily*, not wet. Ellen had injected it with peanut oil, and Serendipity inhaled it. Probably took a really big, deep drag on it. I know that's what I do when I'm grabbing a quick smoke."

"But Serendipity's quit smoking," said Raj. Serendipity blushed.

"Serendipity has been visiting Lizzie to *help* her quit, Raj, and I applaud her for it. Lizzie's hypnotic process allows the person who's quitting to still smoke cigarettes that are already alight, though they won't light them up for themselves. Ellen *knew* that. In fact, she was the one who told Lizzie that she'd seen Marcel at C'est la Vie do exactly that—pick up smoldering butts and puff on them. All Ellen had to do was to inject a cigarette with peanut oil and leave it where Serendipity would be sure to find it—like in the big ashtray-pot at the side of the building here. She could easily just keep repeating the process all evening. After all, what smoker would pick up a discarded butt and puff away at it? *No one.* Only someone for whom that was their only option. When Serendipity ducked out to the loo, and then for a breath of fresh air, she saw a lighted cigarette, couldn't resist, and smoked it. We all saw how extremely swift and violent her allergic reaction was. It's one of the most dangerous and deadly ways to experience an allergen—in the lungs like that."

I turned from the "Soul" table and addressed the MacMillans next.

"Colin—if it hadn't been for your heroism, Serendipity would probably have died. That's what Ellen didn't expect: *you* weren't due to be here tonight, Colin, and she'd already lifted Serendipity's Epi-Pen from her pocket. I have to acknowledge, here and now, that, while you might not be 'The Doctor,' you certainly *are* a hero. You used your brain, and you put another person's life ahead of your own, even though you were reeling from the news of your Dad's death."

"What happened to my Colin? Why was he taken badly too?" Sheri's voice was frail, though she was patting her son's hand, proudly.

"Well, to be fair to Suzie, I think it was quite natural for her to react as she did. All she could see was Colin launching himself at her daughter, and stab at her leg with something metallic. Serendipity would have been exhaling peanut fumes all over him and, being sandwiched between Serendipity and her mother, Colin was pretty close to those fumes. He'd have received a much lower level of the allergen than you, Serendipity, but enough to kick his response to it into overdrive. It's *such* good fortune that you had the spare Epi-Pen with you, Sheri."

I looked around. Pretty much everybody looked as drained as I felt, except Ellen.

She leapt from her seat and confronted me. "*None* of this is true! *No one* believes a word of it. Besides, *there's no proof of any of it!*"

"Actually, there is, Ellen. I have the cigarette with the peanut oil in it, safely preserved for the police. I'm sure they'll be able to match the oil in the cigarette to the bottle in your fridge, *and* the residue on your hands."

Ellen Newman's eyes involuntarily flickered toward her hands. *Gotcha!*

"Earlier on, I had an irrational desire for Reese's Pieces. It was the smell of peanuts that made me want them. I can still smell it on you now. It's tough to get off. That should be enough for attempted murder. You know what, Ellen? I'm sure there'll have been *someone* who saw you with Stacey Willow, and, now that the cops know what they're looking for, they'll find something that ties you to her. And if there's an investigation into the disappearance of 'Jane,' I'm going to bet that you left some trail of evidence there—it's likely you were sloppy. She *was* your first, after all. Unfortunately, I do accept that there might not be any *physical* evidence to put in front of a jury to prove that you killed Annette, but I think that the circumstantial evidence is building up around her death quite nicely. There might still be some evidence to tie you to tampering with the Wisers' brakes. So, to respond to your first point, Ellen, there *is* evidence. *Lots.* And to respond to your second observation—that no one will believe it—well, just look around you. These people have known you for years. Some for your whole life. It looks to me like they *all* believe you could have done, and indeed *did do*, what I've accused you of doing. And if they've made that journey in a few, short minutes, imagine the way the case will build against you over days, or even weeks, in court. *But*, hey, that's not up to me, and it's not even up to the two very accommodating officers from the RCMP who've been listening to all this. It's up to the legal system now." I was exhausted.

As Bud stood guard at one door, the two cops made their way from the other toward Ellen. She had nowhere to go. No escape. She ran across the room and launched herself at Raj.

She kissed him, hugged him. "I did it for you, my darling! I did it all for you. All of them, they were all trying to come between us. I knew it was *me* you really wanted. I could see it when you looked at me. Even when you turned away from me: you didn't want other people to see how much you desired me. That silly girl Jane—she was always flying around on her skates. I sorted her out. I told her you were mine, and she laughed at me! Laughed—*at me!* I pushed her, and she fell. When she was lying there, rambling and bleeding, it was easy. Who knew that skates make such a great weapon? They have such heft!"

Raj was looking in horror over Ellen's shoulder at Bud, who was making *stretch it out* motions at him.

Raj played along. He put up with Ellen's caresses, and kisses, though I could tell from his micro-expressions that he wanted to gag and run away.

"But I never had nothing to do with *Stacey*," he said. Bud gave him the thumbs-up.

Ellen pulled back. "She was all over you, Raj. All over you! I knew she was after you, it was as clear as day. All I did was send her to sleep. I didn't *hurt* her. Like I didn't hurt Annette. All I did was get her to go to sleep too. Her *and* the baby. *Nighty-night.* I didn't like the feeling that I'd *hurt* Jane, you see. You *do* understand, don't you? *That* started as an accident, and then she was dead. But when I *planned* it, I didn't plan to *hurt* people."

Suzie could stand no more. She leapt up and grabbed Ellen's hair. "You *planned* to hurt my baby! We all saw the agony she was in. You didn't care! *You mad bitch!*"

Suzie dragged Ellen off Raj, held her by the hair, and started slapping her with her free hand. Her fingernails raked Ellen's face. Suzie was screaming incoherently. She was a tiger, protecting her young.

It took the two officers at least a minute to detach Suzie from Ellen. Suzie had lost most of her fingernails, and Ellen had lost a large patch of hair. Finally, it was all over.

Ellen was escorted to the waiting police car, weeping, and wiping blood from her cheeks.

Sheri held her boy close, then pulled back, looked up at him, and said, "You know he used to hit me, eh?" Colin nodded, slowly and sadly. He looked grim. "Well," she continued with a forced brightness, "now we're on our own, and no one will ever hit me, or make me afraid again. We'll get through this, Colin, you and me *together. You're* the man I want in my life. I am so proud of you!" He bent down to her and let her kiss him. "Now, let's get you to the emergency room. On the way you can tell me all about this 'doctor' that Cait mentioned."

As the MacMillans left, I couldn't help but mentally wish Sheri luck with the journey she was about to undertake. When Angus died, it had taken me about five years to stop blaming myself for how he'd treated me. It took another five before I'd allowed the walls I'd built around myself for protection to crumble just enough for Bud to peer in, and save me.

I smiled at Bud as I silently sent these wishes to Sheri. I knew very well he wouldn't be able to read the expression on my face, other than to register that I was tired, and relieved

In the corner of the room, the Souls had a group hug, and included Raj. "Man, I love this family!" said Sammy, and he beamed.

At their table, the Jacksons and their two employees had all joined hands and were chanting something, swaying to and fro. They seemed preoccupied.

Standing alone near the exit, close together, the Wisers looked at each other like teenagers, despite their advanced years.

The Corrigans were discussing what they should do about the business. Lauren calmly pointed out that it was the beginning of the busy season, and they shouldn't let folks down. Pat didn't disagree, but I wondered how long it would be before Pat and his world-famous sausages were the draw at another venue. Not long, I suspected. *I mean, who can resist sausages?*

I was tired. Completely done in. All the adrenalin that had deadened my aches and pains for a while was finally draining away, and I was throbbing, quite literally, from head to toe.

Bud reached out and hugged me. Gently.

"Cait Morgan, I love you, and I am *very* proud of you," he said, smiling, "but it's the hospital for you. Now. No more stalling. You're done. Go!" He pointed to two paramedics who were waiting to put me into a chair to wheel me out.

"It's okay, I'll walk," I said.

"No, you damn well won't. Sit!" Bud can be *very* firm.

Three hours later, Bud and I were *still* sitting in the waiting area of the emergency room: a pile up on the Bennett Bridge had produced several casualties, all of whom were, sadly, more serious than a broken wrist and a twisted ankle. Colin and Serendipity had already been assessed, treated, and released.

It was just Bud and me and two pretty uncomfortable plastic chairs.

I sipped the Cup-a-Soup that Bud had managed to wrangle out of a vending machine. He *said* he'd pushed the button for "chicken," but I couldn't taste anything remotely like chicken about it.

"Just a few more questions," said Bud, "if you're up to it?" I nodded.

"Am I right in thinking that if you hadn't got locked in the apple store and found that other photograph, you wouldn't have worked this all out?"

"I was leaning toward Ellen—her hoarding and the traits that it indicated; her 'connection' to Raj. The pregnancy was what made it all fall into place. I should have *seen* it in the photo you gave me last week. I told you that one photo is tough to interpret. If I'm brutally honest about it, it wasn't the *photo*, it was *me*. I was *judging* what I saw, not questioning what it *meant*. Immediately I saw that original photo, I should have asked myself *why* a woman so obviously proud of her appearance would wear an ill-fitting bra. Instead, I simply dismissed her out of hand as just another woman who couldn't take the time to be fitted for the right size. Then there was a lot of talk about Annette buying baggy clothes at the thrift store. In the photo you showed me, Annette was well dressed, if casual, and that's probably why her shirt and bra were too tight on her. She was still wearing her own clothes rather than the bigger sizes she knew she was going to need in the months to come. So I won't be so quick to judge like that again—especially after two glasses of champagne and in the company of the man I love. If people's lives are going to depend on it, I should be more thorough. More dispassionate. *Less judgmental.* Though you have to admit, my summation of Ellen based upon the way she wrote those notes was pretty accurate."

Bud smiled and squeezed my good arm. "True," he admitted. "I'll give you that. Why *did* Ellen lock you into the apple store?" he continued. "I guess that's what she did? I know she was alone while I was getting dressed to be able to give her a ride."

"You know, Bud, I believe she had become wary of me, and didn't want me around tonight. With a killer's instincts, she knew it was better to split us apart. Keep us from working as a team. It was clear that her attempt on her 'rival' tonight was premeditated. I think that my reaction to her denial that there was anything going on between Raj and Serendipity might have made her think that I knew more than I did. When she locked me in the apple store, she didn't know I *hadn't* worked it all out. But—and here's the wonderful, fabulous, and quite worrying, irony of it all—you're right, Bud, if she *hadn't* locked me in, I wouldn't have stumbled on that second photo. Actually, if I hadn't gone back to pick up my cigarettes and lighter I wouldn't have found it—but I'm guessing you don't want me to mention that, right?"

Bud tutted, and I carried on regardless.

"So, yes, if I hadn't been locked in, *or gone back for my smokes*, I wouldn't have twigged to Annette's pregnancy, *or* have extrapolated how that played with Ellen's obsession with Raj. I wouldn't have warned you to stick close to Serendipity when I did, shortening Ellen's window of opportunity to a timeframe when Colin was there with his replacement Epi-Pen. Sheri had a spare one in her purse, but I'm not sure she'd have thought of it unless it were her own boy in need. I *would* have got there in the end, but it might have been too late to save Serendipity."

"Well, that's where *I* almost let everyone down—especially Serendipity," said Bud quietly.

"No!" I held up my hand "*Don't* start that again! You *couldn't* go into the loo with her. You *told* her to not leave your side, but she chose to. She *is* her parents' daughter, after all. It wasn't *your* fault. It was Ellen's doing."

"Would-have, could-have, should-have?" he smiled.

I nodded.

"Did they have any other flavors?" I asked holding up the Cup-of-*sort*-of-Soup. Bud shook his head. "Probably just as well," I muttered. "It might just taste worse." I sighed, and looked into the eyes of the man I loved, and knew I would always rely upon. "Bud, when they've fixed my wrist, can we please go back to Anen House, get some sleep, then drive until we get home? *Please?* I don't want to *be* here anymore. I want to be in my own little place, with a giant pizza—with extra cheese and pepperoni, and, okay then, maybe a glass of wine. But nothing from the Mt Dewdney Family Estate Winery, *right*! However good it might be—never again."

"Okay, we'll get you sorted here, catch a few hours of sleep, then hit the road. We'll have to arrange to collect Marty on the way, and then we can pick up a pizza, or *two*. Because you're not very good at sharing, *right*? Not pizza, not wine, not information pertaining to a crime . . ." Bud was shaking his head.

"Sorry about that," I said.

"A heads-up a bit earlier on might have been useful. After all, I couldn't possibly have been expected to suspect Ellen, could I? Not when she was the only one crying 'murder,' eh?"

"That's *precisely* what put me onto her in the first place," I replied, as patiently as I could.

"Yes, so you said." He nodded.

"You're right. I did."

"Hey—here comes the Doc to fix you up," Bud rose to meet the short, dark-haired woman walking toward us. "She looks like she'll take good care of you," he observed.

"Yes, you're right, she does," I replied.

Bud's always right.

Well, except when he's wrong.

And that's what he's got me for, right?

Acknowledgments

WHENEVER I HAVE VISITED THE Okanagan Valley, especially the area in and around Kelowna, I have met only wonderful people. Those who work at the wineries, in the bookstores, at the lake-front facilities, hotels, bars, and restaurants are fully aware that they are living in a beautiful part of the world that offers the chance to live an amazing life. And they do. So I'd just like to emphasize that the characters in this book are total fictions, created by me in such a way that they work within this book, and within this book alone. If you visit this area, you'll meet an eclectic mix of folks. It's just one element in the complex recipe that gives this region its unique flavor. In other words, this area is more beautiful than it's possible to convey and it certainly deserves its reputation for fine wines, liquors, and foods, but it's not peopled by such alarming folks as you find in this book!!

My thanks to Pinki Gidda and the entire team at Mt Boucherie Family Estate Winery in Kelowna. Pinki was a great help during the writing of this book—she checked facts and gave me wonderful insights. I also want to thank everyone at the winery for allowing me to use elements of the descriptions of some of their wines: I only drink reds, and can attest that they are all just wonderful. (I'm sure their whites are just as good!)

My thanks to Andy Cave, coroner at the BC Interior Region Coroners' Office in Kelowna, BC, for sharing his professional insights in such a timely, pleasant, and professional manner.

My thanks to my Mum and sister: if not for their support and encouragement, I might never write another sentence. They read what I have written and give me the most honest feedback it's possible to give someone you love. Because I write, my husband puts up with a lot. Only he knows just how much, and he never mentions it. Thank you.

The entire "TouchWood Team" is wonderful: my thanks to you all. My special thanks to Ruth Linka, the publisher who allows Cait and me to have these adventures and solve these puzzles; Emily Shorthouse, who publicizes the fact that Cait's on the case again; and Pete Kohut, whose cover designs sing out on the shelves of bookstores and libraries. Of course, my thanks go to Frances Thorsen, whose fabulous bookstore Chronicles of Crime in Victoria, BC, provides the perfect setting, and background knowledge, for her to be a wonderful editor, and to Lenore Hietkamp, without whose copy editing there'd be flocks of misplaced punctuation flying about the place.

Thanks to all the printers, distributors, booksellers, and librarians who play a part in bringing this book from me to you, the reader, and, of course, my thanks to you, for taking the time to enter Cait's world: I hope you enjoy your time with her. I know I always do!

Welsh Canadian mystery author CATHY ACE is the creator of the Cait Morgan Mysteries, which include *The Corpse with the Silver Tongue* and *The Corpse with the Golden Nose*. Born, raised, and educated in Wales, Cathy enjoyed a successful career in marketing and training across Europe, before immigrating to Vancouver, Canada, where she taught on MBA and undergraduate marketing programs at various universities. Her eclectic tastes in art, music, food, and drink have been developed during her decades of extensive travel, which she continues whenever possible. Now a full-time author, Cathy's short stories have appeared in multiple anthologies, as well as on BBC Radio 4. She and her husband are keen gardeners, who enjoy being helped out around their acreage by their green-pawed Labradors. Cathy's website can be found at cathyace.com.